# Moorland Lass

# Acknowledgements

The story of Hester and her friends, although fiction, is loosely based on the memoirs of Dr RWS Bishop, who practiced in Kirkby at the end of the nineteenth century. His book, *My Moorland Patients*, was published in 1921, some years after his death. I owe much to his record of High Side life.

Thanks to Peter and Irene Foster of Thorpe, my brother and sister-in-law, for their support and encouragement, and also to the previous generation of our family, whose memories and stories supplied so much authentic detail.

Ann Cliff
March 2006

# Moorland Lass

## Ann Cliff

ROBERT HALE · LONDON

© Ann Cliff 2006
First published in Great Britain 2006

ISBN-10: 0-7090-8075-1
ISBN-13: 978-0-7090-8075-6

Robert Hale Limited
Clerkenwell House
Clerkenwell Green
London EC1R 0HT

2 4 6 8 10 9 7 5 3 1

Typeset in 11/13pt Janson
by Derek Doyle & Associates, Shaw Heath.
Printed in Great Britain by St Edmundsbury Press,
Bury St Edmunds, Suffolk.
Bound by Woolnough Bookbinding Ltd.

# CHAPTER ONE

## 1894

'Doctors! Useless doctors! A new grave every week – and they still get paid . . . might as well get witch-doctors in! Not that I should complain, it pays me well enough.'

Pebbles rattled on to the path and a tousled red head sprouted in the churchyard grass, leering at the girl who stood beside the grave.

Throwing back a tangle of dark hair, the girl revealed tears. 'Ay, Jim, but it wasn't doctors killed our lad. My little brother was dropped. On his head!' she said, biting off the words brutally. 'And now you're digging his grave . . . only six month old, he was.'

Jim went on digging, and the young woman sighed; it was common knowledge. She knew that folks were sorry, but they were used to this sort of thing from her dangerous father. Brushing away the tears, head down, she turned her attention to something else. Anything, to stop the pain of her thoughts.

Here came a pair of boots. They were clean and shiny boots, fine leather, and approaching at speed. 'New doctor, most likely,' she said to Jim.

The girl watched, as the owner of the boots peered down into the half-dug grave. 'Good day. You're busy – you've plenty of work? But with gravediggers, perhaps it's tactless to ask.'

The man peered up at him, red head on a level with the boots. 'You could say we've plenty of burying . . . three bairns this month. And more to come. There's a new village doctor starts today, there'll soon be a run on buryings.' He smiled grimly.

The newcomer stared for a moment, then grinned, and looked suddenly younger. 'So you think the new doctor will fill the church-yard, do you?'

'Ay, boss. Life up here isn't easy,' the gravedigger grunted as another shovelful of earth appeared.

'I'll do my best to keep the village out of the churchyard – your-self included! I'm the new doctor that you seem to have so much faith in.'

The sexton grinned, unimpressed. 'Four hundred folks in Kirkby last year – that was 'ninety-three. We'd best set about breeding a few more, to give you work, doctor.' And the pebbles rained down harder than ever, as the man went back to whistling.

The girl remembered that she'd heard the new doctor was a Ripon lad, he'd been to the grammar school. He would know that moorlanders were a rough, independent lot. But he wouldn't last. They never lasted long, up here on the High Side.

Wherever she was, Hester was aware of the brooding presence of the moorland above Kirkby. The windswept landscape rose from the river valley, a place where folks were tough and spring came late, and where a great many of this doctor's future patients scratched a living from the little High Side farms. Some wouldn't be able to pay him, in a bad year.

The doctor turned to the dark-haired girl, standing there so still, and she wiped her eyes on a sleeve.

'We've never had a decent doctor at Kirkby! Lasses die, babies die and big strong men get trouble in the lungs. There's nowt but death up here. . . .' She sobbed suddenly, and walked away. He wouldn't be able to help. No one could.

As the doctor moved towards the church the girl followed, trying to stem the tears by watching to see what happened next. The vicar had been peering discreetly from the vestry, hoping for a word with the gentlemanly person in the boots. Trust him, thought the girl grimly as she watched.

The stranger swung round at the swish of the cassock as the vicar padded down the aisle. 'Vicar? Pleased to make your acquaintance. I'm the new doctor. . . . Bishop's the name.'

'Welcome, Dr Bishop.' The Reverend Grimshaw knew how to be stately. From the porch the girl could only hear a few words, even of the vicar's beautiful, carrying voice. '. . . could have wished

6

for a better reception . . . Jim Bradshaw and Hester – oh dear!'

The girl Hester winced, then smiled an unholy smile. She wasn't likely to get approval from the vicar. Didn't want it.

'Typical villagers, I'm sure . . .' That was the doctor's deep voice. Hester moved a little nearer.

'Hester Kettlewell is a wild girl . . . ungodly family. A young child died there, buried tomorrow. . . .'

They came out into the porch and Hester quickly retreated behind a buttress. The vicar was in full flow. 'However . . . I hope you will be happy here, and stay awhile. Kirkby has great need of a competent medical man. Shall we see you and your good wife at church? Good, good. I had been sure you would be Church of England!' he fluted. 'And if there is anything I can do . . .' His voice died away.

Ungodly family! Well, thought Hester, if you're talking about my dad, you're dead right, Mr Reverend Grimshaw.

There was a silence, then Grimshaw smiled primly. 'I'm afraid that this little area – we're between Wensleydale and Nidderdale – is a backwater, forgotten by most. Far from polite society.'

The doctor looked up at the architecture, as if seeing it for the first time. 'Very nice church you have here!' And he wandered out into the sunshine. 'Beautiful little church.' For a few moments he lingered, running long fingers over the blurred Norman carvings round the doorway, feeling the centuries of weathering in the honeyed sandstone, lit by the sunset to a blaze of light.

He looked round and saw Hester watching him. 'Eight hundred years of weddings and funerals. Think of that!'

Eight hundred years! 'It's a lot of folks . . . do you reckon they're all piled on top of each other?' She couldn't see how all those coffins would fit in. But even so, for the girl the thought of the centuries made her grief a little easier to bear. She thought of all the people who'd buried their folks there, over all those generations. She wasn't the first to shed tears on this spot. And she wouldn't be the last, either.

The doctor strode along the village street to his house opposite the church. The girl watched from a distance as his wife met him at the door.

'I've been idle too long . . . wonder if we'll see any patients tonight, Mary!'

The wife was small and neat, and Hester thought she looked pretty. There didn't seem to be a maid about. Wonder if they'd give me a job? A wild idea flitted through Hester's head. That would be something, to be maid in the doctor's household. They'd have to respect her then . . . it might be best to ask the wife, not the doctor.

Mary Bishop looked flushed. 'First impressions are important. I've checked the surgery to make sure that it's in order, all the instruments in full view. But the curtains aren't ready yet. . . .'

'You're wonderful. What can I do, dear?' her husband asked guiltily, and they closed the door.

Hester was staring at the closed door, wondering how much cough medicine would cost, when a hand tapped her on the shoulder. And here was Reuben, with problems of his own.

'Found a place yet?' she asked him. She remembered herself, at six or seven, being often given a biscuit by Reuben's jolly wife at the village shop. But that was before Marjorie died . . . they'd been good to her then, given her a bit of the affection she lacked at home.

The little man grimaced. 'Nay, there's nowt doing at the moment. And it's hard being out of work. I'm lodging with the Wilsons, but I don't fancy staying there too long.' His thin, angular face softened as he looked at her. 'Sorry to hear about your little Billy . . . I'm right sorry, lass.'

She nodded. There was nothing to say, the baby was dead. Then a thought struck Hester. 'That's the new doctor, opening tonight. Why don't you ask him if he needs a man for the horses? It would be a grand job, just the job for you, Reuben.'

The groom looked interested. 'Might be worth a try.'

What would be the best way to impress a doctor, though? Maybe with good health. Hester looked at Reuben's lean and wiry frame. That was it. The girl looked round, then lowered her voice and gave Reuben some urgent advice. He'd always been an honest man and a good horseman, and he and Marjorie had been her friends. 'So – there's a chance, Reuben – take it!' He listened intently.

The church clock struck six with slow majesty as Bishop opened his surgery door for the first time. In the spring twilight a small group of villagers filed past the new brass plate and into the waiting-room, where there was a bright fire burning. One of them was Hester, having made up her mind to ask for the medicine.

In the house she sniffed at the smell of polish and disinfectant. A proper doctor's smell, she thought. Not like when old Smithers was there . . . you could smell the whisky in the waiting-room in those days. And, often, a whiff of pigs from the yard. She was beginning to be impressed.

Hester came straight to the point. 'Now, Doctor, our little Susan has a bad cough, had it all winter. Don't want to lose another bairn in our family. You'll know how to treat a bad cough. Got a bottle of cough mixture?' She held out money in a grimy hand, not waiting for the formality of the consulting-room. Hester had jumped the queue, but nobody objected, and eyes were averted, as the other villagers pretended not to listen.

The new doctor looked at her with sympathy, which made her want to cry again. 'Well, yes . . . Hester, isn't it? I have some medication, but I should really see the little girl, you know. Perhaps I can visit – where do you live? And how old is she? That's important for the dose.'

The captive audience in the waiting-room coughed and looked at the ceiling. New doctor offering to go to Hagstones! Didn't know much, for sure. Wouldn't last long. Not many people would tangle with Roger Kettlewell.

'I doubt me dad wouldn't pay for a visit,' the girl admitted. 'That's why I've come.' And she was in the village, she might have added, to pay the gravedigger, because Roger wouldn't do that, either.

As Hester went out with her bottle she looked hard at the little man in the cap who had followed her in. 'You'll do it,' she whispered.

The small wiry man bounded into the surgery ahead of Bishop, and sat down uninvited, cap on knees. Alert blue eyes followed the doctor's movements. 'Name of Reuben Short,' he offered briefly. Another queue-jumper, it seemed.

'Good evening, Short. What seems to be the problem?' Bishop assumed his smooth surgery manner and sat back to wait for the tale of woe. Villagers wouldn't pay a doctor unless they were worried.

Bristly eyebrows shot up into the sandy hair and the patient replied briskly: 'Nay, Doctor, it's not for me to say. That's your job.'

One up to the patient. Bishop grunted. 'What's your job, then? Take off your coat, man. Let's have a look at you.' He reached for the stethoscope.

9

'Hosses.' The word was said with all the pride and satisfaction of a good horseman. The little man took off his jacket and flannel shirt with rapid movements, unbuttoned a wool vest and presented a skinny chest.

'Heart? Lungs? Teeth? Eyesight?' They were all in order.

'I can read yon paper from here,' the patient offered, pointing to the *Darlington and Stockton Times* on the table. Through the window he could see a shadowy shape; it was Hester, watching and waiting.

Hester was willing the doctor to take Reuben on, to give him the little cottage in the stable yard. She envied the groom his ability to go for a place, to offer his expertise with horses. Now, if she could do the same . . . but she had nothing to offer – except that she could learn quite quickly.

Bishop stood back and looked down at the man, considering. A comfortable silence followed and then the doctor sighed. 'As far as I can see there is nothing wrong with you at all. You should be very healthy indeed.'

Reuben Short smiled for the first time, and it transformed his face. 'Ay, Doctor, that I am. Never had a day off work in me life.' He buttoned up his shirt.

'Why did you come to see me, then?'

The man was not the least put out by the close scrutiny. 'Hester says you've got a job for me. You'll be needing a right good man to see to the hosses. And fetch you home across the High Side on a dark foggy night. It's not a place for strangers in winter . . . what with the weather and the villains. Now you've looked me over, you know I'll do.' Those clear blue eyes were fixed on Bishop's face.

Hester again . . . this was her idea. 'Perhaps you could tell me how to find Hester's farm? I would like to visit there soon.'

Reuben almost shuddered. 'Nay, Doctor, most folks stay away from Hagstones. I must say, Hester's a right good lass, but that father of hers is dangerous. You'll need a good man to go with you!'

'Well, Reuben Short, you've found an odd way of presenting yourself for employment. But I'm not yet convinced. Do I really need a groom? Haven't bought a horse yet, you know.' He thought a while. 'I'll be honest . . . in fact, a horse is an urgent necessity. The practice seems to be spread out across miles of moorland. I'm not sure yet how far I will need to travel.'

Reuben's mind was still on his job description. 'And take medicine out, take Missis to town for shopping, keep yard in order and groom horses. You'll likely need two. No horse yet? I know the very one for you. Nice little mare, ride or drive, drop of racing blood. She'll do seventeen mile an hour when you're needed in a hurry – babies and things. Quiet as a lamb, sound in wind and limb . . .' He jumped up in excitement.

'Nay' said Bishop firmly. 'Don't bring a horse in here for a medical examination!'

The horseman looked at him with amusement. 'You might survive. You'll know what's what, and stand up to the High Siders.' He shot the doctor a warning glance. 'Think on!' he said sharply, with none of the deference due to a prospective employer. 'Kirkby folks has turned agin the last three doctors – driven 'em to drink. You'll likely have a fight on your hands.'

'I'll think about it.' Bishop opened the door.

'Ay,' said Reuben as he disappeared. 'Check up on mare and me, you'll find all in order.' He seemed quite confident that Bishop would hire him.

Meanwhile, Hester had decided to give it a try. She nipped smartly round to the back door of the doctor's house, to interview the Missis. Mary Bishop, somewhat flustered, was trying to conduct some sort of holy conversation with the vicar, while sorting out beds, sheets and pillows. They had just moved in, and Mary Bishop did not wish to be interviewed. Hester took it all in with one glance.

'Please ma'am, I'm Hester Kettlewell and I wondered if you was – were – wanting a maid.'

There was plenty to do. The iron frame of the maid's bed and the ornate brass bedstead for the master bedroom stood in the passage in pieces, visible in the light from the paraffin lamp. But when Mary looked at Hester, besides the bold black eyes, she saw grubby, worn clothes and tangled hair. And the vicar was shaking his head.

'Thank you, but we have room for only one maid.' Mary was gentle, but her words were obviously final. 'I'm sorry . . . perhaps you'll find a place with someone else. Have you any experience of domestic service?'

'N-no, only farm work . . . and I can make butter . . .' Her voice died away. In that moment, Hester realized how much she had to learn. She seemed to have stood still since leaving school, dodging her father's blows and trying to cheer her listless mother.

11

Then Reuben came round the corner, cap in hand, winked at Hester, and stood up straight in front of Mary Bishop. 'Does the beds want putting up? I can help, if you like.'

Should she struggle on, or accept the offer of this unknown villager? In her dilemma, Mary raised her eyebrows at the vicar in the unspoken conspiracy of the servant-owning classes; can I trust this man? Hester saw the exchange.

The vicar nodded slightly. Yes, said the nod, you'll be safe with him. Reuben thus approved by the church, Mary gave him a long look. Then she made up her mind. 'Come in.' She smiled at Hester. 'Good luck' she said quietly, as the girl turned away.

It had been just as she expected: no good. It was a waste of time trying to better herself. Hester knew that as a Kettlewell she was not likely to get a job with anybody who had lived on the High Side for more than five minutes. Only new folks would take her on her own merits, and they hadn't been enough. Maybe she should have cleaned up a little – but she hadn't expected to try for a job, today. She'd rushed out of the house, just as she was, to catch Jim before he went home, and pay him. Little Billy wasn't to be buried in a grave that was not paid for.

When Bishop came through from the surgery he found Reuben working away like an established member of the household, the lamp throwing strange shadows on his craggy face.

'He seems very useful,' whispered Mary. 'You'll need a groom, Robert . . . he could have the cottage in the stable yard, and help with the garden. What do you think?'

# CHAPTER TWO

The first stars were pale against the night sky as Hester strode home, bottle of medicine in her pocket. It looked as though Reuben was set fair for a place. For a while this had taken her mind off her grief and her own disappointment at not being even considered for a job.

The girl looked down at her muddy boots. After all, she just couldn't see herself in a little white cap, opening the door to patients, talking with a plum in her mouth, and remembering not to swear.

It was true that if she didn't believe in a respectable Hester Kettlewell, nobody else could be expected to believe in her, either. But – how did people better themselves? She didn't know where to begin. But she did know that getting away from home would be a start.

Hester's mind now turned to her present danger. Would her father reach home before she did? Roger Kettlewell was unpredictable. Sometimes he went straight home from the cattle-dealing of the day, at others he drank in the Moorcock Inn until midnight. Of course, with the funeral tomorrow, he was likely to drink more than usual.

As she reached the soft turf of the moor, the girl increased her stride.

Caught coming home after dark, she'd get a belting. Dad had this daft idea of marrying her to a rich man, to solve his own problems. Keeping her in after dark was supposed to make her a better catch, though she couldn't see why. If he were a better farmer and gambled less, they'd all be happier. But the drink made him violent. Best get home quickly.

Hester's luck was out, that night. As she crossed the Pateley road she saw a shawled figure stumbling along, one of the neighbours. Something must be wrong. The older woman came up to her, panting and anxious.

'Hester! I'm right glad to see you! Dan's ill, desperate bad, and we need doctor . . . he's come, the new one, hasn't he? And I don't like to leave Dan, all purple he is, and breathing that bad. . . .' She peered cautiously at the girl. People stayed away from the Kettlewells as a rule.

Hester took a deep breath and squared her shoulders. She was wary of neighbours, since she had learned what it was to be a Kettlewell, but she felt sympathy for this poor woman in trouble. She'd seen enough of it herself. 'Don't worry, Mrs Thirkell, I'll go down and fetch doctor . . . he just started today. He might not be so bad.' She gave her precious bottle of medicine to the woman. 'Keep this for me.' And she turned and strode off with the long moorland lope, down to the village again. Bugger Roger Kettlewell.

'Were you abed, doctor?' said the hollow-eyed Mrs Thirkell at the farmhouse door, as Hester and Bishop walked in some time later. The doctor sighed and consulted his fob-watch.

'At this time of night I was thinking about bed! But that's a doctor's life . . . where's the patient?'

The woman took a candle and led the way up a creaking, twisted staircase to a bedroom under the eaves. Hester followed them up, knowing nothing of privacy, and wanting to see what the new doctor would do. It wasn't often she got inside a neighbour's house.

In the four-poster bed lay a heavy man of about forty. He was sweating in spite of the chill air, moving uneasily on the pillows. 'Must shift bullocks tomorrow,' he muttered.

Bishop opened his bag near the candle, while the patient rather fearfully watched his tall shadow on the wall. There was tension in the air, and unspoken questions hung in the room. Would the new doctor be any good?

In a silence broken only by harsh breathing, the new doctor fished out a thermometer and stuck it under the patient's arm. 'Keep it there.' The victim looked surprised, but also rather proud to have such treatment. He kept glancing down at the unusual gadget as Bishop questioned them both, slowly and patiently. 'How long have you been like this? Has there been any treatment? Does it hurt . . . here?' The farmer was calmer now, but they were both eying the stranger nervously.

The man was far too hot; his skin was burning to the touch. 'Shall I try aspirin?' The doctor took out a small bottle and gave two tablets to the woman. He smiled into the woman's anxious face. 'Give him these, with plenty of water, as much as he'll drink. He'll probably improve by tomorrow.'

Hester doubted whether any pill would work. A rattle like that meant lungs; might turn to pneumonia, a known killer on the High Side. And a lost case now would be a grave setback to the doctor's new career. She suddenly found that she was on his side, willing him to win. The new doctor wasn't bad, he'd talked to her as if she were a real person.

The rooms of the old house smelled of damp as the visitors creaked past them and down the stairs. The place was oppressive. Fevers could be oozing from the dank stone walls as the candle flickered over them. Hester could almost feel the clammy clutch of death, her enemy, which had taken little Billy. Perhaps the man would die, just as her baby brother had died. Could anybody stop folks from dying?

Back in the kitchen, the woman said without looking at him: 'Will ye take a drink, Doctor? It's a long way home.' She gave him a bowl of cold water to wash in, from the pump over the stone sink.

Shivering as she waited, Hester glanced round at the massive sides of bacon, hanging suspended from the beams in their muslin shrouds. The candle guttered. It was miserable and damp. It must seem even worse to someone used to working in an orderly Bradford hospital.

It was time to go home. 'I'll come back tomorrow,' the doctor promised, and went out into the night with Hester. 'Just put me on the right road, will you? At the moment they all look alike to me!'

Arriving home, a rather weary Hester let herself in quietly by a side door, the hinges of which she frequently oiled for just this type of occasion. She padded up the stairs, boots in hand.

Then the worst happened; a raucous shout from below made her jump.

Roger had heard her and he came pounding up after his daughter. Drunk, as he was so often, stumbling on the stairs. But not too drunk to catch up with her by the bedroom door. She could see his looming shape in the flickering light of the candle he held. She was used to scenes like this, but even so, her mouth went dry with fear.

Her father had a horsewhip in his other hand, and he got in two cruel cuts across her back, before she tripped him expertly and he fell, legs tangling in the whip. Under her dress, Hester could feel the trickle of blood. With the speed of long practice, she grabbed the candle, slid into her room and locked the door. You had to watch the candles when he was drunk.

You could never reason with Roger, even when he was sober. He would not be interested in why she was late. Better keep quiet and hope he'd have forgotten about it by morning.

There was salve in the cupboard, and a bowl of water on the washstand. The girl undressed and tried to bathe the wounds, but they were hard to reach.

Had it been worth the pain? Not if old Thirkell died. And he probably would . . . everything was dark, depressing. She sank down on the bed and sobbed, for the little brother who would never play in the sunshine, for Dan Thirkell, fighting for breath and for his life. And for herself, hopelessly trapped in a house on the cold moor.

The next day Hester rose early, washed more thoroughly than usual and took the road again, fearing the worst for poor Mr Thirkell. But in the morning light the world looked very different. Larks sang buoyantly in a clear sky, and the moorland was taking on the first green tinge of spring. In spite of the funeral in a few hours' time, the girl felt a slight lift of the spirits.

The comfortable smell of ironing greeted Hester in the farm kitchen. Grey-flannel shirts were being smoothed with a flat-iron fresh from the fire, and above them the woman's face was calmer, less hostile.

'Come in, Hester, he's better this morning. We were right glad of your help last night.'

On the table was a spread of ham, pickles, cheese and a big teapot. They were going to feed the doctor well when he paid his morning visit.

On her way back Hester met Bishop, on his way to visit Dan Thirkell.

'You'd better eat real hearty, they've got breakfast laid out for you!' she told him with a hint of a smile. 'You know the rules up here, don't you?'

Hester pointed out that his character would be judged by whether he tucked in and ate heartily. One wrong move could spoil his reputation – and refusing hospitality was a grave insult. It looked as though you didn't like the stuff they offered, or you thought the folks were too poor to afford it, or that you were too grand to eat with them . . . or all three.

'So – you've got to get your feet under the table, see.'

Skinny Lily Metcalfe put on her hat and patted her hair under it, a little flustered after her examination. Bishop turned away tactfully, washing his hands to give her time to recover.

'There's nothing much wrong with you, Mrs Metcalfe, as far as I can see.'

Lily felt work-worn, tired out. She was scrupulously clean and neat, anxious about everything; you couldn't help worrying with so much to do. Their butter and cheese were the best in the parish, and that took some doing. But you were only as good as the last batch.

'I'll bet you have too much to do. Three bairns, a big house to clean and farm work as well. Does that husband of yours hire a labourer for the summer? These farmers work their wives to death, I know, and then what do they do? They get married again and spend all your hard-earned brass on a young lass.'

This doctor sounded just like a moorlander, but Lily Metcalfe was still very nervous of him. 'We've not hired any help this year, because we wanted to save the brass.' She hesitated, caught between money and self-preservation. She looked after the money very well indeed, and she'd told Ned that they could manage the work between them. Hands twisting nervously into her long black dress, she looked at Bishop. 'Well, Doctor, he gets a man for sheep-dipping and hay-timing. But there's calves and butter and cheese. . . .' At the thought of all the work waiting for her, she stood up. 'Time I was off. Nearly milking time.'

Bishop got down a big bottle of tonic from the shelf. 'I think you may be short of iron, it's a frequent female problem. Black pudding will be good for you, when you can get it.' He poured the liquid into

17

a smaller bottle. 'Get a strong young lass then, to do some of the housework and help on the farm as well. There must be plenty of girls looking for a place. What would it cost you? Twenty pounds a year and her keep? Well worth it, I should think. Your health is more important than the last penny, you know.'

The woman shuddered at the thought of spending money, then turned her plain little face to him earnestly. 'Nay, doctor, I doubt as good village lasses wouldn't bide on the moor. It's too quiet, not enough company. And a lot of moor lasses are mucky tykes as wouldn't know how to clean.' She looked down at her work-worn hands.

Bishop paused for thought. 'There's Hester Kettlewell, a big strong girl who might very well want to leave home and earn some money. You know who I mean . . . the lass at Hagstones. She'd need training, but I think she's intelligent.'

As the doctor opened the door for her Lily felt a little confidence returning. 'Ay . . . well, I could go over one day to see Kettlewells. I could just do with a lass in the kitchen. Hester's mother and me were at school together. But they're a rough lot. Any lass of Lizzie's will need a sight of teaching. She'll know nowt, that's for sure.' Clutching her bottle of medicine, she went out with a new purpose.

A few days later Lily Metcalfe went off, face set with determination, to visit Hagstones in search of Hester. There was faint sunshine as she left, but a heavy mist hung over the moorland above the Metcalfes' farm.

Lily was nervous, but she meant to see it through. She was going several miles through the cold spring weather to a place which decent people avoided if they could, and she only hoped it would be worth the effort. She fervently hoped the father would be out. He was a terror, that man, big and strong, and everybody went in fear of his foul temper.

The watery sun disappeared as she climbed the moor road, and an ominous gloom hung over the dank farmyard at Hagstones as she picked her way round a foul heap of manure. The mist hung low on this part of the moor, and the rainwater was dripping monotonously from the old barn roof as it sagged out its days at the end of the yard. This farm was losing money, you could see.

Water ran down the back of Lily's neck as she peered cautiously into the farm buildings. A skinny fowl ran out of the stable and made her jump. The place was eerie. Ned had warned her before she left about the perils of Hagstones. 'Every soul that visits there, and they aren't so many, looks into the stable first. If horses are stabled, master's at home.' And only when she was satisfied that the stable was empty did the little woman rap quietly on the scratched farmhouse door.

The door opened a crack eventually, and a hopeless female face appeared, peering through wispy hair. She glanced at Lily. 'It's you. Come your ways in.' The voice was lifeless.

Once inside, Lily peered hastily round, wrinkling her nose at the smell. It was a pungent mixture of wet dog and thick peat smoke, laced with cow-dung.

They were in the living-kitchen, a low-beamed room with a slate floor. Little Susan Kettlewell, a thin child of about four, sat in a window recess, playing with a rag doll. Not much light struggled through the grimy windows. A ragged side of bacon, much cut away, shared a nail with a string of onions. Lining one wall was a scratched oak settle and in the middle of the room there was a huge table, littered with horse harness.

Lizzie Kettlewell waited, without visible emotion, to see what happened next.

The object of the visit, the daughter, was not there, Lily decided after peering into all the corners. Through in the scullery could be heard the rhythmic sounds of churning; swish, thump as the cream thudded from one end of the churn to the other. Probably Hester at work.

The visitor cleared her throat nervously. Small-talk seemed out of place, so she came straight to the point. 'Well now, we were wondering if Hester might be looking for a place. There's over much work for Ned and me, with three bairns as well.' Her mouth shut tightly in case any mention of money escaped her.

The other woman shrugged. 'Hester must please herself. If her father'll let her.' There was a silence. Swish, thump went the churn in the scullery. At least, the girl knew how to make butter.

Lily looked at the fireplace, where cooking was done over the open fire or in the side oven. The peat fire was low, throwing out very little warmth, and the hearth was piled high with ashes, and fringed with dirty dishes. She looked at the grimy teapot on the hearth, and hoped they wouldn't offer her a cup of tea. It didn't seem likely, in this frigid atmosphere.

Looking down at the muddy floor, Lily tried again. 'She'll need to know how to scrub, and serve calves . . . can she milk?'

Hester herself appeared in the doorway, with a rather sulky face, one hand pushing back her dark hair. 'Butter's slow today, Mam. Time you took a hand. She saw the visitor and looked surprised. 'Now, Mrs Metcalfe.'

'She wants to know if you want a place – they're looking for a dairymaid,' Hester's mother said tonelessly. She looked too depressed to care about what happened to her daughters. And of course, Lily remembered, she had just lost her baby son.

Hester could hardly believe her luck. The offer of a place! She'd been dreaming about it for so long . . . but her father wouldn't hear of her going out to work for somebody else. She suppressed her pleasure, in case the job fell though. She had to get it past Dad, first, and he wasn't the sort of father who cared what she wanted to do.

Roger had long planned to marry her to some well-off old farmer, who could help to pay off the Hagstones' debts. She was quite aware that to him, her chief selling point was her youth and strength. Looks didn't come into it. Nobody had ever suggested that Hester was beautiful. But time was going by, she was twenty now, and he would soon be making a move.

As Hester turned away to hide her excitement, there was a commotion outside. The yard was suddenly in uproar; cattle bellowed, dogs barked and long horns emerged from the fog. Kettlewell had come home from the market.

Little Susan hid her face as the door flew open and the master of the house strode in. He had a shotgun under one arm and a fierce scowl pinned to his bearded face. His loving wife slunk into the scullery and went doggedly on with the churning, without a word of greeting. The old dogs disappeared under the settle again, and Lily Metcalfe pressed back into the shadows. It seemed that only Hester stood her ground – although she had a nasty bruise on her face.

The farmer saw Lily, and the scowl deepened.

'Bloody visitors . . . too many folks up here with nowt to do. Where's my dinner?' shouted Kettlewell, standing with his back to the meagre fire. A well-made man, he could have been handsome in a dark way, but for his mean expression and small, darting eyes. The big black beard terrified Lily Metcalfe, who couldn't look at him.

Hester opened the oven door and brought out a dish of mutton stew. The dogs caught the scent of meat, and moved forward under the table. Kettlewell kicked them ferociously, and then glared at the visitor. 'What does she want?'

'Mrs Mecca's come to offer me a place. To go to work for them.' Hester spoke calmly, not flinching as her father towered over her. She was suddenly resolute; this was what she wanted to do, and this time, he wouldn't stop her.

'You're not to go to work for Ned Metcalfe and his scratting wife!' he roared, shaking her roughly. Her arm came up to shield the bruised face; Hester knew her father's moods and could calculate his degree of drunkenness. Little Susan hid behind her doll.

Hester's mother looked through from the scullery, but said nothing. Lily Metcalfe wished she'd never come to Hagstones, and Hester went to stand between her father and the little woman. She smiled faintly at Lily.

The farmer swayed and sat down suddenly in the high-backed chair. He picked up a knife from the table. 'You shall not go!' he shouted, obviously half-drunk and unpredictable. He proceeded to eat his dinner, cursing at the same time.

In the scullery, Hester's mother finished the butter-making, her movements those of a woman with no pride in her work, and no hope of anything better.

Lily Metcalfe, for all her fear, thought of her own bright butter at home in her spotless dairy, each perfect brick with a different pattern on top. She spoke up bravely. 'Hester's young enough. A change might do her good.' She looked at Lizzie. On her way to the door she looked round again, fascinated by a scene so different from her own orderly life.

'Thank you for coming.' Hester was as polite as she could be. It seemed odd to hear a normal remark in that setting. 'I'll come over to see you next week,' she added quietly, at the door. Her father appeared not to hear.

Hester's mind was racing. This might be a last chance to get away from this miserable place. She had learned something, last month, organizing Reuben into his new job. Just what he needed, and it was due to her that he'd nipped in and got it. Well, maybe it's my turn, she thought. And a farm job is more in my line than a doctor's maid could ever be.

# CHAPTER THREE

'Now this here is calf-meal, and that hay is special for calves, it was well got on a bright sunny day.' Ned Metcalfe was instructing his new dairymaid in the routines of a well-run cowshed. 'I'm trying to remember everything you'll need to know, which is quite a lot.' Hester's upbringing at Hagstones, he seemed to be saying, was sadly lacking in many respects.

Hester was concentrating, and her brow was furrowed under severely tied-back hair. 'Your byre's cleaner than our kitchen!' she said in wonder. The stone walls were neatly whitewashed, the floor was scrubbed and the wooden divisions between the cattle stalls shone white in the spring dusk. There was a faint fragrance in the air, of good hay, fresh milk and the breath of contented cows.

It was getting dark. Ned lit a paraffin lamp and hung it on a nail, the pool of light catching the quiet eyes of the cows, and turned towards Hester in mild enquiry. 'They know you're a stranger.' He patted his favourite cow affectionately.

Hester had never before seen a man who liked cows and enjoyed working with them. 'At our place . . .' she was still contrasting the Metcalfes' farm with her squalid home, 'it's all swearing and kicks. Dad hates cattle, and they're scared of him.'

The mercenary Roger Kettlewell had, in fact, been hard to convince that he should allow Hester to work at Shaw's Farm, the Metcalfes' place. But Hester was determined, and she had his own stubborn streak.

Catching him at a comparatively sober moment, Hester had persuaded her father that she'd be a more marriageable commodity if trained by the famous Lily Metcalfe, the best cheesemaker and the thriftiest housewife on the High Side. Of course she had no intention of marrying any old codger, just to pay Dad's debts. But it was a good argument. Hester certainly needed some kind of polish; even Roger could see that. So, here she was, thank goodness.

His hair glistening gold in the lamplight, Ned handed the girl a bucket of warm new milk, straight from the cow. 'Do you know how to teach a calf to sup?'

' 'Course I do. Which one?' This was her first test, but she mustn't seem to be nervous.

They moved down the long shed. In a corner pen was a small, red-brown calf, curled up asleep in a ball. Hester hitched up her skirt, and hopped over the gate into the pen. 'Lost your mother, then?' she said to the calf, waking it gently.

'Have ye got patience, lass?' asked Ned with a grin. He sighed gently. 'I'm not sure as we can afford a dairymaid.'

'Why not?' Hester looked up in alarm, the lamp casting a soft glow on her face. She didn't want to go back to Hagstones. 'I know how careful you have to be with money, of course. But I was hoping that this would be a new start for me. . . .'

Ned looked doubtful. 'You'll cost brass, all right. And you're ower good-looking to be a real worker,' he added mischievously. 'Plain lasses work hard. Good looks are dangerous.' The look he gave her was frankly admiring.

The girl looked at him in surprise, not used to compliments, however double-edged. 'Maybe I do look a bit better for a bath, and this frock of your sister's. But I can work, never fear.'

Lily Metcalfe had tidied up Hester considerably. Her hair was clean, and her skin now had a healthy glow.

With the girl's encouragement, the calf was beginning to realize what was in the bucket. The little red head went down and drank. Then it gave a sudden lunge, tipped up the bucket and showered Ned with milk.

Ned laughed, brushing the milk from his jacket. 'That's grand. Just a pint or two at first . . . it's a right good lass we've gotten ourselves, I can see.' Then he thought of his critical wife. 'With a lot of teaching, of course.'

Hester eased her aching back.

'Do you like a joke?' He looked at her with an impish smile. 'I'll tell you one. Parson says to beggar, "Are you not ashamed to be begging in the streets, my man?" Beggar replies, "I'd rather do it in the pulpit or church bazaar, but Fate's agin me." '

Hester giggled. 'We never had jokes at home about anything . . . you ought to do a turn at village concert.'

Ned threw back his fair head and laughed. 'I bet life's a serious business at your old man's place. We'll have a thing or two to teach thee, young Hester.'

One evening, at the end of the girl's first week, she was bathing the children in the scullery, when she heard Ned and his wife talking about her. She strained to hear.

'You were right, lass!' Ned was saying. 'Hester's going to be a good worker . . . we'll treat her right, so she'll stay.'

'She's on the go from cocklight till murking.' The little woman liked the old farm words.

'And clean enough now to let near the bairns. She looks forever better in those old dresses of your Betsey's. Poor lass never had a chance at home. Tell you what, Ned, I know one thing. My life's a lot easier now.' Lily spread the cloth for supper. 'And the bairns like her as well. We'll send her home on some Sundays after dinner, to see her folks, it's only right.' She smiled her thin little smile. 'And come hay-time, we needn't hire a man this year.'

A Sunday came, a few weeks later, with the sort of calm spring airs when the moor is at its best. The skylarks sang for joy as they ascended, the lambs skipped beside their more stately mothers, and Hester skipped and sang as she walked.

Happiness was a new experience. True, she was going back to Hagstones, but only for the afternoon. Servant-girls were expected to visit their mothers, and life was so good that even the prospect of seeing the Kettlewells didn't depress her. She was a new woman; she hadn't had a beating for a month, and it surprised her how different she felt.

In spite of her long skirt, Hester strode like a true moorlander over the short, sheep-nibbled turf. She waved when she saw Kit Horner, whose grazing rights spread over this side of the moor.

Kit turned aside to join her. 'Hester lass, you look well today . . . how's the new job going?'

Everybody on the moor knew about Hester's place. And anything that happened to Kettlewells was bound to attract attention, Hester knew only too well. They were a dramatic lot, and provided a sort of entertainment for the law-abiding. Unless, of course, you happened to get one of Roger's bad deals.

Kit was a gentle, silver-haired shepherd, a bachelor who lived on the moor with his two sisters. He'd always been a favourite with Hester. He was one neighbour who didn't judge people, even her family, and who did a kindness when he could.

'It's all right, Kit. Too soon to say,' said Ned's dairymaid cautiously. And that was all Kit could get out of her.

Tactfully, he changed the subject. 'Shouldn't really be shepherding on a Sunday.' Kit had a high, gentle voice. 'But it's a grand day to be out of the house, so I'm looking round the sheep. I can't feel godly, somehow, in church. Do you know what I mean?'

Hester was only half-listening. 'Ay, I'd rather be up here,' she agreed. 'Can't stand sermons anyway – all that shit about hell-fire – ooh, sorry for swearing, Kit. It's just to frighten us into doing what they want. But our family never went in for church much.' The young pagan looked round with enjoyment at the wide expanse of moor and sky, thinking that she must remember to watch her tongue if she was going to be respectable.

Little silver rivulets hurried down the gullies, sparkling in the sun, gurgling their way down to the river in the valley. From her perch on a boulder Hester could see that the heather was taking on its first pale bloom of spring green. She jumped down from the rock and smoothed her dress. 'Must be off!' She braced herself to face the atmosphere at Hagstones as she set off down the track leading to her home.

A dog came to meet her on the road, and Hester knew the animal. 'Now, Moll!' she stooped to pat the soft fawn head. 'You brought that Josh visiting again. I wish he wouldn't bother.' Her face set, and she lost the spring in her step. Josh Bell must be waiting for her at Hagstones.

The gloom and grime of the Kettlewells' kitchen looked worse than ever as she went in, contrasting starkly with the bright spring world outside. But thank goodness, Roger wasn't at home. Hester's brightness faded as the despair of Hagstones closed round her again. She hadn't realized how bad it was until she'd experienced something better.

The kitchen was stuffy and dark, and most of the light was blocked out by the large body of Joshua Bell on the settle, sitting upright with cap on knees. He looked at Hester, his breathing fast and shallow. 'There was something I wanted to say to you, Hester.'

Joshua had crisp dark hair and an open, ruddy face; he looked gentle, amiable and completely out of his depth. The strong young body twisted in embarrassment as Hester said coolly: 'How did you know I'd come home?' Silence.

Little Susan sidled up to Josh, and he took her on his knee. Lizzie Kettlewell put more wood on the fire. Hester looked across at her little sister. 'You need a good clean up, our Susan. I feel ashamed ...' she looked round at the dirty kitchen. Painfully, she saw the contrast with the neat farm where she worked. A few weeks at Metcalfes' had taken her a long way.

Josh was sad. 'We were good friends at school, Hester. Remember we shared a desk? But since we left school, it hasn't been the same.'

They had held this conversation several times in the last few months. Josh had been like a brother to her, a best friend, protecting her from the taunts of other children. But she couldn't imagine him as a lover; he wasn't exciting enough. And however desperate she was to get away, Hester wasn't going to marry a man unless he swept her off her feet, in truly romantic style. She felt it would be dishonest to marry Josh, just to get away from home.

Hester looked at him. 'A Kettlewell's not good enough for the Bell family. Your lot are respectable, I'd never fit in.' She knew it was true. The Bells were yeoman farmers with their own land, held for generations. She'd seen their beautiful old house, full of oak beams and polished antique furniture.

Josh moved restlessly. 'Hester ... it's always awkward for a farmer to think of marrying. ... Some wait for their folks to die! But there are other ways. I'm looking to rent a farm when my brother gets married. Or – there's Canada and Australia wanting farmers, and with both of us together ... I can't find the words.'

To get away from the Kettlewells Australia might be a good idea. But not with Josh. Hester tried not to be impatient. 'We were only kids at school, Josh. Real life is harder. And I don't flirt. With me, it's all or nothing. So it's nothing, between me and you.' She turned away.

Josh tried once more. 'This new job, now – it might cheer you up a bit ... and maybe I could visit at Metcalfes', once in a while. I don't flirt either, lass. I'm serious.'

That's the trouble, Josh, Hester thought. You're far too serious.

Josh stood up. Now for it. 'I'm taking the trap to Pateley Fair,' he said huskily, his voice strained with tension. 'If you'd like to come with me, Hester.' He was a slow speaker, a big, well-proportioned man with faithful brown eyes. He dropped his voice and moved a little nearer. 'It'd mean a lot to me, Hester, if you'd come.' It was a long speech for Joshua.

They faced each other in the gloomy kitchen. 'No, thanks. I'm not going to the fair, too busy.' Hester shook her glossy head, with the hair now neatly tied back. 'Know any jokes? No, didn't think you would. Well . . . better see what Mother's doing.'

It was all over. Josh sighed, and slowly took from his pocket a small, crushed bunch of primroses. He put them on the dirty table and looked once towards Hester. Then he walked out. 'Goodbye,' said little Susan sadly. Josh didn't hear her.

One day Dr Bishop called in at Shaw's Farm where the Metcalfes lived, partly because he was wondering how the girl was surviving in her new environment. He felt responsible, having suggested the move. He was greeted warmly at the farm, and was pleased when he looked at Lily. 'Yes, Mrs Metcalfe, the tonic is doing you good.'

'Ay, doctor. There's them in the village says it's only coloured water, but I'm sure it's a drop of good stuff, and worth anybody's hard-earned brass. And I shall tell them so, myself,' she ended with a sniff. 'There's ways of spreading news at chapel teas, and I'll make sure it gets round.'

Laughing, the doctor said: 'Typical moorland praise! But some of the credit should go to your new dairymaid, I'm sure.'

'Hester's a right treasure, doctor,' the farmer's wife agreed, as she poured Bishop the inevitable cup of tea. She looked round the spotless kitchen with pride, and moved the apple pie a little closer. 'Reach to and help yourself. Well, it must be admitted that this is a far godlier place than Hester's home, and a sight cleaner. So she'll be the better for it, and I'm teaching her what I can. Hester made this pie, Doctor, try a piece. Her dad's drinking heavy again, and losing money, they say.'

'How does he lose it?' Bishop's eyes were bright with interest as he looked across the table.

'Gambling – at Moorcock pub away on top of moor. We Methodists are dead set against public houses, as you know ... drinking morning, noon and night. Cattle- and horse-dealing, sometimes lucky but more often not – that's dealers for you. And there's cock-fighting up there still, they say.' Lily shuddered at the waste of time and money. 'I'm thankful none of mine ever took to that company.'

'Where is Hester at the moment?'

'She's away over the moor, looking at a batch of ewes with lambs as we turned up the hill last week. She's good with sheep – saves us a lot of time. You might see her on your way back.'

By the time Bishop turned his horse's head on to the road over the moor his thoughts were on evening surgery. But as he trotted along he was jerked back to his surroundings by the sight of Hester. There she was, a lone figure among the sheep, in a vast landscape of rolling moor and sky.

Hester was trying to catch a ewe that seemed to have lost its lamb, but the animal was evasive. Even though she had Ned's dog with her, Hester had no luck, until suddenly a shape appeared, and sent the ewe flying towards her. Hester caught it and hung on grimly.

The man came closer and together they turned the ewe on to her haunches for a closer inspection. It was Joshua Bell. To Bishop, they were etched on the skyline like a frieze; he could see their movements but not hear their words.

They released the ewe eventually, and watched her trot away.

Josh walked along beside Hester. 'You like working for Ned Mecca?'

'Ay, I do.' The girl avoided looking at him. 'Better than being at home. It's that miserable, since baby died. And Ned's funny, he's always laughing and joking. Good company.' She laughed, and her dimples appeared. 'Now don't come no further, Josh Bell. I haven't time to talk to you, I'm supposed to be working.' She called the dog and turned towards the Metcalfes' farm.

'Don't you want my company at all, Hester? It's the last time I'll ask. If you're shy ... of being courted, I'll understand. I'm shy, as you well know. But if there's a lad you like better ... tell me straight.'

'It's no good, Josh.' She looked at him then, but remotely. 'Give your primroses to village lasses, there's plenty of girls in Kirkby would be right pleased to see you. Cheer yourself up a bit.' Hester

# Ann Cliff

felt numb when she looked at Josh. She felt sorry for him, she could see he was suffering, but there wasn't much she could do about it.

Hester bounded away through the heather as Kit Horner came towards them with Bess at his heels. Ned's dog went immediately to the attack, and a vigorous dogfight ensued, with snarls and growls and flashing teeth. It was some minutes before peace was restored, and when Hester looked round Josh had disappeared.

'It's thronged with folk up here today, and noisy, too!' Kit smiled as they stood watching the dogs in their uneasy truce.

Hester's grim expression softened a little. 'Too many folks up here at times. Well . . .' she shrugged off the memory of Josh's miserable face. 'Tell us a story, Kit. Something to think about.' All the village children loved Kit's stories.

Kit hesitated. 'Story? Nay, you're too old now for fairy-tales, lass. I'll tell thee a bit of history.' His eyes were fixed dreamily on the horizon. 'The Body in the Peat.'

In the afternoon light they sat together on a big stone outcrop, looking around them at the sheep nibbling the short turf.

Kit Horner raised an arm. 'Just over there now, at Castiles, well – it must be fifty years or so ago – two lads were digging peats for the fire . . . and they found a body in the peat.' He prodded the spongy turf at their feet, exposing the underlying peat. Hester's eyes widened then.

The shepherd paused. He had just spotted a distant figure: Hester's father driving a cart over the moor, and he was sure they'd been seen. Why should it matter? 'Folk called him a Roman soldier,' he went on, turning so that she wouldn't see Roger Kettlewell. He was not likely to drive over to wish them good-day.

Kit's dog got up, sniffed about and took off after a rabbit. 'Come here, Bess . . . but they never found a weapon, or a shield.' He leaned forward earnestly. 'Nobody knows what happened to him!'

A cold breeze sprang up and Hester shivered. 'It's milking-time by the sun. Thanks for the story, Kit!' With a quick change of mood she bounded off down to the farm with the dog at her heels. Kit smiled as he watched her go.

Ned was waiting for Hester in the cowshed, with all the cows tied up in their places. Coming into this clean and fragrant shed was beginning to feel like coming home.

Sitting with her pail underneath a cow, Hester struggled with

30

Agatha. 'Will you milk this one, Ned? She's not easy.'

'As long as you milk two others while I'm at it. No good being too soft with dairymaids,' Ned told her, grinning. 'Nay, lass, don't let a cow beat you. She's only hard because you don't sing to her. Try it and see.'

So Hester tried again with the boss cow of the herd, the big roan Agatha. The massive head turned, the tail flicked, the large eyes looked at her from under ferocious horns. Instead of the usual spurt of milk into the pail, Agatha let down only a thin trickle. Then she moved a foot as if to kick the pail. The tail flicked, again and caught the girl across the face.

Hester flushed. 'Come on then, you great horny bugger!' she shouted in a voice coarser than the Metcalfes had yet heard her use.

'Now then, young Kettlewell. We'll have none of your father's language here!' The boss was quite in earnest. 'We don't swear here. Missis says it curdles the milk.' Then he smiled, realizing the girl was close to tears. 'Never mind, lass, I'll sing for the old girl.'

As the sun went down over the moor, the roan cow was serenaded. Gradually, Hester realized that the fearsome Agatha was milking out just like any other cow, standing still, placidly munching. So Ned was right, and you could sing to a cow and calm it down. Ned had a pleasant baritone voice, much practised at chapel on Sunday mornings.

When Agatha was done Ned put a casual arm round Hester. 'You did well.' He gave her a squeeze.

Unused to affection, Hester melted. Then she backed away, and blushed. 'Oh, Ned, you shouldn't!' It was pleasant, all right, but he was a married man. . . .

Ned laughed and patted her. 'Just a bit of fun, my girl. You're a bonny lass, you'll have to get used to that.'

Milking over, Hester carried the frothy pails into the house. In the big, cool dairy the shallow setting-pans waited on their stone slabs. There the milk would stand, the cream slowly rising to the top while the house slept.

Hester poured the milk into the pans with a steady hand. Lily Metcalfe watched her placidly, candle held high, the shadows leaping over her sharp face. 'We'll have supper now, when you've had a wash. There's your apple pie, as Dr Bishop said was fit for a king.'

They sat round the table in the warm glow of the brass oil-lamp, talking about the day's work. Then Mrs Ned made a suggestion. 'We could take Hester to Pateley Fair. She could look after the bairns.' Hester, her mouth full of bread and cheese, looked up brightly. Pateley Fair, with the Metcalfe family and in their smart pony and trap, would be a treat.

# CHAPTER FOUR

Following her plan of being good to Hester, to keep the wages down, Lily Metcalfe had decided to give the girl a change of scene and company when she could squeeze some time out from the busy farm routine.

'Living on a moor farm, with an old married couple isn't much company for the lass,' Hester heard her say. 'I'll take her with me to chapel tea on Wednesday.' The tea was a monthly event, and a social focus for the godlier members of the community. Maybe they would have a civilizing influence on the dairymaid, who was shaping up well, but still showed a few rough edges, she implied.

Hester was pleased enough to get washed and changed on Wednesday afternoon, and to go rolling down into Kirkby in the Metcalfes' trap. But the idea of tea-drinking and hymn-singing didn't appeal to her at all, partly because she knew very well that the Methodists openly disapproved of Roger Kettlewell and all his ungodly brood. Even with Mrs Ned beside her, noses would be elevated and tuts would be tutted. Hester didn't fancy that.

The moors were still austere under the spring sky, but the hawthorn blossom foamed to meet them from the lower hedges as they rolled down the hill. Spring came to Kirkby much sooner than it did to the upland, and the village, sheltered by the ridge of moor, was full of blossom.

As they approached the village the maid thought of a solution. 'Old M – my Aunt Maud's ill in bed. Maybe I should visit her instead?' she suggested demurely. So Mrs Ned put her down by the aunt's house, and promised to pick her up to go home in time for milking, as she shook the reins and moved off.

Maud Thompson was sitting up in bed, clean and neat and ready for a chat. Aunt Maud, who appeared incredibly old to Hester, was her mother's elder sister. Although she heartily disapproved of Roger she evidently felt sorry for Lizzie, and said she was pleased to hear that Hester had managed to get away from Hagstones. And now she seemed glad to see the girl.

'Came down with Mrs Mecca – she's going to chapel,' Hester explained, seeing the aunt's surprise.

The older woman looked at her. 'So you're dodging the Methodists, eh? Don't blame you. Our family's always been Church of England. Oh dear . . . the rheumatics has got me and very painful it is. Ow! Sat on a twig again. They're rowan-twigs, for a cure.'

Hester laughed and sat down by the bed. 'What good are rowan-twigs? You might be better off with the new doctor. Mrs Mecca says he's right enough . . . and Reuben works for him now.'

'Well, Reuben's local, and steady enough. Doctor must have some sense. I don't know this new doctor, but Molly wants to ask him to come. But it's rheumatics, and what can doctors do about that?'

Maud twitched the patchwork quilt. 'Sometimes I can hardly move for pain. Meg White's due to call about now, with some herb stuff. Now, tell me what really happened to poor little Billy.'

In a few minutes there was a light knock at the door and Meg White came in. Composed and quiet, thin and brown, she sat down by the bed and looked at Maud, then at Hester.

'Now, lass, you're looking a sight better these days,' she said with a smile.

Hester smiled back happily. 'Yes, Mrs White. I've got a place, working hard, day and night. It's a good job, and Mrs Mecca's good to me.'

Aunt Maud said firmly: 'Now Hester, you go down and help our Molly to make a cup of tea.' She obviously had no intention of taking the wise woman's advice with Hester listening.

Hester was pleased to go down to Molly, who was about her own age, and leave the two old lasses to talk. Meg White knew a lot, of course, but herbs were boring.

It was turning into a busy afternoon at Aunt Maud's. No sooner was the tea made than the vicar came to call, puffing up the stairs to offer a prayer for the sick.

The vicar looked startled to see Meg White, but after all, Hester knew, she did no harm, and she always went to the harvest festival service. She was a sort of fringe Christian. Hester herself was another matter, a young pagan with a wild streak. And she never forgot that he considered her ungodly.

'And how is ... ah ... your family?' the vicar asked Hester, painfully polite, evidently trying to set a good example.

'My family? Talk of the devil!' the pagan said cheerfully, pouring the vicar's tea and rushing in where angels feared to tread. 'Me father's a raging devil. I'm better off away from that lot ... and trying to improve meself.' It didn't sound quite right.

The Reverend Grimshaw's eyebrows were raised, but he said mildly: 'Well, Hester, the first step to self-improvement should be ... to attend church on Sundays.'

Hester faced him squarely. 'Vicar, if a lass doesn't go to church, does that make her a bad woman? There's plenty bad folks go to church every Sunday.'

Maybe she shouldn't have said that, but it was honest. She closed her mouth firmly, in case anything else escaped.

There was a shocked silence. Her aunt started to talk quickly about her roses, meanwhile giving Hester a look that was supposed to quell. The moment passed, the girl went thankfully downstairs again, and the vicar presumably recovered.

This polite conversation was harder than it looked.

Hester was thoughtful as she helped Molly to wash the tea-things. Small-talk was something she'd had no practice in at Hagstones, and the good example of her school teachers had worn off long ago. She decided to watch what she said, to think before she opened her mouth; easier said than done. But, Hester decided, she wouldn't tell lies just to please other folks.

It was lucky for Hester that Mrs Ned arrived to pick her up while the vicar was still there, and Auntie Maud was only able to say: 'Have more respect for your betters, lass!' as the girl picked up her skirts and ran.

'Got to go, it's milking-time. I'll come again soon,' Hester promised. Aunt Maud shuddered.

While they were milking Hester told the boss about putting her foot in it, down at her aunt's. She felt rather worried, thinking back. As they changed cows Ned put his arm round her waist. 'Don't fret!' he said lightly. And she blushed, and laughed.

Hester had slightly guilty feelings about the way Ned treated her;

he was careful to make sure they always got the work done, but he liked to touch her; he was affectionate, and this was new to Hester. At Hagstones there was no affection. Josh had been friendly, but had never shown his feelings. Hester really felt she'd missed out on affection. But Ned's was different, too. It held a dangerous excitement.

'You're such a bonny lass!' Ned always said when she tried to pull away. 'Don't worry, I won't get up to anything – too near home!'

The girl was not sure what he meant by that, but she wondered what Mrs Mecca would think. Ned never put his arm round his wife, not when Hester was there, at any rate.

The trouble was, Hester thought as she milked, head well into the cow's side, that Ned was so attractive. She thought about him a great deal of the time. And it was hard to resist when, just before they went into the house, Ned slid both arms round her and pulled her against him. 'Stopped worrying, honey?' He laughed. She didn't want him to let her go.

The next week Ned asked Hester if she'd like a trip to Larton, a village near Kirkby, where the little River Laver flowed under a bridge on its way down to Ripon.

'You know Meg White's cottage? It's not too far to walk for a strapping lass like you. Take the evening off, fetch me some cow-salve from Meg's, and Missus and me will do the milking.'

Meg's ointment for sore cows was effective and cheap, and made the life of many a moorland cow more comfortable. It was good for the milkers' hands, too.

Hester had hardly missed a milking since she started work at Shaw's Farm, so this was a little holiday. She washed and put on a clean dress, and walked out into the calm evening with a light heart. A change of scene and company was still a novelty to a girl who had been shut up on her father's farm since leaving school.

Meg White's stone cottage was rather isolated, on the outskirts of the village, and Hester had never been there before. The 'wise woman' was regarded with some sort of awe by the folk of Kirkby and Larton, and Hester wondered why a few herbal remedies should earn her such respect.

There was Meg in her garden, using the sunset light to plant a row of beans. 'Plant with the waxing moon,' she said mysteriously; then she opened the gate and they walked together up the flagged path. The air was heavy with the scent of lavender, and the buzz of late bees. 'And what can I do for you, Hester? You look healthy enough.' Meg was in her sixties, ancient in fact, silver-haired and with a serene sunburned face and quiet blue eyes. 'Gave the vicar a shock last week, didn't you?'

Hester had tried to forget about the vicar. 'Ned Mecca wants some cow-salve, please. And, well, vicars mean nowt to me. I don't hold with religion and all that stuff. There's plenty of rogues go to church and chapel every Sunday. And I stopped thinking about saying me prayers, after our little Billy died – you know, me little brother. Dad dropped him. God should've looked after little Billy. . . .' She wiped away a tear.

Meg listened sympathetically, those calm blue eyes making Hester relax a little. 'Well, it's not always wise to say what you think, lass.' She seemed to understand just how Hester felt. 'And it's better to respect other people's views – even if you don't agree with them. Especially leading figures like vicars!' She spoke lightly.

They went into the dark of the cottage, which smelled of sage and rosemary. Meg took down a jar of greenish ointment from the shelf and gave it to the girl. 'There's your salve . . . and you've walked a long way, would you like a cup of tea?'

There was a loud knock at the door. Hester started up, as if to go. 'Best be off, you're busy . . .' but Meg motioned her to sit down. 'Stay there, Hester lass,' she said calmly. 'I expected this visit, and I want you to enjoy it. It was lucky you came by just now. Sit in the shadows and don't make a sound.' Rather uneasily, Hester sat down, wondering what would happen.

The woman opened the door. With a clatter of boots on the path four men moved towards her, solemn and stiff in their Sunday suits. 'We are the chapel mission, come to save your soul,' one of them said with a hint of a nervous quaver.

Meg stood in the doorway among the clumps of rosemary and marjoram, letting them look into the room, with its mysterious jars and bunches of herbs. Then she pushed them in, and closed the door behind them.

Behind the men was the glow of the sunset, and as they stepped inside they could see little. A dull peat-fire and a couple of rush-lights hardly relieved the gloom, and huge bunches of drying herbs obscured the corners of the room. There was no chance of their seeing Hester, hidden in a deep recess, but she could see them, through a small gap in the screen of dried herbs.

The boots scraped nervously on the stone floor. Leaning forward confidentially and fixing Meg with an unwinking stare, the leader of the mission smiled in forgiveness. 'We have come to bring happiness to your heart, Mrs White.' Thomas Johnson sounded as if he'd been used to some success with this approach.

The small woman looked up at him. 'Your teeth fare badly, Mr Johnson. No doubt you suffer from terrible indigestion, as well as bad breath? I've a remedy for it.' Hester grinned in the darkness, stifling a giggle.

'Will ye turn from the Devil?' he tried again, more earnestly. 'The Lord has power to save, even poor sinners like you. . . .'

Meg picked up a sprig of rosemary and waved it at them. For some reason she looked sinister. Johnson went pale.

From the shadows a pair of large unblinking eyes made Johnson jump as he looked uneasily around. 'Only Blackie,' said Meg soothingly. The shadow purred and the black cat stretched lazily, flexing his claws.

'What have you got to do with a poor old woman?' Quietly, Meg locked the door behind them and put the key in her pocket. 'D'ye think that I'm one of your black sinners?'

'Let us consider . . .' said Johnson, teeth clicking as he leaned towards Meg, his sparse hair a faded yellow.

'Let's consider what fits you for a mission,' Meg interrupted smartly. 'You, Thomas Johnson, an elder of the chapel. We,' she looked round at Blackie, 'we have not forgotten, as you maybe have, how you cheated your brothers off the farm and took it all for yourself. Altered the will as your father lay dying, didn't you? Ay, and only last week you took a good hay-fork from Robson's barn. The Devil's in ye yet.'

Blackie arched his back, and Hester'e eyes widened.

Billy Robson rounded on Thomas. 'I've looked high and low for that fork!' His divergent vision made him look even more annoyed. Thomas couldn't meet either of his eyes.

With a gesture, Meg silenced them. The rushlights guttered as she moved, and her shadow flickered on the wall. 'Not so fast, Billy, you're no better. There's three bairns in Kirkby who get their red hair from thee, and their squint eyes, poor mites. Shall I tell thee their names? There's Mally Sykes's Joan, and. . . .'

Hester laughed silently. This wise woman was clever!

'. . . Lizzie up at mill,' went on Meg quietly, 'and that child as was born to the poor little servant-girl at Larton Manor. An orphan, she was, with nobody to look after her, or point out right from wrong. Mission to Kirkby!' Disgust showed in her voice. 'So the orphan girl came to Sunday school, for a bit of company. No harm there, you'd think, but she fell into your hands. You took her down by the river . . . the poor bairn was too young and ignorant to know the danger. By the time she came to me, it was too late.'

There was a silence.

'I suppose it's news to you, Billy Robson, that when the baby showed, the poor lass was turned out of her place, with nowhere to go. What did you care? It's always the woman who suffers. If it hadn't been for Miss Bramley that poor child would be dead by now. She was too young for child-bearing, and she was desperate. As it is, she's got a new place, and a fresh start. But it's no thanks to you. You are a disgrace to real Methodists. They are godly folk.'

The men breathed out, carefully. Perhaps she'd finished.

But Meg moved back into the darkness, leaving them standing by the fire. She spelled out in detail the crimes of each of the other two. Hester could hardly believe her ears.

The mission was in a state of collapse, much to Hester's delight. They would take a long time to recover. Meg opened the door, and they slunk away into the dusk. There was a laugh from the corner.

'How did you know they were coming?' asked Hester, with a new respect. But Meg smiled and stirred the fire and drew the kettle on for a cup of tea.

'You know what, Mrs White? You told those folks exactly what you thought – which you said was wrong!' The girl smiled triumphantly.

Over the tea the two women talked easily, and Hester began to realize what a store of knowledge Meg had gained over years of helping the moorlanders. The wise woman knew her limitations, and treated minor problems like sprains and bruises, listening all the time, but seldom offering advice.

'Sometimes people just need to talk.' She looked at Hester with her peaceful expression. 'They know their secrets are safe with me. I've never told on them, before tonight. But it was time somebody stopped that ungodly crew. There's a time and place, Hester, for saying just what you think. You . . . may have learned something from this evening.'

Hester thought for a while. 'Well . . . some of village folk are as wicked or worse than High Siders, I can see. I never thought . . . that folks could be as bad as that, when they're sober.' She'd always blamed the drink for Roger Kettlewell's sins.

A young owl screeched as Hester walked home and she shivered, thinking of those poor girls with unwanted babies. Good job she had more sense than lasses like that. She'd have known better than to go down by the river with a dirty old man.

It would be good to have children, she supposed, with a decent husband . . . somebody like Ned. She could imagine herself with Ned . . . but he was a married man. It was dangerous to have thoughts like that.

Hester loped swiftly over the moor in the gathering darkness, feeling that she had been away for a long time.

Ned looked up and smiled a heart-stopper as she walked in. He was a Methodist of the godly sort, a genuinely pious man who liked to sing hymns as well as tell jokes. She wondered what he would have made of the mission to Kirkby.

'Here's your salve. Mrs White gave me a cup of tea.' That was all she said.

# CHAPTER FIVE

The day of Pateley Fair dawned bright and cloudless, but Hester could feel the cool wind that often lingered on into a moorland June. The ewes, their fleeces ruffling, curled protectively round the lambs at their sides.

Hester was up before dawn as usual, going round the sheep as soon as the sun came up over the rim of the Vale of York. Ned groomed the pony more carefully than usual, hissing through his teeth. His little wife peered anxiously at their best cow. Beauty was due to calve, and she was uneasy. The deep red short horn's tail swished to and fro, and her feet were paddling.

When Hester came humming into the byre Lily Metcalfe shook her head. 'I doubt one of us will have to stay at home,' she said glumly. 'Beauty's the best cow we've got. We can't afford to lose her. If she needs help, and she did last year, we've got to be there.'

Hester's smile disappeared. 'I was right looking forward to the day—'

'Nay, not you, lass. You've never had much enjoyment in life. I'll stay with Beauty – and you go with Ned and look after the bairns. It won't be the first time I've helped a cow to calve, and I'll have a quiet day at home.'

At last all the morning jobs were finished. Up in the little white-washed bedroom Hester brushed her black hair until it shone. She washed thoroughly, with much splashing, at the marble washstand and she grinned at the thoughtfully chosen text on the wall.

May virtue guide my inexperienced youth
And lead my footsteps on the path of truth.

The words wobbled in uncertain cross-stitch over a faded canvas.

41

Mrs Ned had obviously spent a virtuous youth doing needlework. Had she enjoyed her youth? For a moment Hester felt sorry for the skinny, unattractive little woman. Then she ran lightly down the stairs in her new print dress, the best she'd ever owned.

The dress was the result of a lot of thought and labour. It was perhaps rather thin for the cool moorland but, as Mrs Ned said, you could wear a shawl over it. The women had made it together, under the lamp in the evening after supper. The older woman was horrified at Hester's lack of any sewing skills. While Ned read the paper and shook his head over the sheep prices, the pretty green cotton was cut and sewn, with only a little blood shed when Hester pricked her finger.

Hester was proud of the dress, and of the new personality she was developing. She felt happy, standing young and darkly glowing in a patch of sunlight in the kitchen. Poor Mrs Mecca looked pale and thin by comparison; the good little farm her father owned had been Lily's great asset, and Ned, by marrying her, had become a farmer instead of a farm worker. He'd gone up in the world, and her thrifty ways kept him happy.

Hester had worked all this out for herself, and she knew that, according to Lily, good looks didn't last, and they only caused trouble. Hester's dad had been a good-looking youth, but no doubt her mother had often regretted marrying him.

'Behave yourself, Hester!' Lily shook her head. 'There's many a one is too bonny for her own good.'

Elated by the prospect of a day off, Hester swung the three children into the trap. Ned jumped up and shook the reins, and they rattled out of the yard, hoofs drumming on the hard ground. Ned was in his second-best suit, face shiny with soap, and in the best of moods. Another farmer was taking their sheep to the fair in a cart, so they had no worries for the day.

When they reached the open moor on the winding road to Pateley, Ned broke the silence. 'Doesta like poetry, lass?'

Hester giggled. 'We did that at school. It lasted too long. . . .'

'Ah, the one I have in mind is a rhyme of Pateley Fair. Steady, Charlie, don't fall out!' Ned restrained his young son, who was leaning out to watch the wheels go round.

Hester's dark hair blew over her face, and she swept it back and laughed at Ned. 'Tell it now, Ned, while we're going to the fair.' It seemed natural to call him Ned, but his wife was always Mrs Mecca. 'D'ye mean to say that a poet knew about Pateley?'

Little Emily raised her golden head. 'Is it a story, Father?' Charlie and Edward looked interested. Ned coughed, furrowed his brow to remember the lines, and urged on the pony to overtake another trap.

The other vehicle had two people in it. As they passed on the narrow road, with Ned's pony's mane and tail streaming, Hester caught sight of the other driver's set face. It was Josh Bell. He didn't look at her, but she could sense his agitation.

Josh was taking good care of his mother's horse, and didn't offer them a race. Beside him, bag on knee, was Dr Bishop, and he looked as glum as Joshua. He gave Hester and Ned a thoughtful look as they passed.

'Here it is, written by Thomas Blackah, a Pateley lead-miner.' The other trap was left behind and Ned relaxed.

> Old men that's fowerscore summers seen,
> Wi'hairless heads and sparkless een
> Cum toddlin' hither.

'That's me!' he offered, looking at Hester. She shook her head at his golden hair and sparkling blue eyes. Ned knew that he was handsome.

> There's lots of bairns that just can walk
> In brats an' frocks as white as chalk
> An full-grown lads and lasses stalk
> About together.

'Ay, that's it. You've a pinny as white as chalk, our Emily.' Hester was busy thinking of Ned and herself as the full-grown lass and lad. She could feel his warmth beside her on the bench. They should be sweethearts; he was younger than his wife, nearer Hester's age in his ways than Lily's.

Ned drove carefully down the long, steep hill into the little town of Pateley, set in a hollow beside the River Nidd. Its full Sunday name was Pateley Bridge. By now they had joined a procession of traps, carts and wagons, all winding down the hill, some of the horses sliding a little. The wagoners put their brakes on.

As they turned into the main street Hester caught her breath. The pavement was thronged with people in their best clothes. Flags fluttered from windows, dogs barked and from an open window came the sound of an accordion. Music floated out over the crowd.

The rhythm of Ned's verses seemed to pound through the town, as the crowds surged down the steep and narrow street to the fairground by the river. Here he took the pony out of the shafts, and tethered it under a tree in line with the others.

> A hundred different voices rise
> Such bawling, hoarse, discordant cries,

chanted Ned, as more verses came back to him. 'Hang on to the bairns, young Hester.'

There were some admiring glances for the good-looking young farmer and his bairns, and a few for Hester, glowing as she was from the ride. Looking through the crowd, Hester saw nobody to equal the ruddy splendour of her boss.

They were all enchanted by the fairday atmosphere, in such a contrast to the quiet moorland, with its lonely calling curlews, where they spent their days. It was a sale, a show and a circus all in one. There were little stalls selling toffee-apples, ribbons, fairings for sweethearts. . . .

Little Charlie was heavy and their progress was slow, but everywhere they went, as Ned stopped to speak with neighbours, there was a kindly word for his dairymaid. 'Lass must've had a rum time at home,' she heard one farmer say to his wife. The goodwill was new to her and it belonged to the Metcalfes. As a Kettlewell, she'd always been an outsider.

Hester saw a girl she had known at school and, to her own surprise, she turned aside to speak. 'I've got a place!' she said proudly.

Mabel beamed back at her. Happiness is catching. 'You look right well, Hester!' And she told some of her own news. She was engaged to be married, to Josh Bell's brother.

When Hester caught up with Ned again, he held out a red ribbon. 'Here, lass. Summat to remember the day.' Blushing, she took it from him and tied it in her hair.

There were sheep and pigs and calves for sale, in lines of pens by the river. This was a great exchange centre for the High Side and part of Nidderdale, a day of business as well as a holiday. Folks were pleased, too, that the winter was over and the grass was turning green.

Leaning over a pen nonchalantly, Ned nodded slightly and Hester realized that he was bidding for a little black sow.

'Are you sure she's in pig?'

'Ay, right enough. How much luck money do I get?' asked the vendor promptly. There was a mumble, then a smack of hands meeting as the bargain was struck. 'Done.'

Ned turned to Hester and winked. 'Good bargain,' he whispered, but with a straight face. It would never do to look too pleased. 'I'll get Chandler to take it home.'

Hester was relieved that they wouldn't have to share the trap with a black pig on the way home. But the day was golden and nothing could upset her too much, not even the sight of Josh Bell's unhappy face, glimpsed in the crowd.

Meg White passed them with a big basket. She was selling herbs, quietly as she did everything, not advertising her wares, but having a word with people here and there. Hester sniffed the aromatic basket, remembering the evening of the mission to Kirkby. 'Mrs Mecca wants some sage, for cooking rabbits,' she told Ned.

As Ned bought the herbs, Hester saw her father lurching out of the beer tent, and she turned back quickly, saying nothing to the others. Ned didn't drink, thank goodness.

'We'll give you a ride home if you like, Mrs White,' Ned offered.

Hester hoped they would not have company on the homeward ride.

At noon they went back to the trap and unpacked the wicker basket for a picnic in the shade. There was white Wensleydale cheese and scones, milk for the children and a slice of fruit-cake, because it was a holiday. Hester sat back and watched the crowds, realizing that she'd never enjoyed a day like this before. 'Lovely cheese,' she said with her mouth full.

Ned agreed; Lily made excellent cheese, which sold well at Ripon market. 'You'll have to learn to make Wensleydale soon. As part of your education!'

The afternoon passed quickly, too quickly for Hester. Ned's

sheep sold well, which was good news to take home with them. Then it was time to yoke up. As they trotted back across the moor they waved as they passed Meg White, riding serenely in another neighbour's trap. Hester sat beside Ned with Charlie on her knee, utterly content. 'Give us another verse,' she said dreamily.

Ned concentrated. 'There's a bit about day's ending – how does it go?

> No matter how our time we spend
> There's ne'er a day but what mun end
> Time keeps advancing.
> At feast and fast it moves away
> And many a one were there that day
> At will not, I'll be bound to say
> Next feast be dancing.

Hester sighed. Where would they be, next fair day? The pony went steadily on, advancing like Time through the shadows of evening. The sun was nearly setting before they saw the roof of home.

Hester changed into her working-clothes in the little bedroom, but everything looked different. The day spent with Ned had changed her, body and soul.

With eyes enormous in a white face, Hester went about the evening duties: tying up cows, milking, feeding hungry calves. But she did the work mechanically, with none of her usual light-hearted zest.

Hester had been fired with a burning passion for Ned. The Kettlewell intensity was surging through her blood with an urgent rhythm. The day at the fair had brought out some deep instinct, and she hardly knew what she was doing.

Mrs Ned had spent a restful day, cleaning out the pantry. Her hair was full of whitewash and her heart with job-satisfaction. Intent on getting the tired and drooping children to bed, she was not aware of the dairymaid's strange mood.

Ned himself was just as usual. 'What's up, Hester lass, you're never tired?' he asked in a rough but kindly way. 'Never! A big strong lass like you, and just had a day off? Come on then, let's get finished. Beauty hasn't calved yet, but mebbe she won't be long.' The little cow was even more restless, but not yet in the last stages of labour as far as he could see.

Supper was a quiet affair. Mrs Ned fried some liver, but Hester could hardly eat. She tried to hide her churning emotions, crumbling her bread and looking across the table at the lamplight shining on Ned's golden hair. Ned talked quietly of the day's prices, and the people they'd seen at Pateley.

Gradually the inner turmoil subsided, leaving Hester tired and rather empty. Heavily, she took her candle and went upstairs. In the privacy of her little bedroom she unpinned her dark hair slowly and let it fall. Her face looked back from the mirror, mysterious and changed, so that she would never be the same young girl again. She smiled faintly at the image, blew out the candle, and got between the cool white sheets, clutching her red ribbon.

From the deep sleep of youth, Hester was awakened by the rattle of the door-latch. Ned, candle in hand, put his head round the door, but didn't look into the room. 'Hester!'

The girl sat up, pushing back the heavy hair.

'Wake up, lass! Cow's calving and I need a hand.'

It was the first time she had been asked to do such a thing, but it was reasonable. Hester was bigger and stronger than Lily Metcalfe, and when a calf was to be pulled, strength was needed. He'd evidently decided not to wake Lily, asleep in the big brass bed at the other side of the house.

Throwing on her working-dress, Hester hurried down the stairs. The byre was still warm with the memory of cows' breath, and silvery with moonlight. While the rest of the herd slept outside under the moon, or cropped the moorland grass, Beauty was awaiting her big event.

Blinking in the light of Ned's lamp, Beauty was lying on her side and panting, with now and then a groan. Hester clenched her hands, hating to see the animal suffer.

'What can we do?'

Seeing Hester looking worried, Ned tried to cheer her. 'Job's half done, lass. All she needs is a good pull.' He lit another lamp, which made things seem a little more normal. The red cow looked round at them pathetically, and Hester could see that she was afraid.

Ned now brought two thin ropes, each with a loop at the end.

Kneeling down by the cow, Hester could see that the calf's feet were visible. He looked round. 'Fetch a bucket of water, and some soap.'

Hester ran into the little dairy and snatched bucket, towel and soap. Impatiently she waited for the water to run from the iron pump. By the time she returned with the water Ned had his sleeves rolled up and was kneeling at Beauty's side. He washed and soaped his hand and arm and felt gently round the feet. 'Yes, it's a big 'un. . . .'

His assistant shuddered. Ned turned and looked at her sternly. 'Not afraid, are ye? Hold this rope and pull when I tell you.' The loops were placed round the calf's forefeet. 'We only pull when she pushes, so we're helping her. And we pull downwards. Ready, now?'

Hester was ready to faint. For the first time, her boss spoke sharply to her. 'Come on, woman, earn your brass, you get good wages. Lily-livered lass!' He caught her as she slumped and slapped her face, not too sharply. She cried out, but she revived.

Ned took a deep breath. 'Get on, Hester, this is a gey good cow and I'll not lose her for a daft taking. Come on, woman!' He was angry now, as well as anxious.

With a great effort, Hester picked up the rope. Ned took the other and they waited. Beauty pulled herself together and strained to get rid of the calf. 'Now!' said Ned and together they pulled until their arms cracked. The calf slid forward a little, and the tip of a nose appeared.

Beauty seemed to know that they were trying to help and she did her best, tired though she was, to rally for a last effort.

The calf came clear, a long inert form lying on the straw under the lamp, with no sign of life. Ned tickled its nose with a piece of straw, and Hester held her breath. Suddenly the eyelashes flickered and the new calf sneezed. It started to breathe and lifted its head slightly, looking round for the first time at the world.

Exhausted, Beauty lay quiet a minute or two while Ned watched her anxiously, but then she saw the calf and raised her head. Beauty sniffed the little body and then began to lick it with her long tongue.

Ned stood up and stretched. 'See that, Hester? What a grand cow! And you did well, lass, I'm proud of you.'

Hester glowed with pride. She looked at Ned, sharing his triumph. Ned took a step away, but the floor was wet. He slipped and fell, clutching at Hester as he went down. And Hester fell with him. Down they went together into the soft yellow straw, laughing with triumph and weak with the long tension. 'We've got a good calf, lass, it's bound to be a winner!' Ned was saying as he pulled Hester to him.

Ned and Hester found themselves lying on the soft oat-straw beside the calf, with Beauty watching them in mild surprise. Ned did not let her go. He kissed her gently, and she found herself responding.

Then she struggled, tried to get away, willing herself to be a good girl, not to give way to her feelings. 'Steady, Ned!' she gasped. He was a married man, and though she was a pagan, Hester had standards of honesty. She couldn't make love to Lily Metcalfe's man.

And then the tide of warmth overwhelmed them both, with the fragrance of Hester's hair.

That was the end of being sensible. As the new calf found its way to its mother's teat and took a first mouthful of milk, the two who had brought it into the world took no further notice of it for a time. Locked together, they lay in the straw, absorbed in each other. Outside the byre, owls hooted in the soft summer night.

# CHAPTER SIX

'You'd better work with me today,' said Mrs Ned sternly, the day after Pateley Fair. Hester gave a guilty start. What did she suspect? A guilty blush went unnoticed; Lily's mind was on her work. 'We'll do a batch of show cheese, and you can learn the job, lass.'

'Ooh, yes, please, Mrs Mecca. I'd love to do that.' Hester was quite honest; she wanted to learn from a champion cheesemaker.

And so it happened, almost against her will. Hester began to live a double life, against her principles and her better judgement. She hated to be less than open and honest, but she was deeply in love with Ned, and she wanted him with all the force of her passionate nature. She was sure, now, that Ned loved her.

In the house she was a good girl, one of the best; butter wouldn't melt in her mouth. She was learning all she could of dairy work and housecraft, and, as everybody kept pointing out, she had much to learn. Cheesemaking, just one of the tasks, had been a slovenly affair at Hagstones, and her mother's cheeses had often been bitter or rancid. But Lily Metcalfe took a pride in everything she did, and Hester was learning attitude as well as skills.

In the byre, the dairymaid was less demure. She worked well and swiftly, but Ned knew by now how to seduce her, to overcome her conscience. By the way he looked at her and the things he said, he could excite her, even while they worked. She was waiting until the moment when they moved away, up into the dark hayloft or down among the heather, to be together. And the glow of it, the triumph, stayed with her when she went back to being a good servant. Surely this couldn't be wrong!

Hester worried about Lily, but Ned told her that his wife was happy enough.

Ned said he was crazy for her, he had never known an experience like this. One day, up on the moor when they were lying at peace on a bed of heather, he described how Lily took out her teeth at night and put them on the washstand, scrambled from her dress into a flannel nightgown, knelt down to say her prayers and then blew out the candle before getting into bed. 'Turns you off,' he said.

The young farmer said he'd never before made love to a woman in broad daylight. He'd never seen Mrs Ned without her shift. Naked bodies, he'd been told, were snares of the Devil. But now he didn't believe it. 'This is natural,' he told Hester. 'This is how folks ought to live.' And when he pulled her towards him, she believed it.

Hester was sure that Ned belonged to her. In time, she planned to have him all to herself.

The summer dawn was breaking over the moorland, pink mists parting as the sun rose, to reveal the great sweep of Nidderdale under the summer sky. The slight breeze was scented with clover and new-cut hay. Smoke was beginning to rise from the village chimneys down in the valley, and a cloud of another kind was travelling fast along a bumpy farm track. Hester was driving a light cart at breakneck speed, flushed with exertion and tight with anxiety, concentrating fiercely, but glancing up frequently. Where are you, Doctor, when you're wanted?

Spotting a horse and trap on the road, Hester dashed up to it and skidded to a halt, throwing dust all over the doctor.

'You're risking life and limb, young woman!' Bishop passed a tired hand over his face.

Hester noticed the gesture. 'Have you been out all night, Doctor?'

'Another case of pneumonia,' he said wearily. 'Crisis passed, patient sleeping. I was hoping for a spot of sleep myself . . . I can tell I'm going to be unlucky.'

'It's Mrs Robinson . . . I've been down to Kirkby to fetch you. Pains have started, you promised to come . . .' Hester was willing him to come. Delivering calves was one thing, babies were quite another, and she didn't feel equal to it. And it was their first child, after ten years of marriage. Mrs Robinson seemed quite old, to Hester.

'Yes, she's Mrs Ned's cousin, and so the Meccas sent me along to help!' said Hester importantly, flashing Bishop a look from those dark eyes to see whether he was impressed at such evidence of respectability.

'Good. Well, try to keep calm, Hester, and spare the horse! I wish I had the nerve to drive like that!'

He sounded like a grandfather to Hester. Bishop shook his head as she set off again in a cloud of dust, whirling back to the farm to tell them that help was on the way.

Hester unyoked, stabled the horse and got back to the house before the doctor arrived at a more sedate pace. The panic was over, the doctor was here. Brushing the dust from her skirt, she bounded upstairs to tell Mrs Robinson.

Hester was enjoying her new role, and her part in the drama, in the lovely old sandstone house, smothered in roses. This morning, Garth Farm seemed like paradise to the girl: bathed in sunshine, surrounded by a fragrant garden full of mint and thyme. It was a little pocket of civilization on the edge of the uplands, and she could tell by the ancient trees that it had been here for hundreds of years.

Only a few miles away over the moor, at Hester's home, a baby had died. At Hagstones, there was no garden, no roses and not much trace of civilization. Why was there such a difference between families? She shook off the thought of Hagstones, and helped the maid to serve the farm workers' breakfast.

The doctor came down from his patient, and Hester gave him a sizzling plate of thickly sliced ham, two eggs and a wad of crusty bread, spread with deep-yellow butter. Strong black coffee completed a satisfying meal. She wondered why all the coffee was black; on a dairy farm there should be plenty of milk. But here, all the milk was kept for cheesemaking – it was their little economy.

'But it's a good meat house,' grinned one of the men, winking at Hester. 'They get more work out of us that way.' This was a bigger farm than Ned's, with three or four men employed, clattering into the stone-flagged kitchen for breakfast, dinner and tea.

Bishop was looking better for the meal, Hester noticed. As she cleared the plates away he looked at her. 'And what is your role in this affair, apart from galloping about at speed?' His smile took the sting from the words.

Her answering smile was full of pride. 'I'm to make the cheese, Doctor!' Hester said with satisfaction. 'Milk won't wait for anybody. And Mrs Mecca said I'm good enough to work on my own, till Mrs Robinson is downstairs again.' She pulled a slight face as she thought of the many instructions the farmer's wife had given her.

Breakfast over, Hester was swathed in a big apron, and pails of milk appeared on the kitchen table. The milk was warmed in a cheese-kettle over the open fire, hot work on a summer day.

On his way back to the patient the doctor paused to watch. 'Are you confident, Hester?'

'Not really,' the girl confessed. 'Mrs Robinson's cheeses win prizes at Leyburn show. She and Mrs Mecca are best cheesemakers on the High Side!' She turned back anxiously to the milk, testing the temperature with an elbow.

As she worked Hester thought about the woman upstairs, and hoped that she wouldn't be in bed for too long. It was a big responsibility to take over all this work – and also, she wanted to get back to Ned. But . . . should she? Away from the Metcalfes, things looked a bit different.

How would she feel if another woman stole her husband? But then the memory of Ned's smile came back to her, and she sighed. It was too late now to turn back. Maybe Mrs Mecca would be happy enough to manage without Ned. She'd got her bairns, which were much more important to her.

An hour later the cheese was well on the way. Hester wiped her sweaty face as the doctor came in quickly, looking serious. 'Hester, I need your help. I'll have to use the ether apparatus – thank heaven it's in the trap. Do you know what that means? It's a difficult birth and she's in great pain. You can help me – I need another pair of hands.'

Hester went white. 'Nay, doctor, I've never done anything of the sort before! I can't—'

'Nonsense!' Bishop was sharp. 'If Reuben can do it, you can too. Reuben helped me to deliver a baby by the light of a tallow-dip, not so long ago. All you have to do is to obey instructions.' He went out to get the apparatus.

Wasn't there anybody else? Hester looked round in panic. Mr Robinson had been so anxious that Bishop had told him to go out on the farm; the little maid was about fourteen, and young for her age. There was nobody else to help the doctor. It was up to Hester Kettlewell.

Taking a deep breath, Hester made up her mind to do her best. She took off her apron, scrubbed her hands and went upstairs.

Mrs Robinson was suffering, trying to be brave. The doctor was reassuring, confident. 'Well done so far, Mrs Robinson,' he said in his gentle way. 'You're a healthy woman and things should go well! It's a grand morning for hatching another moorland chick.' He was preparing the apparatus. 'How did Hester know that the time had come?'

'Look out of the window, Doctor, and you'll see.' Hester pointed.

Mrs Robinson gasped as another pain hit her, and Bishop looked out to see a large white sheet suspended from a tree above the house. Several miles away on the opposite slope, he could just see the roof of Shaw's Farm, where Hester worked. The Metcalfes had been keeping watch, and sent Hester along to help as soon as the signal appeared.

Quietly, he gave Hester instructions. The ether dose was critical; too much would kill the patient, too little and she would suffer pain.

The farmer's wife slipped into oblivion and Hester, listening and watching carefully, had no time to be afraid. Afterwards, she thought of the two lives in her hands, and shuddered. But now there was a job to do and soon she could hear the anxious father, returned from the fields and pacing up and down outside the door. Fathers were not allowed in until it was all over.

In a four-poster bed with white hangings, on a glorious summer morning, the little Robinson came into the world. He was a big baby, and caused Bishop some anxiety, having the cord wrapped tightly round his neck. But eventually all was well. Hester stretched, and heaved a big sigh of relief. She had not let them down; she, a Kettlewell, had done a good job and the doctor told her so. And the baby was alive!

'Doctor, is it . . . a boy?' The woman was exhausted.

The baby was carefully washed and dressed by Hester, everything was tidied up and the mother revived before Mr Robinson was allowed in, looking very shy and uncomfortable. This experience was new to him. 'Marmaduke!' he said, enraptured, holding the infant in huge hands.

'Marmaduke?' To Hester, it seemed a heavy load of a name for this scrap of an infant to carry. The new mother whispered that it was the name of a rich uncle, one who could leave the little lad some brass.

They went back to the kitchen, now full of farm men eating mutton-stew and mashed potatoes. Hester was weeping as she finished putting the cheese into the moulds. Bishop went across to her. 'You did well, my girl. Why the tears?'

'Oh, damn,' Hester said, in a whisper. 'The baby . . . when I washed him, I remembered little brother Billy. . . .' It was just the strain, she supposed.

Bishop smiled his kindest smile and said: 'Well, Hester, you have a good future ahead. You'll marry a young fellow, and have a baby of your own to care for.' She felt better for that. Maybe her dreams would come true, one day.

They were all called into the parlour for the next important business. 'You must cut the baby-cake,' said Mr Robinson firmly, handing the doctor a knife. Bishop muttered something about saving the cake for the christening, but Robinson insisted. 'A sight of good eggs and butter went into that cake.' The maid came in, wiping on her apron the dust from a bottle of home-made wine.

The proud father, some of his tension now gone, raised his glass to the light. His hand trembled a little from excitement. Hester and the maid held their half glasses expectantly and Bishop raised his glass for the toast; it was a solemn moment. How would he welcome the little stranger?

There was a short silence and then the farmer spoke. 'It's turned out clearer than I thought!' It was a splendid wine, clear and ruby-red; the bramble-wine of Garth, made from last autumn's berries and very hard to beat. Hester suppressed a giggle.

Since there had been no toast yet, Bishop produced one as he cut the cake. He looked out from the dark parlour to where the hills and valleys of the High Side soaked up the afternoon sun. 'I wish the baby good fortune. I hope,' and his voice was pitched to carry upstairs, 'that the boy Marmaduke will grow up to be the father of a large family, and so keep the doctors out of the workhouse.'

Hester smiled and sipped her wine thoughtfully, distrustful of any type of alcohol, thinking of her own future. Meanwhile, upstairs in the master bedroom, Marmaduke was taking his first drink of milk.

# CHAPTER SEVEN

As the summer went on, Hester convinced herself that one day she would marry Ned and they would go off and find a little farm together. What would happen to his wife and children was not quite clear, but apart from this, she had the future planned. All she had to do was bide her time, do excellent work, and time would solve everything. Ned wouldn't be able to live without her.

It was the sort of plan her father might have made, but for one thing. She wanted to marry for her own farm, but she also wanted Ned because she loved him. It was much more than infatuation, or physical attraction. It was true love, and much stronger than the attraction of a good farm and a wife and family.

Hester knew that it was not respectable to have a love affair with your boss, under his wife's nose. Even if it was his idea, she should have had the strength to resist. She still wanted to be respected; one day, to be honest. Sometimes, when she woke in the middle of the night, she felt guilty. Wicked. What harm had Lily Metcalfe ever done to her? She was a better person, she was the girl whom Ned loved, because Lily had helped her to better herself, when she hadn't known where to start. Lily had been patient with her rough ways, and generous with everything but money. And now she was planning to steal Lily's husband, the father of her children.

The guilty feelings lasted until she saw Ned again, and felt the healthy young blood coursing round her body, and forgot her guilt in the warmth of Ned's smile.

Hay-time came and went, the farm work following its ordered, seasonal pattern. Mrs Robinson called at Shaw's Farm one day. Proudly driven by her husband, she came to show off the new baby, and to tell cousin Lily Metcalfe how good Hester had been when the baby was born. 'It must have been five or six days she made our cheese, Lily, and nobody but me can tell the difference. That Hester'll make somebody a right good wife one day.'

'But not just yet!' said Lily firmly. 'She still swears when a cow kicks her – Kettlewell blood, you know. We're used to her little ways, but she wouldn't do for everybody. Too rough.' She poured the visitor a cup of tea.

'Well, she doesn't go after the lads – very steady for her age.' Nellie Robinson said she'd seen enough trouble with flighty maids. Taking the cup, she added: 'Never looked at our farm lads, so of course they left her alone. That was a blessing, with me upstairs and out of the way. She's a bonny enough lass . . . but very steady.'

This remark relieved Lily's mind a little. With Hester looking prettier by the day, she had been wondering whether Ned might be taken with this bright young woman. In the past she'd quietly but firmly discouraged his attentions to other females, and she believed he'd taken the hint. Lily knew she was plain, thin and not very exciting. But the farm was hers, and when it came to the point, that was why he'd married her. His part of the deal was to stay true to his wife.

Mrs Mecca was thoughtful as she washed the best china cups after the visit and put them back carefully in the cabinet. Theirs was a marriage of convenience, but Lily thought they managed to get along quite well. The only problem was that Ned's good looks and happy disposition attracted more notice than was good for him. She knew that.

Lily shook the lace tablecloth and put it away. But surely, a dairy-maid who'd just been rescued from a slum would know which side her bread was buttered on? Hester was obviously trying to better herself, she was doing well and liked the work, and she was hardly likely to risk getting into trouble. And a girl like that would know how to look after herself and keep herself nice. She was twenty, and had never been in trouble of that kind. When lasses got themselves into trouble on the High Side, it was usually when they were too young to look after themselves.

On the whole, Lily Metcalfe thought that Ned would be sensible enough. But she hadn't realized, when she went over to Hagstones to find a maid, that the lass would turn out so bonny. A plain girl would have felt safer, somehow. The original Hester, with her scowl and tangled hair, would never have caused her a moment's unease.

When Hester came in from the sheep, Mrs Robinson had gone, but she'd reminded Lily that a good worker should be looked after a little. 'We're off to Ripon market tomorrow,' she said. 'Would you like to come with us? You can look after the bairns while I buy some material, and then you can go off for an hour yourself.'

The first tinge of autumn was gilding the trees as the Metcalfes clopped down to Ripon, along eight miles of winding lanes. Ned drove with Lily beside him, and Hester was with the children on the back bench. The trap gleamed, the brasses shone, and the whole family was bright with cleanliness – and some of them with godliness. Hester wore her green dress, and with her hair neatly tied back she felt the picture of a good farm servant. Ned didn't look at her, nor she at him, but she was aware of him in everything she did.

It was good to be in Ripon's ancient streets again, to have a glimpse of town life. And to have an hour to yourself, at nobody's beck and call, was a rare luxury. Hester wandered through the stalls, enjoying her freedom.

In the middle of the bustling market-place, there was a small oasis of calm. Meg White stood at the foot of the obelisk, a basket on either side of her, the thin brown face serene. Hester watched as she quietly sold herbs to the townspeople, bunches of mint and thyme, sage and rosemary. Farmers and their wives bought salves for bruises, cough-remedies and tonics. The square was noisy with the sounds of much vigorous trade, but Meg said nothing, except to give some quiet advice when asked about herbal remedies.

Hester exchanged a greeting with Meg White and with one or two other High Siders, revelling in her holiday. She mentally added a trap and a smart pony to her list of requirements for the future life, so that she could drive out and see a few people sometimes.

Meg smiled at her. 'Now lass, you're looking bonny today. Have you seen Reuben about? He's taking me home, I hope. Ah, here he is!'

Giving her his grim look from under the cap, Reuben sighed. 'Reckon you've gotten me into a right pickle, Hester, telling me to go for the job with doctor.'

The girl was alarmed. 'Why, Reuben, I heard doctor say as it was the best thing he ever did! Don't you like it?'

The blue eyes gleamed. 'Ay, I like it right enough. But it's turning out to be for life. Bishops can't do without me – I'll never get away, to better meself.' He looked round at the crowded market-square, and then back at the girl. 'And another thing. I can tell folks nowt, these days. Everything's confidential! Where we go, doctor and me, who we see, what's up with them. And sometimes, other folks should know!'

'Well, Reuben, what would you tell me – if you could?' asked the girl mischievously.

The groom looked at her keenly. 'You're a bright lass. Well . . . I would think about going to see your old Uncle Tom up at Hill Top, if I was you. That's all.' His mouth closed in a characteristic straight line and of course, that was all.

Tom Sutton had been Hester's favourite relative when she was a child, a courtesy uncle and a kindly old man. He and Aunt Susan lived on a little holding at the top of the moor, miles from the beaten track. They had no children of their own. When she was a schoolgirl, Hester had sometimes spent the holidays up at Hill Top, but as her home life deteriorated the visits had ceased. She still thought of those weeks as the best of her childhood.

'I'll do it,' she promised Reuben. 'Soon as I can.'

On the way home Hester thought about her meeting with Reuben. It was a long walk to Hill Top from where the Metcalfes lived, and the visit would take some planning. She decided to ask Mrs Mecca, not Ned. That night, over the washing-up, she confided to Mrs Ned that she thought the old man must be ill – what else could Reuben have meant? And that she should visit.

'I thought maybe – if you don't mind – I could have a day off, it's quite a long way. Please,' she added. Good manners did not always come naturally.

Lily Metcalfe said she knew Tom Sutton, of course. 'He must be eighty, if he's a day, maybe more. I'll ask Ned if you can borrow young pony, you could ride him bareback, save you time. That way, you'll only need half a day off, and we can move some cattle in the morning.'

The next afternoon was cool and windy, with cloud low over the moor. Hill Top Farm was lost in mist above her as Hester cantered gently over the short moorland turf, riding Darkie, only just broken in and rather skittish. Ned had warned her to be careful with him.

She felt guilty that it was so long since she'd seen or even thought of the Suttons.

Aunt Susan was just as usual, gently welcoming, snowy-white pinafore over her long black dress. Uncle Tom was in bed, frail but composed.

'My time's over, lass,' he said quietly. 'Dr Bishop's been, and he agrees – me heart's winding down, that's all.'

The couple were evidently pleased to see her, exclaimed at how she had grown and how bonny she looked, and were glad that she'd been able to get away from Hagstones.

'Is there anything I can do for you?' Hester asked.

The girl sat by the bed, young and vital, exhilarated by the ride. The thought crossed her mind that you have to enjoy being young, being in love, and healthy. In the end, you'd be old and wrinkled like the Suttons. She shivered at the thought.

A light rain was falling across the moor and Hester watched rain-drops trickling down the window. The sadness of the situation came to her: Uncle Tom was dying. It was the end of his days at the farm, and another death. But this time, a gentle one.

The old man's hand, almost transparent, lay on the quilt, and Hester took it gently. 'I loved coming here when I was a bairn, Uncle Tom. You were so good to me,' she said, choking a little. 'I hate to see you like this.'

'Nay, don't be sad, love. Death is natural, y'see, we all come to it some time. . . . Yes, lass. There is summat you can do for me. I'd like to see a parson, before I go. But – which one? They never know what parish we're in, just here.'

Aunt Susan smiled. 'We went to church sometimes . . . Christmas and Easter. To whichever one we could get to – folks used to give us a ride. . . .' They were on the borders of three parishes up here, with rolling views of each, when the mist lifted.

After the inevitable cup of tea Hester mounted the pony again, and promised to try to find a parson. She didn't hold with parsons, but she had to put that aside now. And she'd better do it right away. Aunt Susan had whispered: 'Larton's nearest, you could try there.'

Lamps were being lit in the Larton cottages, and chimneys smoked in the damp air as Hester walked her pony sedately into the village on that dark and rainy summer evening.

The Reverent Grant was the parson here; she'd better try to

61

smooth down her wet hair before she knocked at the door, and tie the pony to the garden fence. Hope he's home.

Mr Grant was at home . . . he nearly always was. His hair gleamed white in the lamplight.

'And what can I do for you, my child, on this rainy evening?'

Hester spoke up. 'Visit Tom Sutton, before it's too late. You'll be burying him soon, like enough. Up at Hill Top,' she added, seeing the vicar's mystified expression.

The pale eyes grew wide. 'Oh, but it's not my parish, you know. Come. I'll show you the map.' Shuffling to the wall, Mr Grant pointed out on his map. There was the Larton parish boundary, a thick red line, with Tom Sutton for ever outside it.

'Not that I care for wordly boundaries, of course, where a soul is concerned. But it's also a matter of etiquette. We don't trespass into other men's parishes, you see. . . . It's a sin.'

Mr Grant tried again. 'I will pray for him.' He smiled at this solution, brought out a small notebook and wrote it down, and then his eyes wandered to his chair by the fire.

Hester strode out into the deepening dusk and the rain. Kexmoor was the next parsonage, on the way to Kirkby. But the Reverend Scott-Jones didn't even ask the wet little figure inside. 'Hill Top? Not my patch, I'm afraid. Please keep that pony off my lawn.' He obviously knew that peasants didn't mind the weather. Hester forgot her new manners, and blew a raspberry as she trotted away.

By the time Darkie and Hester plodded wearily into Kirkby, it was dusk. The Reverend Grimshaw, Vicar of Kirkby, warm in his study, was drinking an after-dinner coffee. He seemed amazed to see the wet and weary girl. 'Hester! What brings you here? Come and get warm by the fire – such a wet night!' It was a more Christian welcome, at least.

'Tom Sutton up at Hill Top, he's dying and he wants to see a parson. Will you go?' Hester came straight to the point.

The fire crackled in the quiet room, while Hester dripped on to the carpet. Grimshaw smiled primly, just as usual. 'Hill Top does not belong to my parish, and Tom Sutton has only rarely been to my church. But . . . I will go.' Fussing a little, he gulped down his coffee, took his hat and a big cape and prepared to face the night.

Hester smiled. 'Thank you, Vicar, it'll mean a lot to Uncle Tom.

I have to get back to my place now. Do you know the way up there to Tom's?'

'I know a farm lad who'll guide me over the moor. Bless you, Hester, it was well done.'

A blessing from a parson! She could hardly believe it.

A couple of farmers, with the violent complexions of fair Viking skins exposed to the weather, strode through Kirkby some days later. Arriving at the vicarage, they rang the bell there with some force. Hester also appeared, and Grimshaw's dragon housekeeper ushered them all into the house together.

Cuthbert Fisher and Edward Banks looked at the girl with some sympathy. 'You didn't have to come,' Cuthbert said, not unkindly.

But Hester was not to be dislodged by a couple of second cousins. 'I promised Aunt Susan.' Her mouth shut in a firm line.

Cuthbert Fisher, cap twisting in huge hands, spoke first. 'It's like this, Vicar. Sorry to intrude, but we haven't got all day. We've walked ten mile to see thee, about Tom Sutton's burying. He's our uncle, you see.' Hester nodded.

Grimshaw's face flushed, and the prim mouth tightened. 'When I have finished writing this letter, I will talk to you,' he said precisely.

'Nay, Vicar, it won't take long. We have just come to say that we'll carry the old lad along over the moor in the old way, it's more respectful. And we should be at church by three tomorrow, or a bit after. You'll have to be ready to bury him then.' Edward Banks had the unhurried, rhythmic speech of the High Side. He was not deferential, but neither was he rude. He was explaining the situation to an outsider who was ignorant of local customs, and it offended the vicar considerably.

'Thanks for going to see him,' Hester volunteered. But the vicar was not to be placated.

'You cannot dictate to me when a funeral is to be held, my good man! Tomorrow is out of the question,' said the vicar icily.

'Well, Vicar,' Cuthbert was deliberate, 'we shall fetch the old lad along in his box, like we said. We shall upend him in church porch . . . and if you're not ready when we come, you can side him yourself, whenever you've a mind. Good day.' They turned to face the door.

Grimshaw was beaten. 'Very well. Three o'clock tomorrow, don't be late.' Hester saw him reach for a diary on the desk and strike out an entry, but this was lost on the cousins as they clattered out. They hadn't waited for a reply.

Back on the street, Cuthbert turned to Hester. 'Don't you worry about coming down with us – just come to church.'

It was Hester's turn to be assertive. 'Thank you, Cuthbert, but I want to come. Uncle Tom was good to me . . . and Aunt Susan is too old to walk the way. I'll walk behind you.'

A light rain fell as the bearers eyed the coffin awkwardly at Tom Sutton's door. Their clothes were a compromise: working boots for the tramp over the moor, and shiny Sunday suits. Hester wore a black dress and a cape for the rain, borrowed from Mrs Ned. She had time off for the funeral.

The awkwardness was partly because of George, Hester could see. George was an old friend of Tom's, but since he was only five feet tall, his size didn't match that of his neighbours.

Cuthbert thought for a while. It was his job, as the oldest nephew, to do the thinking. He looked round the solemn faces and black ties. 'Which of you can tell me whether, if dip a coffin must, it should dip in front or behind?'

Nobody knew. So they put George at the front, so they could see where they were going. Boots creaked as they shouldered Tom and prepared for the long walk, the four bearers, and Hester, pale and determined, behind them.

It was the old way, the traditional moorland funeral: hard and slow, but more fitting for a man who had lived all his life on the moor, and had loved the old ways.

Hester felt a curious mixture of emotions. Sadness for Tom, regret that she hadn't seen more of him when he was alive. It wasn't that far, she could have made an effort. And also, in spite of her ungodliness, Hester felt the rightness of the slow procession, on foot across the moor, to take a moorlander to his grave.

They walked in silence for a while, each in their own thoughts. Then Edward spoke up. 'Let's have a hymn, lads – Jesu, Lover of My Soul.'

Wavering at first, but with increasing power, the men started up the old hymn.

'. . . While the nearer waters roll
While the tempest still is high. . . .'

Hester shivered as the rain clouds rolled around them and the
autumn wind carried the deep voices into the vastness of the moor.
She felt a lump come into her throat as the hymn wafted over the
heather.

'Other refuge have I none,
Hangs my helpless soul on Thee. . . .'

The moor was so vast, dwarfing all human effort.

Awed by the sanctity of the occasion, the party dwindled into
silence. On they walked, and on. When they reached the Kirkby
track, they lay down the burden reverently and stretched their arms.

Speech came back slowly; Cuthbert asked George reverently
about sheep prices. Edward looked disapproving, but Cuthbert
cheered him gently.

They picked up the coffin and plodded onwards, a little lighter in
spirit. The talk continued as they went.

As they rounded a bend, a small boy ran up to the party. 'Mother
is expecting you to step in.' The rain had settled to a steady drizzle,
and they were all wet.

Jenny Little's cottage came slowly into sight, chimneys first and
then the heather-thatched roof, which blended in with the sombre
colour of the moor. The woman came out to meet them, shawled
against the rain and with a smaller child on her hip. She held a small
posy of garden flowers, which she put gently on to the coffin as they
lowered it.

'Tom Sutton was good to us, may he rest in peace. Blessed are the
dead that the rain falls on.' It was an ancient ritual.

They crowded into the kitchen, and gathered round the low peat
fire. 'Would ye take goat's milk?' offered Mrs Little with composure, still playing her part in the ritual.

Hester was the first to react. Mrs Little had been widowed about
a year ago, and life must be hard for her. 'Nay, Jenny, we'll not take
bairns' milk. Let's have a sup of water. Best water in the district,
Uncle Tom used to say.'

So the woman brought to each of them a cup of cold water from the spring, and a piece of oatcake. Hester smiled at Jenny Little, and thought how thin and pale she looked. 'It's good of ye, Jenny . . . Uncle Tom would've been pleased.'

The woman smiled. 'He'd have been pleased to see you here today, Hester.'

Four miles on and with the rain still falling, they reached the village. When they came to the church, the lamps were lit, and the vicar was in the porch, waiting for them. Hester went to support Aunt Susan, who looked old and fragile, and there were other relatives and friends waiting in the church.

Hester was wet and weary, but she was satisfied. All was as it should be, and the job was well done.

# CHAPTER EIGHT

Josh Bell had made up his mind to leave the High Side. Without making a fuss about it, he would go away from Kirkby, his friends and relations, the little community in which he'd been born. He loved their farm and had lived there all his life, but his brother was soon to be married, and his new wife could take Josh's place.

One evening in September, Josh stood on the green at Kirkby, wondering if he'd ever play quoits with the village lads again. The scene was golden in the setting sun, and the players squinted against the light as they threw the heavy iron rings.

Josh suddenly realized how attached he was to this place and these people, his everyday world, taken for granted all his life – until now. But the misery of thinking about Hester didn't go away, although he was ashamed of so much emotion. He desperately needed a change of scene.

Then the church clock boomed the hour from the other end of the village, and Josh turned to go. It was time for evening surgery, and he wanted to see the doctor.

Josh felt his heart thumping as he walked along the village street. He'd only met Dr Bishop once, when the doctor visited his mother. Mrs Bell had liked the new medical man, but Josh was rather shy of strangers, especially professional men. He'd got into a fine sweat about seeing the family solicitor when his father died.

There were a few people waiting, but all too soon it was Josh's turn.

'I'm sorry to see you here, Josh – a fit young lad like you!' The doctor was trying to lighten the atmosphere, but Josh's gloom was settled on his thin brown face. 'What's up, then?' he said more gently.

Now for it. 'I'm . . . going to apply for the police force. In Leeds.

67

So . . . will you sign the papers and give me a character, Doctor?'

Into the silence a blackbird poured its evening song from a bush outside the window. The brief moorland summer was giving way to autumn. It was a pleasant time of year, a brief respite between the hard work of summer, and the yearly struggle against winter weather.

Leeds! The very name made Josh feel sick. But he'd heard that they were short of coppers in Leeds. And that they liked country lads, who were more resourceful than young men from the city.

Bishop seemed at a loss for a moment. 'Well, I suppose many a farmer's son has had to go out to earn a living. Farming hasn't paid so well lately.'

'Farm's doing all right.' This much Josh had to say, for the family honour. 'But I need a change. To get away.' Josh had been to Leeds once or twice, and knew that it was like plunging into a battlefield after living on the moorland. It was never quiet, it was crowded, rough and dirty.

The doctor stood up. 'Let's do the thing properly,' he said with a sigh. 'Where's the form?'

Josh produced a crumpled envelope and the doctor spread out the sheets. 'You need to pass a medical examination, of course. Name: Joshua William Bell. Occupation: farmer. Age: 22. What's next? Ah . . . character reference. "Sober, industrious, honest. . . ." '

The doctor wrote rapidly and then, pulling out a stethoscope, he approached the victim. 'Coat off, Josh, let's get on with the medical. It will need to be thorough for the police to be satisfied.'

Under Bishop's matter-of-fact approach the young man's breathing had become nearly normal. But his hands still shook a little as he replaced the shirt and jacket. The doctor smiled reassuringly. 'You'll pass, as I thought you would. Now, you have to fill in this bit, and sign the form as well.' He went to the desk and found a pen.

Josh went hot as he took the pen in one fist, and the paper in the other. The blackbird sang on heedlessly as he lumbered over to the table and spilt the ink.

Josh bent over the paper, sweating.

'You're blowing a bit for a young man – maybe you're not as fit as we thought?'

The doctor smiled, but Josh didn't think it was funny. He laid down the pen, took off his coat again, rolled up his sleeves and made a manful attack on the form. 'Oh Doctor, this writing is hard!' he groaned. 'I haven't done any since I left school!'

Bishop looked at him. 'Are you sure this is the right thing for you? To work in a big, dirty town – and to have to write on bits of paper? Policemen have to write reports and take notes, you know.'

Josh winced, but his mind was made up. 'I'll just have to get used to it.'

'But do remember – think before you go, Josh. The pavements of Leeds are hard and grey, and the tall buildings shut out the light. And the smoke hides the sun . . . you'll miss the sunset, and the trees. I did, when I worked there. City folk, too – they are different, you know.'

Josh heard him in silence, but he felt the sympathy; this was a man he could trust.

The interview was over. 'Thank you, Doctor.' Blinking back tears, Josh walked out into the evening without turning his head. He didn't see that the next patient in the queue was Hester Kettlewell.

Josh walked back to his home and lingered at their farm gate with a view over to the west, where the sun was going down over the moorland. Rabbits were popping up for the evening feed all over the slopes. At the edge of the field, where a wood climbed up to meet the skyline, a fox barked. A flight of snipe whistled over his head and looking up, he saw the evening star.

Well, the thing was done now, and Dr Bishop would post the application. If only he could have stayed, if only he could have rented a little farm and married a dark-haired lass. But Hester had changed.

The problem was that Josh had grown up first, and had wanted to plan a future with Hester. But he could see she wasn't ready for that, so he made sure they kept in touch. They saw each other in the village, at cricket and quoits matches. In winter, there was some-times skating on the pond at Thorpe.

The real pain had started when Josh turned twenty-one, a year ago. He had inherited some money, held in trust until he came of age. Not enough to buy a farm, but he could stock a rented one with care. That led to serious thoughts of marriage, and he'd never been able to imagine a life without Hester. When she held him off, and finally turned him down and, worse still, was obviously taken with Ned Metcalfe, it was like a light going out. So now he had to get away. The memory of seeing her at the fair, laughing with Ned, tormented him.

The twilight had deepened and it was absolutely quiet, as night settled on the little valley.

Squaring his shoulders, Josh set off briskly as dusk fell. The moorland breeze, warm for once, blew softly round him, laden with the scent of the flowering heather. There would have to be a survival plan.

Josh thought hard as he strode along the lane. He'd give Leeds a year or two, learn the job. He'd try to be good at it. . . .

And then, he told himself as he reached the farm track, he'd ask for a transfer to a little country police station. Not Kirkby, that would be too near home. Somewhere the other side of Pateley . . . the West Riding force covered a large area, there should be plenty of choice. And maybe, one day, he'd be able to forget Hester and find a decent wife. But the thought did not excite him.

As Josh went out, Hester also went into the surgery that night with agitation, and much on her mind.

'Ah, young Hester! What can we do for you? Is it cowpox spots, or a sprained wrist? Dairymaids often get cowpox! But Dr Jenner has proved that this is why you don't get smallpox, so that's a good thing. I have an ointment for it.' The doctor was talking fast and he looked a bit ruffled, though she couldn't think why.

Hester went straight to the point, as usual. 'I . . . I might be expecting a bairn,' she said pleasantly, with a hint of embarrassment. 'Thought I'd better come and see you, Doctor, to make sure.'

Well, that seemed to hit the doctor hard. There was total silence, while Hester bit her lip, not feeling as confident as she'd sounded.

'Oh, Hester,' the doctor said slowly, as if to gain time. He looked serious. 'If that is so, as an unmarried mother you're bound to have a very difficult time. That is, unless a marriage is likely – and the father can support you.'

She'd been trying not to think like that. Hester knew quite well that in the villages it would be impossible to live as the mother of a bastard. The scandal had killed many a girl. She remembered the sad stories she'd heard that night in Meg White's cottage. But of course, once again the moorland folk were different. There was many a bairn running round the moor who didn't know who its father was, and a lot of quite respectable folk left it rather late to publish the banns in church. But even then, a girl would need the support of her family to survive, and the Kettlewells did not function as a family should.

The outlook was bleak, to say the least, but Hester believed that Ned would marry her. Only she knew how much he loved her.

The doctor frowned, obviously worried for her, but Hester smiled and said nothing.

Bishop tried again. 'It has nothing to do with Joshua Bell, I suppose?'

He thought it was Josh! Who'd never even kissed her since they were seven! Hester was scornful. 'Josh? Wouldn't look at him. Too soft for the likes of me.' Josh's quiet persistence had become boring, especially once she knew Ned.

'What does your father say?'

That brought her down to earth, a little. 'Dad doesn't know yet. He'll play hell . . . I don't care! He wanted to marry me off to make money. I'm going to live my own life!'

The girl sat upright, with sudden energy. 'It's Ned Mecca's bairn. And I'm glad. Glad, I tell you!' Her father's violent nature flared in her face, fierce and possessive. 'That wife of his is no good for Ned. He'll want me instead when he hears about this.' She was willing it to happen; this might be a way of getting Ned for herself.

Bishop said wearily: 'Moralizing is no doubt a waste of time. But Hester, do you not realize the terrible stigma attached to children born out of wedlock? Do you really think that Ned, a staunch chapel-goer, can get rid of one wife, and she the owner of their farm, to marry another? I'm speaking frankly to you – I feel some responsibility, of course. It was my idea for you to work there.'

He loves me, the girl told herself. That's all that matters.

As Hester left the surgery Ned was going by in the trap. He had been to Thorpe for a bottle from the farrier for a sick ewe, and had left Hester at her aunt's. Rather surprised, he stopped to pick up their servant from the doctor's door. 'Does anything ail thee, lass?' He looked anxious. They couldn't very well manage without Hester now.

With a smile, she swung up beside him. 'Do you want to hear a joke?' But she didn't tell him one. She sat smiling to herself and swaying with the trap, until they were half-way over the moor. How long would it be, before the baby was born? Would it be a boy, or a girl, with Ned's bright hair and laughing blue eyes?

The setting sun lit the moors with a rosy glow, and turned Ned's hair to copper. He looked magnificent, she thought.

'I need time to talk to you.' Her face was alight with joy as she turned to him. 'Ned . . . I'm expecting your bairn! Aren't you glad! I am!' This was the final bond between them. It would mean that he belonged to her!

Ned sat in stunned silence.

A minute later he was raving, with the pony wandering all over the road. Ned was hysterical. Hester was trying to ruin him. She'd seduced him, he was only flesh and blood, flaunting herself whenever they were alone. She was a wicked woman who had tempted him to sin, at dead of night and under the warm summer sun. It was a sin, he could see it now, to lie in a hayloft with a servant-girl. He wanted nothing more to do with it.

Then Ned started to cry.

'Hester! It'll be the finish of me. The Missis will kill me! And it's her farm. . . .'

Hester was crushed. 'I was hoping that you'd come away with me and we could be together. I thought you'd be pleased! Don't you love me, Ned?' She was frightened now, and cold. An evening breeze blew chilly round them. She thought of the night the cow calved, and the weeks since then, when they had been together. His caresses had seemed like love to her. The sun sank out of sight, leaving them in a grey world where nothing would ever be the same again.

'It was a sin,' Ned kept saying. 'You tempted me with your body!'

'Sin! Temptation! You're talking like a parson!' Hester was rallying now. 'It wasn't sinful, to me. I thought it was true love, for ever. I was true to you, Ned. I was glorying in carrying your bairn. That is not sin.'

The man did not hear her. She could tell he was preoccupied with his own position, feverishly working out how to keep this from Lily.

To the girl, the realization of his attitude made the pain bearable, after all. Ned was not the man she had imagined as her hero. Meg White had been trying to warn her, that night in her cottage when the men were exposed as villains. And that night Meg had said: 'It's the women who get the blame.'

'It'll ruin my life,' Ned moaned. 'I'm beholden to the Missis. It's her farm, and she's worked and scratted to make it pay.'

So she had, thought Hester bitterly. To make brass was her chief interest in life – and now Ned was turning out to be of the same mind. 'And the bairns, I can't leave 'em behind. They need me.' He looked at her for the first time. 'Hester?'

For wild moment she thought he might change his mind. 'You can have more bonny bairns, with me.'

The farmer shook his handsome head. 'Be a good lass. Go away quietly, without saying anything, not straight away, but in good time. But don't tell who the father is. Don't ruin me, Hester. I'll try and find some brass for you . . . to get rid of it. Nobody need know.'

Silently they drove into the farmyard. Ned unyoked and led the horse away.

# CHAPTER NINE

The dark waters of the River Laver were swirling round the bridge, sucking at the stones and offering a dreadful temptation.

Hester longed to jump in, to surrender to the current, and to end all her problems at once in a final solution, down in the dark depths . . . so easy.

A chilly autumn wind stirred up the dead leaves, and dark clouds were scudding over the moorland. Hester shivered. It would soon be dusk, she'd better make her mind up.

What was there to hope for? Life as a social outcast once again, with no chance of getting away from it, this time. Hester had thrown away the chance of a normal life with the Metcalfes.

Respectability was all, at Kirkby. Most folk were loud in condemnation of immorality, which was only too evident when a bairn had no father. The mother was always blamed. And whose fault was it? Ned had seduced her, with his handsome face and laughing ways, but she could have refused to steal another woman's husband. Even though she had thought it was true love, not just Ned's bit of fun. Yes, it was partly her fault.

Hester leaned forward over the peat-stained water. The river was full, gushing down to Ripon, swollen with recent moorland rain. It would be easy to do, just a short struggle, then – nothing. Nobody would care if she disappeared; Ned would be thankful, that was all.

The girl thought of the alternative, and shuddered. Letty King, the old lass who dealt in poisons, would give her a bottle of something to rive her insides out, the unborn baby included. Did she want to do that? Or – did she want to die?

It was becoming clearer, as she gazed into the cold waters of the Laver. Now, when it was too late, Hester wanted an honest life, with a man of her own, and children she was not ashamed of. But no self-respecting farmer would marry a fallen woman. Her brief hour of happiness was over.

An honest life. The girl realized gradually that she wanted to do the right thing, to do what decent people like Reuben and Meg White would do. It was a strange time to start, she thought wryly. Was it too late to be honest?

There had been few moral standards at Hagstones, and she'd never been to Sunday school, but Josh and some of the teachers at the little Kirkby school had given her an idea of what was right. It was not harming others, and doing what felt right, inside yourself. She had been harming the Metcalfe family, and living a lie. So, what now? What was the decent thing to do?

It was time to face up to things as they were, and accept her responsibility.

It was time to turn away from the river, to go quickly back to Shaw's Farm for milking. She would not take her own life, and she had another life to think of now, in addition to her own. Hester turned her back on Larton and the dark river, and went heavily down the road.

At Shaw's Farm there was no help at all. Ned was utterly silent. It was easy to go about her work, avoiding talk, with Mrs Ned too busy getting ready for the winter to worry about the moods of a servant girl. She noticed that Hester was quieter, but that was all. There were plums to bottle, apples to lay out in the loft and many pounds of blackberry jam to boil up and put into stone jars. There were hams to cure and eggs to 'put down' in waterglass, for when the hens stopped laying. It was a busy time; but all seasons on a well-run moorland farm were busy. Work occupied most of Lily Metcalfe's thoughts.

At her home nobody had ever taken much notice of Hester, so it was easy at first to keep quiet and pretend that nothing was wrong. She dimly realized that things were getting worse at Hagstones, and that Roger had increasing problems of drink and debt.

Kettlewell must be now a desperate man, and in his more sober moments would be turning over every scheme he could invent, legal or illegal, to raise money for the rent and to keep the business going. A few more months, a good deal or two and he'd be back on his feet again. Hester knew his thinking. The alternative was ruin, to be turned out of the farm, with his family in the workhouse. He'd probably revive the idea of marrying her off . . . but that wouldn't be honest, either. It offered no solution for Hester.

Life at Hagstones was miserable, but at least it got Hester away from the Metcalfes where Ned avoided her and Lily had time only for work and the children. And she felt awkward with Lily, who had shown her nothing but kindness. She had betrayed that kindness, and all her guilty feelings were back in full force. So she walked over the moor to her home on Sundays, the walk giving her a little time to herself.

Lizzie Kettlewell had never been close to her daughter, and there was no one who could comfort her now. Sometimes Hester thought of Josh and wondered whether his despised softness was really a deep, unspoken kindness. He had always looked after her when they were at school. But she had sent him away, and this trouble was no affair of his . . . she'd be ashamed for him to know about it. Good job he'd gone off to Leeds.

Hester had no heart, either, for Kit Horner and his stories. She kept her head down when she met him on the path, on her way to Hagstones, one windy Sunday afternoon. 'We're very busy!' she muttered as they passed, hoping he wouldn't stop.

'Well, Hester, I'll walk a piece with ye. You look a mite down, lass.' Kit was obviously concerned to see her looking so troubled. His sympathy was open and genuine, and it made the girl feel worse, guiltier than ever. When they got to the boulder where she perched when talking to Kit in happier days, Hester sank down and started to sob, weary with trouble. Kit's gentleness was the last straw. But she couldn't tell him, of all people. She was too ashamed.

Kit took her by the hand. 'Nay, honey, don't fret so. Just tell me what's wrong and I'll help thee, bairn.' She could hear all the tenderness in his voice, for the children he'd never had. Hester turned away, her face tearstained and her dark hair blowing in the wind. He held her hand and waited. The feel of it was comforting to her, the feeling that one human being was concerned for her.

A raucous shout made them both turn round. 'Hester, what's to do?' Her father was riding towards them with another man, and the horses had made no sound on the turf.

Kit was embarrassed for Hester. 'Lass is upset about something, but she won't tell me about it . . .' She was unlikely to tell this coarse brute, even though he was her father. Hester said nothing, looking at Roger's black face with fear.

The other man cleared his throat and rode on a little, to distance himself from trouble. Kettlewell's domestic affairs were no concern of his.

Roger Kettlewell shot his daughter a murderous look. 'Follow me home.' She followed him silently, and Kit watched her go.

At Hagstones she was soon found out. Her mother looked at her with distaste. 'Look at your precious daughter. You can see what her trouble is! She who'd never look at a lad!'

Hester stood awkwardly at the table, head down. Her pregnancy was beginning to show.

The dealer stared for a moment, not understanding. Then the truth dawned and he glared ferociously. 'Who's the father? Not yon Kit Horner? He's old enough to be your father!' He would never understand a decent man like Kit, Hester thought, shaking her head miserably.

'Who is then?' He stood over her. 'You've been thick enough with Horner up on t'moor. I'll make you tell me!' He shook her arm roughly. There was silence apart from Hester's sobs. 'It's not Ned Mecca?'

The situation was suddenly clear. Her mother looked disgusted and turned away.

Hester blushed with shame. Gone was her pride in carrying Ned's bairn. She was like any other silly lass, falling for a handsome face and then having to pay for it. These things happened, and nobody felt much sympathy for a lass who was so foolish.

'I'll shoot him!' Kettlewell cursed and stamped in rage. 'It's an insult to the family. And I can't find you a rich husband, you're finished. You're no good to me now!'

'I don't care what you do.' Hester's head ached. She wished she'd had Kit for a father, instead of this brute.

A cheerless meal followed around the littered table, with little Susan trying to understand what had happened. Kettlewell brooded, and as he thought, he became calmer. After tea he seemed almost pleased, his ruddy face creased with a crafty expression. One problem might just solve another. Who suffered did not matter, as long as it wasn't Roger Kettlewell. Hester could see the way he was looking, and tried to guess what it might mean.

The dealer stood up and leaned on the mantelpiece, looking into the fire. 'I've thought on a plan,' he announced. He looked at Hester with his mean and cruel eyes and she knew that it would not be a kindly plan. He was quite capable of killing her, if it suited him. He'd killed her little brother, half on purpose, because he cried too much. She'd never been afraid of Roger before, having inherited his own boldness, but she was uneasy now.

'I shall father the bairn on to yon Kit Horner.' He smiled.

There was an appalled silence. No, thought Hester, not poor Kit, the truly decent man. It's not his fault. She knew better than to say anything.

'I will accuse him of seducing my darling daughter. He's soft as butter, the fool. Whole family's weak in the wits . . . he'd never stand the disgrace, and he wouldn't know how to deny it. And he has plenty of money. He shall pay me to keep my mouth shut about the bairn.' And that would pay the rent. Eighteen months of arrears, a desperate situation, thought Hester. Desperate enough to make him do such a terrible thing. What had she started, when she gave in to Ned Mecca?

The lamp guttered, and Hester trimmed it mechanically. How could she warn Kit? She would go to find him, first thing in the morning, and tell him to stand firm. That she, too, would deny the accusation. She'd never let Roger get away with it.

'He'll marry you' said Kettlewell, improving on his idea, 'and I shall get the farm. Or if not, he'll pay. Five hundred pounds it will cost to keep quiet about his disgrace. A girl half his age!' He smiled. 'We'd get nowt from Metcalfe, he has nowt. Horner's the man. He'll pay.'

'No!' shouted Hester, roused at last by her fear for Kit. She faced the big man defiantly. 'You can't blame Kit Horner. . . .'

Roger Kettlewell stood over her and raised his fist. A hard blow sent her reeling into the fire. Hester was really frightened now, but she didn't cry out, she clenched her teeth and tried to get away. Kettlewell pulled her up and knocked her across the room. Little Susan ran into the scullery, sobbing and even Lizzie went white.

Hester tried to twist out of the room and get away, but Kettlewell was sober for once, and much stronger than she was. Pushing her arm behind her back, he marched her upstairs and gave her one last kick before locking her in her old bedroom.

'There she stays,' he snarled to his cowering wife, who knew how much he enjoyed violence. 'Let her out and I'll kill you. We'll keep her here so we can control things.' He meant it. He might even kill the child.

Sitting on the bed as the evening light failed, Hester realized that she had allowed herself to be cornered. It was a dangerous situation and she'd walked right into it, risking herself and risking the baby, too. There was someone else to consider.

Hester's pregnancy had been easy so far; she was healthy and fit and had been well nourished at Shaw's Farm. And now she was bruised and scorched, but the baby should have survived the violence. It was mainly her limbs that had taken the knocks.

Instead of screaming to be let out, Hester put salve on her bruises and resolved to bide her time. But the next time she left Hagstones would be the last. She hardly dared to think about Kit Horner. Surely he would laugh, knowing that no one would believe such an outrageous story?

That was the last Hester saw of the outside world for some time. As the days passed, she realized that it was vital to Kettlewell's plan to keep her locked up, and unable to deny his version of events. He knew that she wouldn't keep quiet, she would go about shouting that Kit was innocent. Her mother said he'd sent word to the Metcalfes that the girl had gone away, to another 'place' with more money. They wouldn't be looking for her.

Ned would be most relieved, and pleased also that he didn't know where she'd gone. She couldn't expect him to send her any money.

Lily was bound to be angry, after all her efforts in training Hester and trying to keep her happy, that she could go off without a word.

The Metcalfes were worried at first, and then angry when Hester failed to come back. But then, what could you expect from a Kettlewell? And they could train another lass. Neither of Hester's employers asked questions. As Hester had guessed, Ned was profoundly thankful that she'd gone quietly.

After a few weeks of keeping very quiet, Ned began to make plans. He needed to find another woman, one who knew how to keep out of trouble, while having a bit of fun. Hester had let him down badly, allowing herself to get pregnant like that. And expecting him to marry her! She must be off her head.

A young married woman with an old husband would be ideal. Ned didn't intend to go without his pleasure for long, but he'd have to be more careful in future. Maybe he'd look round for a bit of land to rent, so there was an excuse to travel about. . . .

Lily had her own suspicions, which she kept to herself. There was no point in disrupting the family harmony now that the lass was gone. But if she found out that the little hussy had been after her Ned, Lily would make sure that she never got another place. She wouldn't blame Ned; men would be men after all, and it was the women who led them astray.

Lily just hoped it was Josh Bell who had been led astray. Hester might have met him on Sunday afternoons, up on the moor, out of sight somewhere. And Josh Bell had rushed off to join the police in rather unseemly haste, folks thought. The Methodist ladies had reported that his family couldn't really explain it.

Mrs Metcalfe set about finding the plainest, homeliest lass from last year's school-leavers, and one from a God-fearing, church- or chapel-going family, to be the new dairymaid.

On the first day of her imprisonment Hester woke to a clear, sunny autumn morning, the sort of day she loved. Waking in the old familiar room took her back to her childhood. There might be some mushrooms in the horse paddock. She scrambled out of bed, and then she felt the full weight of her imprisonment. Hester went wild, hammering on the locked door, sobbing, screaming. She was desperate to get out into the fresh air.

Nothing happened. The house was quiet, unresponsive when Hester stopped to listen. The walls were of thick stone and nobody could hear her. Then she heard the clatter of hoofs on the cobbles of the yard, and ran to the window. Leaning out, she saw her father, mounted on his big black mare. The horse was thin and scraggy, but on it the man looked intimidating.

Seeing Hester, her father stopped under the window. 'Best get your wedding-dress ready, woman,' he shouted. 'I'm off to tell Kit Horner he must marry you next week!' He laughed, dug in his heels and took off, out of the yard and on to the open moor. And the girl was left to agonize, imagining what would happen next. Would Kit laugh at the preposterous idea? Not many people laughed at Roger Kettlewell and got away with it.

There was a heavy dew, and mist lay on the hills. Spiders' webs hung jewelled in the heather, sparkling in the sunshine. Hester could follow the track in imagination, and work out where Kit and her father might meet.

Kit's dog would see the horse coming, and would growl – Roger had that effect on most dogs. The sparkle would go out of the morning then for Kit. Would he ever get over it? Hester could see the scene as if she were part of it. She was weeping when Lizzie brought up some breakfast for her.

'Now, Mr Kit Horner.' Kettlewell stared down from his gaunt mare at the shepherd, using all the advantage of a mounted man against one on foot. It enhanced his air of intimidation. He went into the attack straight away. 'Maybe you've an inkling of my business, but I'll inform you right away. You have gotten my lass into a sore mess.' He was the injured father, coarsely aggressive.

Kit stared up at the man in astonishment. He looked at the fierce black beard, the slit eyes and the cruel mouth. His first feeling was one of sympathy for Hester. What a man to have as a father!

'But I never found out what her trouble was,' he said reasonably.

Spittle appeared and the corners of Kettlewell's mouth. 'You know quite well, Horner, she's to have a bairn. Maybe you won't admit to being the father, to taking advantage of a young lass. Too much disgrace for the Horner family quality!' He mouthed the words in derision. 'But look here,' and he leaned down from the horse, 'you must either wed the lass, or pay me five hundred pound to lap job up.'

So it was blackmail. Kit stood quite still.

'You may well stare.' The big man was venomous. He was coming to believe in his own lies. 'You can't get out of it. Over many folks have seen you together on the stones yonder. Joplin's a witness, the other day you were holding her hand when we came up.'

'What about Hester?' Kit watched a plover strut across the turf. 'She knows it's a lie.' Surely Hester would clear his name? His hand went to his head.

'Hester?' Kettlewell shouted. 'She swears the bairn is thine. Now take note: I give you a week to chew it over and make up your mind. You must get asked in church, or you must pay.'

Kettlewell went away, leaving Kit Horner devastated.

The moors were vast, impersonal and bleak, to a man as hopeless as Kit was then. They increased the feeling of depression. One day Kit did not return home from checking the sheep, and his sisters set out to look for him. They met Reuben, returning to Kirkby after delivering medicine. The groom sent the women home, and promised to go out with a search party. He had always liked Kit, and he thought it might be a case of injury.

Two gamekeepers, summoned from their suppers, went up the moor with Reuben as dusk was falling. They thought the shepherd might have broken his leg. 'Rabbit holes are dangerous,' they said. It was Reuben who spotted the still figure in the heather, with a shotgun at his side. Kit had taken the only way out that he could.

Reuben's face was wet with tears as they carefully lifted Kit into the trap for the homeward journey. It was all too obvious that a doctor would not be needed. Kit's troubles were over.

# CHAPTER TEN

'What's going on, Mother? Tell me, while Dad's away . . .' Hester begged, after a few days of isolation. She did not think the news would be good.

Lizzie shook her head. 'Kit Horner's dead . . . accident with a gun.' Hester sat with her face in her hands.

'Your dad's taken over Kit's farm.' Her mother spoke in a frightened whisper. 'Old sisters are over the moor somewhere, he said he'd look after them.'

There was a long silence while Hester wondered if she could ever be free of guilt. Kit Horner's death was her fault.

At last Lizzie got up to go downstairs, and in a more normal voice she said that Roger was in a better mood lately, and had money. Folks were busy getting ready for the winter.

'Let's have a fire, Mam, it's freezing!' Hester said as the weather grew colder. And Lizzie made sure then that there was a fire in the little bedroom grate, a fire which warmed Hester and cheered the room. It made all the difference.

At first the baby was not mentioned. But one day the girl said gently: 'I'd like to make some clothes for the bairn. Can you get me some stuff?'

Lizzie brought her material, needles and thread, and some wool and knitting-needles. For a pattern, she had a few baby clothes; poor little Billy had had few clothes in his short life. Lizzie shed a few tears for Billy when she saw what Hester was making. The lass had learned to knit at school, with all the other girls, and now it was going to be useful.

For a few weeks Hester hated herself; then she realized that she'd have to come to terms with the past. Some of the blame was Ned's, as well as hers.

A decent life in the future came down to finding somewhere to go, where she could bring up the baby safely, away from bad influences. She would make sure that her little one was taught the difference between right and wrong, and she intended to keep it far away from Roger Kettlewell.

But when it came to future plans, there was a blank wall. Hester couldn't imagine where she could go or what she could do. She'd have to earn a living, of course, and now she certainly had skills to offer – though mainly farm skills, only suitable for the country. And if Mrs Mecca got wind of what had happened, there wouldn't be a job for Hester within fifty miles of Kirkby, she was sure.

Thirty odd miles away, in another world, Josh was also coming to terms with living in a small room, with not much hope of escape.

It was impossible to ignore the feeling of being trapped. The dull roar of the city came though the window, instead of the moorland breeze. His lodging-house was close to the railway station, with all its clanking, hissing, roaring monsters. He could see a patch of sky, but no stars – the gaslights hid the stars. There were imposing buildings in the city centre, but to Josh they seemed pompous and unfriendly.

Even the sun was hazy in Leeds, a smoky city sprawling by the River Aire, in a valley which collected the fumes from industry and harboured them lovingly. Josh soon realized that the more successful mill owners, making money in Leeds, went to live at Ilkley, high up on the Pennines where the air was pure.

As lodgings went, it was quite good – the police-sergeant had recommended it. 'There's a bonny daughter, too,' he said with a wink.

The tall countryman was rather too quiet for the Leeds folk, but he tried to fit in. Mrs Ackroyd was pleased to get a policeman for a lodger, as being more respectable than a travelling salesman. Widows had to be careful what type of men they took in, she explained to PC Bell.

The room was clean enough, but dingy with city smoke. It was lit by a spluttering gas-mantle, which shed a greenish, depressing light. There was a narrow iron bedstead, a washstand, and a wardrobe. A wooden chair stood before the fire, and Josh asked for a small table. He wanted to practise his writing.

Life settled down into a humdrum round after the first anguish of leaving home had subsided into a settled melancholy. Josh's summer suntan faded, and soon he looked more like a 'Leeds loiner' as the locals were called, although he was taller than most of them. He found that his height was an advantage in the force, giving him a slight air of authority from the start. Senior police predicted a bright future for him. They told him he was intelligent, but too quiet. And he needed to improve his writing.

So now Josh's world was this little room, and the grey streets of Leeds, where he learned how to break up fights, apprehend pick-pockets and give strangers directions. During the day he concentrated fiercely on learning the job. But off duty, his thoughts strayed back to the moorland, and to Hester.

Josh often dreamed about Hester. Sometimes, they were children again, playing in the beck. Once, he dreamed about walking with her, hand-in-hand, on the moorland in the evening light, with the moor wind blowing round them. Then he woke to the little room in Leeds, and he could feel his heart lurch down like a stone, a physical ache as he came back to reality.

For writing practice, Josh copied out passages from the police manual, which also helped him to learn procedures. For light relief, he read the *Yorkshire Post*, with increasing ease as the weeks went by. This gave him some idea of life in the West Riding.

One evening Sarah Jane brought him a bucket of coal, and caught him at the table, writing. She stopped to talk, and Josh though how little and thin she was to have carried such a heavy bucket up the stairs. 'I can do that for you,' he said.

Sarah Jane smiled at him, transforming her small, rather ordinary face. This was Mrs Ackroyd's daughter, only seen in glimpses until now. He noticed that she had grey eyes, peering though mousy hair. 'You can't let lodgers carry their own coals. Got a lot of paper work?' she asked.

Josh confessed that he was trying to improve his reading and writing, for the new job, and that his life as a farmer had not prepared him for desk work. Those clear grey eyes made him say more than he normally would.

'The Mechanics' Institute has books that would help you,' she suggested. 'I'm a teacher, I go there sometimes. Would you like to go down there with me?'

Sarah Jane got him to talk about his interests, and seemed to want to help him. Josh said he liked birds and missed the moorland birds in the city.

One chilly evening they went together to the Mechanics' Institute, a huge building, imposing, a world away from the little Institute they were so proud of at Kirkby. The girl trotted along beside him. She was only half his height, and talked quickly, in the way they had in Leeds.

Sarah Jane found him books about birds. At first, Josh was shy with her; she was a teacher, she'd be far better educated than he was. But the books drew them together. They fascinated him, and opened up a new world of learning. Country folk were always on the look-out for unusual things in the natural world, learning from nature. Josh now realized how much you could learn from books about nature, his abiding interest. For a little while it took away the ache of homesickness.

The job itself he found interesting, although the roughness and cruelty in the slums disgusted him. Josh had a good memory. He could memorize the law, and remember people, too. Firm but tolerant, he had the makings of a good policeman. He knew that. His big drawback was that he felt miserable for most of the time.

Winter came to Leeds with an icy touch and the air grew, if anything, thicker. Josh's mother sent him some woollen underwear, with a letter to say that she missed him. He would have to go back to see her, come the spring. She also sent him bits of news; Mabel and his brother Elijah were planning their wedding; and Hester Kettlewell had disappeared. All the old ache came back for Josh when he read that. Where had she gone, and why? He didn't like to think of the implications.

Sarah Jane was undemanding, she was gentle and seemed to like his company. Josh found himself spending more of his leisure time with her. It relieved the loneliness a little; he could talk about his mother to her, and some of his old life. They sometimes went for walks, but most of their outings were to the big library or the Mechanics' Institute.

'What's the point of reading stuff that isn't true?' Josh demanded one evening. Sarah Jane was trying to take his education a step forward, but Josh was resisting. As they walked down to the

Institute through a thick Leeds fog, he looked down at his small companion. 'Police stuff's useful, yes, bird books are good, but I can't see the use of stories that somebody makes up.'

Josh's duties at the police station were getting easier, and he no longer sweated quite so much over the paper work, although he still preferred to be out on the beat. He managed to keep fit because of the amount of walking he did through city streets. But the air was foul, and he pined for the fresh air of the moors.

Sarah Jane laughed up at him, her face almost invisible beneath a winter hat. 'You can learn a lot from stories, Josh. About people, and about places you've never seen.'

Josh continued to disagree, in a lighthearted way, as they went up the steps of the building. He followed Sarah Jane as she led the way to a different section and waved her tiny hand across the shelves of novels. 'There you are! Mark Twain can take you to America! Kipling to India, Zola to France. . . . Where would you like to go?'

Josh laughed. 'Let's pick Africa, there's some pretty ferocious animals there – and birds, too! Those vultures! But I'd rather read a true story, maybe one of the explorers, or a missionary, even. It's dangerous in Africa, but they must have a grand time! And it's all true!' He'd been reading extracts from a traveller's memoirs, in the *Yorkshire Post*.

Sarah Jane's eyes suddenly filled with tears, which rolled down her cheeks, making her look young and vulnerable. Overcome with pity, Josh put his arms round her and gave her a hug. 'What's the matter, love?' he asked gently.

The girl hid her face in his coat and clung to him for a moment, then gently moved away. 'Sorry, Josh, it's . . . nothing.' She repaired her face with Josh's handkerchief, then shook her hair back and led him along the stack to a different section. 'Let's get on with your education, my boy!' She sounded just like his old school-teacher at Kirkby School. 'Maybe you'd like biography – or science?'

Josh stopped at a shelf labelled Agriculture. 'Fancy seeing farming in here!' He selected a book about sheep improvement and sat down to look at the engravings.

'You're a real country lad, I can see.' Sarah Jane sighed a little. 'I don't think you'd ever settle down in Leeds. . . .'

Heaven forbid, thought Josh, standing up.

The fog swirled even thicker as they left the building, reducing the streetlamps to a fuzzy glow. 'Good job you're a policeman!' said his companion brightly. 'Or we might get lost!' They laughed, because Josh still didn't know his way around the city half so well as did Sarah Jane.

Josh glanced down at the girl as they walked along, thinking that there was a lot about her he didn't quite understand. Maybe he wasn't very good with women. . . .

Mrs Ackroyd was waiting for them rather anxiously. 'It's a terrible night! Come into the kitchen for some cocoa.'

Soon Josh was sitting by the kitchen fire with a steaming mug in his hand, feeling warm both inside and out.

'I'm glad our Sarah has company to go down to the Institute,' said her mother comfortably, when the girl went to take off her coat. 'It's dangerous enough out there on a dark night . . . as I suppose you'll know, being a policeman.' She obviously approved of a police escort for her daughter.

'Ay, there's been a few thefts and bag-snatchings lately, not to mention fights,' Josh agreed. And he thought back to an incident the previous week, when a thief had nearly knifed his colleague.

Jim had given the credit to Josh in his report, and he asked the recruit how he'd done it. 'That was pretty quick work, lad.'

'Well,' said Josh with a grin, 'We used to breed bulls at home . . . you had to keep eyes in the back of your head. They could be dangerous – just like these alley rats!'

Sitting in Mrs Ackroyd's warm kitchen, Josh also remembered how, in the moment of the attack, he'd thought about Hester with part of his mind. He could hear her saying, 'Hit the bugger, Josh!' just as she used to do in school fights. How different from the dainty, demure Sarah Jane. And how he still missed Hester, swearing and all.

Then Sarah Jane came back, and Mrs Ackroyd looked over her cup at him benignly. 'Mr Bell, we were were wondering — would you like to take your dinners with us? When you're not on duty, of course.'

Both women looked at him and Josh blushed a little. 'It might be less lonely for you,' said Sarah Jane.

'Call me Josh, Mrs Ackroyd, please. Yes, it would be good to eat my dinner with you.'

Until now, Josh had dined in lonely state in the parlour, as lodgers usually did. It seemed as though he was being promoted from 'lodger' to something else. Paying guest, maybe?

'That's settled, then.' Mrs Ackroyd got up stiffly and collected the empty cups. She was inclined to stoutness, but was obviously a hard worker. 'We can all eat in the parlour.' She gave him a friendly smile as she moved towards the sink.

He'd been lucky to find these lodgings, they told him so at work. He enjoyed Mrs Ackroyd's dinners, good simple Yorkshire cooking with stews and pies during the week and the lightest of Yorkshire puddings, followed by roast beef, on Sundays. And she made a good apple-pie.

That night, as Josh laid out his uniform ready for work the next day, he felt less isolated. He'd been lonely since the train had steamed out of Ripon station, dragging him from the old life. But tonight, he felt more like he'd always felt at home, part of the community. That was something he had taken for granted, at home on the moorland.

Over the next few weeks Josh began to feel like one of the family at the Ackroyds. His work was becoming easier as he got used to it, and he was trusted to do more on his own. But he still missed the country. The air, the water were not the same. And the people . . . he still missed Hester.

Settling down to make the most of his life, Josh could not be quite at ease. He began to worry about the Ackroyds' friendliness. What exactly was he getting into? The young man found Sarah Jane quite appealing, and he enjoyed her company. But did they see him as a suitor? And what did that mean, for him? He wanted to get married, some day. . . .

As he walked with deliberate tread about the beat, Josh pondered his situation. The lodgings suited him, and the companionship was just what he needed. But was it fair to get closer to Sarah Jane?

# CHAPTER ELEVEN

For years afterwards, people remembered the winter of 1895, the winter when Hester was a prisoner in the stone fortress of Hagstones, on the lonely moor. It was the worst winter for a century.

'Nine months winter and three months cold weather,' was how the moorlanders usually described their climate, and when they went down to the milder Vale of York they said they were 'mafted' in their thick woollen clothes. But this winter was severe, even by their standards. In the worst winters the shy moorland birds came to the farms and cottages for food. And this was one of the worst; Hester saw them from her window, old friends, and threw them scraps of bread. They looked bigger than usual, feathers fluffed up against the cold.

The first snow of winter fell with mixed blessings on the High Side. Cottages and farms, even Hagstones, looked almost pretty under a white thatch, and Hester remembered how down in the villages children lugged out their sledges. She and Josh had loved sledging. The moors gleamed under the moon with a strange beauty, but Hester shivered and thought of the long ordeal of winter, the sickness and death that would stalk them until the spring.

Hester looked out of her bedroom window at the snow, and felt utterly discouraged. Her last chance of escape from Hagstones was gone now. She could just see across the moor to the little wood near Larton. The village was about four miles away, but for ever out of reach. She was always locked in.

Lizzie wasn't sure what Roger intended to do, but letting her go wasn't an option. In the bedroom Hester stayed, and as the weeks ran into months, she would have gone mad, but for her will to survive. She had tried the trick of hanging a sheet from her window, as they had done at the Robinsons', but nobody noticed. The farm was too far from the road, and such was Roger's reputation that even fewer people went there these days.

The knitting and sewing helped to make time pass for Hester. It also made the thought of a baby seem more real. She now thought of the baby as a person, a boy or a girl. She kept the little boots and caps in an old pillow-case. She would have someone of her own to love . . . but what sort of a life would they be able to lead together? She knew that most lasses in her situation had to give their babies away, so that they could earn a living to survive.

Always, Hester came back to the idea of getting away, for the baby's sake, before it was born. She did not trust Roger at all. He had no compassion; he might kill the baby, cover up tracks and try again to sell her to a rich old farmer.

Hester was always trying to think of a safe place – but where could she go? She made a warm woollen dress for herself, just in case there was a chance of escape. Her mother, after a trip to Ripon market, had told her that Josh Bell was doing well as a policeman in Leeds. There was nobody to help. Reuben would have done his best to get her out, but Reuben wouldn't know where she was, and she wouldn't want him to take the risk of being shot.

And now – the snow. Footprints would be seen and could be followed, and it was very tiring to walk in deep snow. It was also dangerous; if you lost your bearings and wandered into a drift you wouldn't be found until spring. Quite a few moorlanders had died that way. Her mind went round, but she reached no conclusions. Except that, if ever they left her door open, she would run for it.

Apart from the lack of exercise, Hester felt quite well. It was a mercy that Roger left her alone, and she hadn't been beaten since the night he locked her up. She tried to do a few exercises, but her muscles felt weak as never before. Hester had always been vigorous, active, used to walking long distances and carrying heavy weights. Now she was cramped up in one room, and she desperately missed her freedom.

The calm at Hagstones was bound to end sooner or later, Hester thought. And one night, the peace was broken. She was sewing by the light of a fat candle, smuggled upstairs by her mother. She was supposed to be making do with tallow-dips. The snow was falling softly outside, piling up gently against the stone walls.

Hester shuddered, as she heard a sudden commotion downstairs: arguments, blows, screams. Her mother's voice, crying: 'You can't do that!' It was nothing new. She had often wondered why her mother didn't leave, get away from Roger and take little Susan with her. But now she understood; there was nowhere to go. By the nature of their lives the Kettlewell women were without friends.

The clatter of her father's boots on the stairs made her jump up in alarm. He was coming upstairs, fast, a little drunk, but not too far gone to inflict damage. Hester was expert at reading her father from the sound of his voice, his footsteps and the way he closed a door. Tonight, she judged he would be at his most dangerous. She grabbed a pillow and held it in front of her. The baby must be protected at all costs.

The door was unlocked and burst open, and her loving parents came in. Her mother was crying. Hester hadn't seen her father since her imprisonment, and he looked meaner than ever. He was better dressed and fleshier, she noticed, trying to keep calm.

Roger came brutally to the point, without a greeting. He looked at his daughter with open dislike. 'The bairn has to be got rid of. I'll not wear the expense of bringing up another brat, nor the shame of a bastard.' His mouth shut with a snap.

So the worst was going to happen. Hester's heart sank, as the man went on shouting. He left her in no doubt of his intentions.

Kettlewell made it clear that he no longer needed Hester as a source of income right then, but he didn't want to be saddled with her keep. He might match her up with a rich man later on, of course. For now, she should go away into service in a big town, as far away as possible, and without talking to the neighbours. But she would only be employable without a child.

'Take this, it'll do the job. Get rid of it.' He was shouting, working himself up into a rage. Worse still, he was half-sober, as she'd thought. 'Go on, you fond bitch. You got yourself into trouble, now get out of it.'

Hester backed away, hands in front of her, shrinking from the black bottle her father held. Lizzie sobbed. 'It'll be for the best, you'd be better off without a bairn. Mebbe get another place. This stuff will do it, Letty King made it . . . herbs and such.'

Lizzie knew about the baby-clothes, the hopes for a better life. Hester looked to her for help, but she could see that Lizzie had no fight left. She'd already taken a beating before they came upstairs, Hester could tell by the red weals on her face. She was trying to tell her that the best hope for Hester was to get away from the place, on any terms.

'No! I won't kill my bairn!' Hester was pale, but with fire in her eyes.

Kettlewell was a big man, and far stronger than the women. He flung his daughter down on the bed and pinned down her arms, motioning Lizzie to force her to drink. But Hester moved her head away, and they could not make her take the poison. She could see his black beard, menacingly above her and she felt suddenly sick.

Hester held out, moving her head this way and that, pleading with her mother. 'Don't make me take it. Don't.'

The dealer paused, his grip tightening painfully. Then he thought of another way. He let her go, took a coal from the fire with the tongs and applied it to her mother's arm in one swift move. Lizzie screamed, and Hester looked at the ugly burn.

'Drink it, Hester,' her mother begged.

The liquid was thick and very bitter, but she had to swallow it, then. If she didn't, her mother would be burned to death. The stuff would kill the child, she had no doubt. The King woman was well known for getting rid of unwanted pregnancies.

Hester gagged on the bitter taste, but far worse was the bitter thought that she would lose the baby. A little life was over, before it had begun.

Then, when it was too late and the draught was swallowed, Lizzie turned on her husband and told him what a monster he was. Hell was too good for him. She was obviously in terrible pain from the burn, but Kettlewell ignored them both and went straight out of the room. Lizzie followed him, still yelling. And for the first time, the door was left unlocked.

Hester was retching, but she noticed the unlocked door.

What advice would Dr Bishop give? He would tell her to try to get rid of the poison. Putting her finger to the back of her throat, she succeeded in bringing up of some of it. Then she had a drink of water, pulled on a cloak and took the bag of baby-clothes. It was risky, but she might get away. While there was still uproar, with her mother crying and shouting, small sounds might not be heard. Was Lizzie doing it on purpose? It was possible. Surely, her mother would want her to escape, even though she would suffer for it.

Hester let herself quietly out of the side door and walked out shakily into the snowy landscape. She felt unsteady and weak, but the cold air revived her a little. Terrified that she would be caught and hauled back, she went through the farmyard.

An owl hooted, and a faint moon showed her the farm lane, where she kept to the trodden snow, so as not to make new tracks. The snow had almost stopped, but a few flakes were still falling; they would hide her footprints. Hester wrapped the cloak more closely round her, and shivered. Her beloved moorland seemed hostile tonight. She might die out there on the moor, and sink into a bog, like the man Kit Horner had described.

A little further on, and Hester told herself not to think about death. A strong young lass could walk a mile or two in the snow, even though she was pregnant. Cheered on by her own will power, she made good progress for a while, and there was silence from the farm behind her. They hadn't noticed her absence, yet.

Then the snow began again, more heavily this time. Soon the moon was blotted out by a driving white blanket, and the distant village disappeared.

A violent pain began to grip her. Would the potion work so soon? The baby would die, and part of her would die with it. But in spite of everything, Hester had decided to survive. She would live to spite him, to spite the Metcalfes.

Should she go back to Hagstones? That would be defeat, but it might save her life, so she could try again another day. But Hester realized that this was probably her only chance. They were not likely to leave the door open again. Roger might keep her there, shut up for years, until he could make money out of her. There was no going back.

The snow thinned for a moment, the shower whirling away over the moor, and she saw the cottage lights of Larton, winking through the dark night. That was the direction to take and she would try to keep to it. Maybe Meg White would help her ... she lived at Larton.

The thought of Meg White and her peaceful cottage was a comfort to the girl, of sorts. But it would be humbling to have to go to her, to ask for help and to admit her folly. Those calm blue eyes would see right through her, see her selfishness for what it was. And then, it might put the old lass in danger. Best to leave her alone.

Hester plodded on, trying to think clearly in spite of the pain. Roger Kettlewell had a long arm, and most of the moorlanders wouldn't risk his anger by helping her. None of the neighbours would dare take her in. Who, in all the High Side, would be strong enough to stand up to him? Only the doctor, but he was at Kirkby, a few miles the other side of Larton. It would be hard in her present condition, but she'd have to try.

The snow made the world unfamiliar, the well-known landmarks became hidden. Hester's muscles were unused to walking, and she soon started to ache. Weak and ill, the pain in her belly getting worse, she went on. She was chilling rapidly in the wet snow, which was getting deeper. Her feet were sore from wet boots.

Her determination drove her on for a while, but after an hour of struggling along, Hester could walk no more. She had to give in, to lie down and sleep. What was there to live for, anyway? It was too late to try to save the bairn, she was sure. The struggle was over, and her tired muscles relaxed. She was relieved to have given up; she'd tried, but it was too much. By now, she had no idea where she was; the driving snow blotted out any signs of civilization.

As she sank into the snow she stumbled on a gatepost and realized dimly that there was some sort of shed in front of her. Her feet rustled on dry straw as she dragged herself in. She fell in a heap. As Hester slipped into oblivion, she thought that a small furry body crept up beside her, and warmed her hands.

The snow fell relentlessly, filling up her tracks. Soon there was no trace of Hester's journey, only the smooth, crisp snow.

# CHAPTER TWELVE

Hester surfaced from some deep unconscious state and opened her eyes. It was getting light. Above her was a concerned face, peering down; a narrow face with a beard. It wasn't Roger, thank goodness – the eyes were benign. It must be a dream. It was bitterly cold, but there was warmth at each side of her. With an exhausted sigh, she went to sleep.

Some time later Hester was awakened by a light hand on her arm. This time the light was brilliant, sun reflected from snow. She felt dizzy and sick, and through blurred vision she saw a woman bending over her. The woman spoke, and it was Meg White.

'Hester, love, whatever's happened?'

The girl struggled to sit up. There was something most important that she must remember. 'My baby! I mustn't lose my baby!' She tried to stand up, and fell over. Then she was violently sick.

Afterwards, Meg could never remember just how she managed to half-drag, half-carry Hester into the cottage. Hester herself remembered very little of the next week or so. She was extremely ill, drifting in and out of consciousness, tended with loving care by Meg White, in a little bedroom under the eaves. The snow continued to fall, and they were cut off, in a world of their own.

As soon as she became able to think clearly, Hester was anxious. 'My dad'll be after me, he'll kill you if he finds me here!'

Meg laughed quietly. 'Roger won't find you, my lass. Nor will anybody else, for a great while. The roads are all blocked; it'll take weeks for the road gangs to clear them. Hagstones will be cut off for a while after that. Time enough for you to have gone to Australia!'

The herbalist had guessed most of Hester's story, and she judged that the lass needed quiet, rest and cheerfulness. So she made light of her problems, and talked about the wonderful fact that the baby had survived. It was still there, and alive. Hester could feel it moving. A small miracle.

Once allowed out of bed, Hester sat by the fire with Meg. There were gaps in her memory that she wanted to fill. 'Meg, how did you know I was out in that shed?'

'Blackie here, he came to the door and scratched and mewed, so I went out to see what the problem was. And there you were, with Bonny the goat sitting beside you. I reckon that goat'd kept you warm, all night. She's a wise old goat, and Blackie's a very clever cat.'

Bonny the goat! That was the owner of the bearded face in the night, looking down at her with concern.

Gradually, Hester told Meg what had happened, simply and clearly, with no excuses. 'I've made mistakes, but I hope I've learned to do better,' she said, stroking the black cat as he sat beside her chair.

Meg suggested that Hester should stay with her until the baby was born. She could keep hidden if they had visitors, although that wasn't likely for some time.

It was Meg's quiet time of the year. In winter she prepared salves and potions from the herbs and fruits she'd gathered all summer and autumn. There was no chance of getting out to Ripon market, to sell her herbs, so she had less work than usual. But there were hens and the goat to care for, and fuel for the fire to fetch in from the shed. Simple tasks, made much harder by the snow.

Gradually, after a few weeks, the snowdrifts began to melt under a watery winter sun. The road gangs made valiant efforts, and one day they dug through to Larton and past Meg's cottage. They were connected with the world again.

On the Sunday after this, Meg and Hester had just finished their Sunday dinner of ham, dried peas and potatoes when Meg looked out of the window and saw Reuben coming up the path. In his hand he swung a brace of rabbits by the legs.

'Will you see Reuben?' she asked Hester quickly, as he knocked at the door.

The girl didn't hesitate. 'I won't hide from my friends,' she said. But she blushed for shame as Reuben came in. She dreaded his judgement of her stupidity in getting pregnant without a husband.

Reuben came in, grim-faced as usual, taking off cap and boots at the door. 'Just brought a coupla rabbits for you to have some fresh meat . . .' Then the blue eyes shone when he saw Hester. 'Why, Hester lass, it's good to see you. I thought you was lost, for sure.'

Hester realized that the little man had come over to see Meg, walking from Kirkby on his half-day off, to make sure she was surviving the winter. It was a cruel time for older folks, and hard and lonely for widows who lived alone.

Meg went off to put the rabbits in the cold pantry, and Reuben winked at Hester, in the old way. She smiled back gratefully. 'It's grand to see you, Reuben, though I could wish to be in better circumstances!'

Over cups of tea and the best fruit cake, kept for special occasions, Reuben admitted that he'd been upset when Hester disappeared. 'They said you'd gone off to another place. My, but Mrs Mecca was mad! But I couldn't just think that you'd go without a word to me . . .' He didn't finish. Reuben had in fact wondered whether Roger Kettlewell had killed his daughter.

Tears came into Hester's eyes. She had some good friends after all. Reuben could see her condition, she was huge by now, but he was exactly the same as he'd always been.

Pouring them second cups of tea, Meg asked casually: 'Any news, Reuben?' Hester knew she was now strong enough to stand it. They had no idea what the news might be, but any mention of the Kettlewells was disturbing.

Reuben must have felt the same. He paused before answering, then looked at Hester. 'Happen you won't want to know about it.'

The girl was pale but steady as she said: 'If it's about Dad, it can't be worse than what I know about him. What's he been up to now?'

The groom flexed his arm. 'Took a shot at us, that's what he did,' he said grimly. 'Through boss's hat – and through my arm.' He actually grinned. 'I'm going to live though, to spite him.'

'Reuben!' Hester felt the old familiar churn of apprehension. 'Tell us all about it.'

Looking at Meg first for permission, the groom began: 'Well, it was before the snow, when two chaps from Bradford came to see boss . . . he actually asked me in, to hear what they had ter say.' Reuben was proud of his place in the medical team, but he'd never been invited to a conference before.

The men were Jim Ashworth, Kit Horner's nephew and heir to Horner's estate, and his solicitor. Plump city men, asking the boss to put his life on the line.

Their story was bleak. Kettlewell had locked up Ashworth's frail, elderly aunts in a remote farmhouse, and was using their money. He blamed Kit Horner for violating his daughter, and there was nobody to deny it. Kettlewell was managing their farm for his own ends. And the only way to rescue the aunts, as far as Ashworth's solicitor could see, was to have a doctor to certify them insane.

'I wouldn't have them locked up, of course, they're harmless enough,' the nephew had said, as if to reassure Bishop. 'But if we could get them out, officially, with police if necessary . . . then I could set them up in a little house in Ripon, with some decent body to take care of them.' He was, of course, trying to get Roger Kettlewell away from them before all his inheritance was gone.

Hester sat with her face in her hands, appalled. The chain of events was clear, all leading on from her selfish affair with Ned. Her pregnancy had caused Kit's death, the destruction of the Horners' peaceful family life, and possibly the insanity of his sisters . . . Kit's death had tipped them over the edge. She was also responsible for putting the doctor and Reuben in great danger, it seemed.

'So you had to go in . . . and doctor had to certify them?' Hester looked up as he paused. She must know what happened.

'Ay. Well, we knew PC Brown had been chased off with a shotgun when he went up there . . . so I worked out when Roger and his lads would be out of the way. Killinghall Fair day, it had to be. . . .'

Bishop had asked rather tartly why Dr Johnson, his more fashionable rival, wasn't handling this case, and Reuben hid a smile when the Bradford men admitted that Johnson had already declined to help them.

So, one wet day, Bishop and Reuben had taken the trap to a spot off the road, hidden it in a ruin, and crawled along wall bottoms to get to the place where the Misses Horner were imprisoned. They couldn't afford to be seen against the skyline, even though they thought Kettlewell was away. He might have left a man on guard duty.

Hester wept to hear of the ancient ruin where they found the women; it looked as though no one had lived there since Queen Elizabeth's day. A great brooding bank of holly grew above the house, shutting out the light.

The doctor had hopped through an open window, while Reuben stood guard. He interviewed the women, who were in a world of their own, and decided he could sign the certificates with a clear conscience. Besides, it was crucial to get them out of that hovel, where they were cold and starved of decent food, dirty and unkempt.

And then, of course, the conspirators were spotted. They had to make a run for it, and got into the trap just before Kettlewell caught up with them. Reuben shook the reins and Dolly the mare flew along the old farm track, faster than she'd ever gone before. And just before they reached the Bramley Lane and safety, shots rang out.

'Were you scared?' asked Hester, fearfully. She could imagine the cool and skilful way Reuben would have driven.

Reuben shot her a glance of the blue eyes. 'Knew harness was up to it . . . well-oiled, and allus ready for a gallop, being a doctor's outfit. Boss said what frightened him most was the thought of having shot dug out of his backside by Dr Johnson!'

And the other piece of news, delivered as an afterthought as Reuben was on his way out, was about Josh Bell. He'd been seen in Leeds, walking out with a young lady. 'A right little lass, it seems, but bonny enough. That's what Willy Thackray said. He walked out of Leeds Central station, and the first thing he saw was old Josh from the High Side. It's a small world! He's doing right well in the police force.'

In bed that night Hester considered the day's news. Why had the mention of Josh disturbed her? It was good to hear he was settling down in Leeds, though she couldn't imagine it, somehow. And if he was walking out with a young lady he wouldn't come bothering Hester again. That was a good thing, too. But somehow, since her childhood, Josh had always been there to rely upon. It was strange to think that he would not be there in future. She'd sent him away, he bored her – but lately she was beginning to appreciate his decency. He was a far better person than she was – and than she'd given him credit for.

Turning over restlessly, Hester reminded herself that Josh was no longer within her reach, in any case. The baby had changed every-thing. It was useless to think about any decent man now.

\*

In a couple of weeks, Reuben was back again to see them on a Sunday afternoon, this time with a bag of warm baby-clothes. Mary Bishop had bought them from a church bazaar, thus raising a few eyebrows. Reuben had told the Bishops where Hester was, knowing that it would go no further. They were relieved to know what had happened to her, as Reuben had been. And Mary – Mary was almost envious. There was still no sign of a baby for the Bishops.

The news, this time, was of a big concert, planned for spring. 'Boss's idea, it was.' The roof of the Mechanics' Institute was leaking, and a big meeting was held to decide what to do.

Reuben described how they sat in the reading-room, with Bishop getting more and more impatient. He chaired the committee that ran the Institute, but their proceedings were too slow for him.

The boss had shocked them by enquiring how much they thought it cost to keep the big coal-fire and two paraffin lamps going . . . and how much their pictures would fetch in a sale. The large needlework picture of *The Dying Douglas* had always been there, it belonged to Kirkby, how could it be sold?

'Does anybody study, at the Mechanics'?' enquired Meg gently. And, of course, they didn't, although it had been built, fifty years before, to help the working classes to get some education. There was a small library and a large billiard table, for those who insisted upon self-improvement.

'It's a grand place for meeting folks, neither church nor chapel,' Reuben reminded her. 'Only spot where church and chapel can meet.'

Working fast, Bishop had suggested a concert to raise funds for the roof, and proposed and seconded the motion before anybody could object. In the minutes Reuben's name appeared as seconder, he later discovered. So now the drive was on to find 'turns' and every possible performer was being winkled out of hiding, some more reluctantly than others.

Hester laughed at the thought of the moorlanders being called upon to perform. But everybody knew that Richard Sayers could sing, and the vicar might recite a poem – he was used to an audience.

'And there's Will the postman, he's offered to bring the handbell ringers. There's forty handbells in Kirkby,' said Reuben, with a mixture of pride and horror.

'Handbells are loud, they're best heard out of doors. From the other end of the village!' Meg had heard them before.

'And then, Ned Mecca always like to tell his jokes.' Reuben looked contrite immediately. That remark came out without thinking.

Hester felt herself blushing, but it was no use – she'd have to face the mention of the Metcalfes some time.

Reuben knew that Hester's trouble had been caused by Ned Metcalfe, and hated him for it. But it was Hester's secret, and he couldn't say anything.

The days lengthened slowly, and the cold retreated once more as spring came to the High Side in a flurry of sunshine and showers. Meg started to dig her vegetable garden, but Hester was too big and awkward to help her. The baby was due any day now. Sometimes she worried about it, and wondered what effect the poison might have had.

One night, as they were lighting their candles to go to bed, Hester felt the first pains. Then followed a time when she tried to relax and tell herself that everything was normal. But when a few hours had gone by with terrible pain but no progress, Hester could tell that Meg was worried. Through a haze of pain, she saw Meg throw a shawl over her shoulders. She was going to walk to Kirkby, to fetch Dr Bishop.

How much later, Hester couldn't tell, the doctor was there, bending over her with the ether apparatus . . . just like the time with Mrs Robinson. Then she drifted off, and knew no more. Her body laboured on for hours, but Hester was under the ether.

The spring dawn was breaking when Hester awoke groggily, floating up through layers of consciousness to find herself lying on the bed. At the foot of the bed, the doctor sat on a stool, shoulders bowed with weariness.

Meg was weeping. And then, in the grey light, Hester saw the still little body on the table. Her baby was dead. Her father and Letty King had won, after all.

Nobody moved for a long time. Then Hester wept, quietly, and the doctor brushed away his own tears. He laid a gentle hand on her shoulder. 'We did our best . . . but he was dead before he was born.'

The girl was in despair. It was her fault that he'd died . . . she would always blame herself, for letting Roger take control. Once she'd known about the baby she should never have gone back to Hagstones again. With freedom, if nothing else, she should have been able to find a safe haven, far from Roger's influence.

Even in her half-drugged state Hester was also bitter about her own lineage. What if her baby had taken after its grandfather, and become a criminal? She couldn't trust even herself to do the right thing, could she? Hester had felt violent emotions: she'd let her passion for Ned rule her head. She could see her father in herself.

It was a terrible thought, but the neighbours were right; Kettlewell blood was bad blood. And there was no getting away from it.

There was nothing to say.

Then, as Hester lay there, she thought she felt a movement, an involuntary contraction. Part of the process, she thought wearily. Then it came again . . . 'Meg?'

Bishop and Meg moved towards her and then, with a rush, another baby made its appearance. A long, slippery shape, not quite inert. Bishop handled the baby expertly, turning him upside down, to clear the airways and start him breathing properly.

For a moment or two the little body hovered between life and death, struggling for breath. Bishop gently pumped the little lungs up and down Then the little scrap filled his lungs, and let out a cry. The tiny fists waved, and the legs started to kick. They checked him carefully, and he was perfect. A small miracle; and he was quite small. The doctor thought he'd weigh less than six pounds.

'Your son, Hester!'

Meg, all smiles, brought warm water and the baby was bathed, then dressed in the little clothes Hester had made.

The atmosphere in the cottage changed dramatically to tears of joy as Hester, exhausted, held her little son. 'Thomas, after Uncle Tom,' she said, looking down at his dark little head.

Never mind that he looked like a Kettlewell; she would make sure that he was brought up right. Little Thomas was going to be happy and secure, as she'd never been. And then, you could say that the Kettlewells had energy, they got things done. Hester decided to be positive about their lineage, hers and Thomas's.

'He's very like you, Hester,' said Meg gently. His mother smiled down at him. She'd rather he was a Kettlewell than a Metcalfe, after all.

# CHAPTER THIRTEEN

'I have no choices left,' said Hester, quite flatly, looking across at Meg White over the baby's head. Little Thomas, named after Uncle Tom Sutton who had died soon after the baby was conceived, was thriving. Hester was too thin, but she too was recovering, and happy except for the worry hanging over her head. How were they to live?

'How old is he – six weeks? Too soon to make a move!' Meg wanted to keep them with her as long as possible. 'You do have a choice, lass. You can either go into a big town to find a place that'll take you and the bairn, maybe a charity for fallen women – as you said just now. Or you can stay with me, at least for Tommy's first year.' She smiled.

Hester pushed the dark hair back and sighed. 'I'd love to stay here, Meg. But I've learned a few things. I can see it from your point of view. You earn your living with herbs and such, but you can't keep three of us. And you won't want other folks in your house for ever – I've been here long enough as it is.'

Early summer was a busy time for a herbalist. Meg was making raspberry-leaf tea, and her hands were stained with green as she waved them at the kettle, boiling on the fire. 'Make us a cup of tea, there's a good lass. And then listen to me, Hester Kettlewell. And I'll tell you what's good for you.' She spoke with quiet authority.

When the teapot was on the table and Thomas back in his cradle, Meg leaned towards Hester. 'I'm glad to hear that you consider me, but let me tell you how I see it. For a start, I've no family of my own. It's been a lonely life here, Hester, and I right enjoy your company. It's been a grand spring, and little Tommy is a joy. So you are welcome to stay here, we've no neighbours. And only friends like Reuben know you're here.' She went to the cupboard and brought out a tin of oatmeal biscuits.

Hester blushed and smiled. She'd known that Meg had saved her life, and had been most kind. But she hadn't realized that the older woman was actually enjoying their company.

'And another thing,' Meg went on, 'you've helped me already, with some of the work. You're a right handy lass, Lily trained you well! And I've got more work for us, if you'll stay.' Her eyes were bright with a new idea. 'Bensons will give us an order for besoms; we can make them here, in the shed or by the fire in cold weather. They can sell all we can make. And with your help, I can double up on a lot of herbs – there's a great call for them.'

Hester considered, her head on one side. 'If we could make enough brass we could buy another goat,' she offered. 'I could milk her. And we could keep a few more hens, for eggs. Ay, Meg, I would like to stay. If you're sure, and as long as Dad doesn't find out where I am.'


'Have you time for a glass?' asked Meg, as Reuben brought a basket up the path. 'Just a quick one?' Reuben often called in these days, with news and small gifts of produce, gleaned from his rounds.

Over the glass of herb beer, Reuben told them what went on in Kirkby. 'Boss is throng, as usual,' he said, meaning busy. 'Oh, and the latest is – village concert. It's next Saturday night, and Missis is playing piano.'

Reuben had said firmly that none of his talents was suitable for the stage, but that he was going to take the money at the door and look after it. Reuben relayed all these small happenings with great satisfaction while watching Hester and the baby. The little lad was growing, they could all see.

Josh was back on the High Side for the first time since joining the police. He'd deliberately kept away from home during the first few months, when he was so homesick that, once home again, he might have decided to stay. Now he felt more confident of his place in the city; he knew a few other policemen and had made one or two friends. It was time to see his mother.

Mrs Bell's rheumatism had got worse; she said nothing about it, but Josh could tell by the way she moved that it was painful. Elijah and Mabel were still talking about getting married, but they'd put it off for a while because Mabel was helping out at home. It was pleasant to sit by the big log fire, and talk to the family. The farm was looking prosperous with the flush of spring grass, and Kirkby village was smothered in apple-blossom and spring flowers. Josh felt he'd never realized how beautiful this place was. You had to go away to appreciate it properly.

Home was safe, home was fine, but out on the moor, it was different. Wherever Josh looked the moorland reminded him of Hester, of the way she laughed, the way her hair blew in the wind. The feeling for her came back stronger than ever, and he hoped that few people had ever known about it. Josh had always kept his feelings to himself His mother had suspected there was a girl worrying him – she wondered if it might be Hester – but they were not a family that talked easily about emotions. High Siders usually suffered in silence, when they hurt.

There were plenty of neighbours who were pleased to see Josh, keen to hear tales of the city and eager to tell him their news, but of Hester, there was no sign. Bishop saw Josh walking over the moor, and stopped for a chat, but he was sworn to secrecy and said nothing about the girl. But he did invite Josh to the concert.

'Come and join us, Josh! You'll see all your old friends on the one night.' And though he had misgivings, Josh agreed to go. He might pick up some news of Hester, although he didn't know what to do about it, if he did.

Josh had long ago decided never to approach Hester again; it would be too painful. But he was more confident now. He could express himself far better and he could see now how simple and hesitant he'd been, with a woman who wanted to be charmed but needed to be led a little. He could have guided her better when they were young. As he jogged down to Kirkby, driven by Elijah, Josh had many regrets.

The night of the concert was sharp and clear. Good weather was essential for success: folks wouldn't walk or drive for miles in the rain. Stars hung luminous, with the Plough above the church, and everybody had turned out to support a good cause.

The big room was nearly adequate and by squeezing a little, they all packed in. Josh arrived rather late, and sat at the back with arms folded. Elijah had gone to join his girl, near the front.

Josh was feeling depressed, and began to wish that he'd stayed at home. He did not feel festive. The last time he'd been in this tiny Mechanics' Institute, so different from the big Leeds one, Hester had been there.

The Metcalfes were all there, of course; Ned loved a concert. Josh felt himself scowling at them, and turned away. He'd already been told by his friends that his pale city face and stern expression made him look less like a moorlander than the old Josh, and more like a copper.

The concert was launched and went smoothly, apart from one or two hitches that added to the fun. Little Emily Metcalfe forgot her lines in a short poem about the evils of drink, but she looked so sweet in her frilly frock that she was applauded loudly, especially by her parents. The baritone sang sweetly, and a few tears were shed as the plaintive notes died away.

Then the vicar read his poem. 'I remember, I remember the house where I was born . . .' Josh felt ready to cry when he got to the lines: 'My spirit flew in feathers then that is so heavy now. . . .'

Then it was over, and there was a call for Ned Metcalfe to cheer things up a little.

Ned climbed up to the stage, his curly hair damped down with oil and his face shining brightly. The glory of Emily's appearance was still with him. 'Tell you a joke . . .' he began.

Josh glared at him from the back row, knuckles slowly whitening. He heard Hester's voice again. *Know any jokes? Ned's always laughing.*

The jokes went down well. They were new ones, Ned himself thought they were funny, and also he was supremely confident. As he finished Ada rolled out the tea-urn and the lads set up trestles for supper. The audience stretched and stood up and Mary Bishop started off briskly at the piano with *Rule, Britannia.*

Moving to the back of the hall for fresh air, Josh noticed that Ned Metcalfe was doing the same thing.

Both men stepped outside, Ned unaware that Josh was watching him. There was no sound in the street except for a faint buzz from the concert room, and the distant tinkle of the piano, now offering *The Last Rose of Summer.*

Josh could bear the sight of that smug, handsome face no longer. He swung round to face Ned. 'Tell me, Metcalfe – where is Hester Kettlewell?' He hadn't planned this, but he couldn't help himself. 'You know something about her, don't you?'

Ned appeared to panic at this. 'Mind your own business, Bell!' His voice was high. Josh took a step towards him, and Ned lashed out with his fist blindly, connecting by chance with Josh.

Someone screamed, and then the doctor appeared. Ned and Josh were facing each other, breathing fast. Josh was bleeding from a cut over the eye. 'I'll ask you once more. Where is Hester? What have you done with her?' Josh had more authority now, police authority. And he was in deadly earnest.

Ned laughed in his face. 'Can't keep track of every dairymaid in the parish. Don't know where she is – why should I? She's nowt to me.'

As Bishop reached them, Josh aimed a well-trained fist and caught the farmer on the point of the chin. All his pent-up jealousy of Ned Metcalfe went into that blow, all his despair over Hester and his anger at being exiled from the High Side. Josh, normally quiet and peaceable, had always been ready to fight for Hester. But until now he hadn't hated his opponents. He'd just wanted to keep them from annoying Hester, taunting her because she was a Kettlewell. Tonight it was deadly serious. Ned Metcalfe had probably ruined Hester, and he didn't appear to care.

Ned went down heavily on the pavement as the music went galloping back into *Rule, Britannia*, Mary feverishly keeping up the volume. Bishop quickly closed the door of the hall. This must not spoil the concert.

Kneeling by Ned, the doctor spoke quietly to Josh. 'Ned certainly deserved a thumping, but a policeman could lose his job for causing a scene like this.'

Meg White came out, sizing up the situation in her quiet way and seeing the danger to Joshua. She went up to him as he stood there, looking dazed. 'Off you go to my house, lad, it's not locked up. Wait until things have cooled down a bit. If this gets reported they'll look for you at your mother's place. Ned won't be much hurt, don't worry.'

Josh thanked her, but stayed with arms folded to watch Ned get rather groggily to his feet.

Without much sympathy, Bishop cleaned Ned up in the Institute kitchen, and applied stinging iodine to the cut. 'You know why he did that, don't you?' he said with quiet ferocity. So the doctor knew something, thought Josh.

Ned groaned. 'No, why should I? Don't tell the missis . . . say I fell.' Then the handbells went into their first peal, and the noise was such that thought was impossible. The second part of the concert had begun.

Josh quickly told his brother where he was going, and left the village.

It was dark in the lane leading to Meg's cottage, the starlight shut out by trees. Josh knew he'd better keep away from home, but this seemed ridiculous. Stumbling along, his city eyes no longer used to the dark, he hoped that Meg had left a fire burning. He was aching, cold and very miserable. It had been a mistake to come back to Kirkby and reopen old wounds, and the pain was worse than he'd expected.

Opening the door quietly, Josh found himself in the rosy glow of a good fire. He was prepared for a presence; Blackie the cat was well-known. And here was Blackie, coming to greet him, and sitting by the fire was a woman.

At first, Josh didn't know her. The light was on her busy hands, leaving her face in shadow. She looked up in surprise, but she was not afraid. Meg's cottage was a safe place.

'Hester!' Josh came to a halt just outside the firelight. She had never been far from his thoughts, and he had fought to avenge her, but Josh hadn't expected to see Hester again. Sometimes he'd thought she might be dead.

'Come in Josh, and sit down. What happened? There's blood on your face!'

The girl was thinner and looked older, but softer somehow, more sympathetic. Giving him a gentle smile, she went on with her task, making a broom from a pile of ling.

Hester's dress was old, but it was neat and clean. Her hair was combed and she looked composed. She was a different woman from the lass who'd lived at Hagstones, but more like the lass he'd imagined she could become.

With a sigh, Josh looked round thankfully at the simple furniture and the bunches of herbs. He felt the tension drain from him, the cloud of depression lift. This was a good place.

Hester laid down the finished broom. 'Threepence each, sixpence for big ones. That's how we live, that and the herbs.' She smiled without embarrassment. 'No wonder they think Meg's a witch, with all these broomsticks!'

Josh sat on a stool, purred over by Blackie, and watched her work. Feeling a little calmer, he said: 'I've just hit Ned Mecca . . . hard . . . but Dr Bishop's there. So I had to get out of the village quick, and Meg sent me here. Unless Mecca reports me, I might get away with it. If he does . . . I'll lose my job in the force.'

'Where were you?' Hester was watching his face.

'It was a bit public – outside the Mechanics'.' He had no idea how many people had been watching.

It seemed easier to talk, somehow, than it used to be. Maybe it was the police training, Josh thought.

Hester poured warm water from the kettle into a basin, added some elderflower-water and took a clean rag to bathe his eye. Her hands were soft in spite of the rough work, and her dress held the scents of herbs and flowers.

'I couldn't stand his jokes. It was high time somebody hit his silly face. If it wasn't for him, you might have looked at me once. It's too late, now.' The water was soothing.

'Yes, it's too late,' Hester agreed. She took away the bowl, and put the kettle on again for tea. Then a cry from the room above made her look up. 'That's Tommy, sometimes he cries in the night.' She ran lightly up the stairs, holding up her dress.

A baby! Josh had wondered whether Ned had got the girl into trouble, but it was still a shock. But if he loved the lass he would have to come to terms with the baby. He sat looking into the fire.

After a while Thomas was brought down to the firelight, his face rosy with sleep and his dark hair standing on end. Josh liked children. He held out his arms, and the baby was soon happy enough on Josh's knee. Holding the firm little body, Josh was relieved to see that Thomas looked not at all like Ned. He would be his own man.

Easily, Josh and Hester sat together in the firelight. 'I'm sorry,' she said gently, 'about . . . that time at Pateley Fair. I must have hurt you. I've had a lot of time to think, since then.'

Hester made some tea, and Josh began to feel better. He realized that his instinct had been right; this was the girl for him, whatever had happened in the past. She seemed to have grown up, just as he had.

'If I got married, the police would give me a good house.'

'Good!' said the girl. She looked over at him like a sister. 'I suppose you have a sweetheart now?'

'Well . . . I do have a woman in mind.' Josh was looking into the fire. 'What about you, lass? Did you manage to get over Ned Mecca?'

Her smile was real, uncomplicated. 'He's not worth a straw. I forgot about him long ago . . . it was my fault as much as his. I can see now how selfish he is.' The girl went on with her task, quite composed. The past was behind her now.

'Do you make a living?' Josh wondered, after a while.

'More or less . . . Meg's been like a mother to me. I've stayed here since I got away from . . . home, and I try to help her all I can.'

Baby Tommy was asleep on Josh's knee, dark lashes on his cheeks. Josh thought for a while, in a comfortable silence. 'I can see you won't want to live on the High Side now – not after everything . . . but do you think we could make a go of getting wed? We could get a house in Leeds to start off, and then I could apply for a country station somewhere.' He took her hand, far more confident than the old Josh.

The besom-making came to a halt, and Hester shook her head. 'Nay, Josh, I'm a ruined woman! Not good enough for the likes of you. You're from a respectable farming family. What would your poor mother say? No, it's too late for me now.'

Josh laughed. 'Don't be daft. If we wed, folks will think that Tommy's mine, and we've just waited a bit too long to make it legal! Nobody's ruined if they've got a good husband . . . and I reckon you'll make a good wife. You're the only lass I've ever wanted, Hester. Or ever will.'

Josh looked at her, a spark of hope in the brown eyes. 'Let's give it time. I reckon it will work out.'

'Well, Josh . . . I think a lot of you, you know. I sort of appreciate you better now. But I won't hold you to anything. You could find a better lass than me, any day. We'll leave it a while, with no promises on either side. After that, we'll see.'

They talked for an hour before Meg came back. Josh learned that Hester was still hiding from her father, and that she was doing her best to help Meg, for whom she had a great affection. And he told her about his life in Leeds, and how he planned to leave the city in a year or two, for a little country station. He didn't trust himself to tell her how much he'd missed her and longed for her.

Meg made up a bed for Josh, but the next morning he decided to go home, hoping there would be no trouble. He was due back in Leeds in two days, and he really wanted Hester to give him some encouragement before he went away. But as they said goodbye at Meg's garden gate, she was still friendly, but still determined that they shouldn't promise anything.

'I don't want to burden you with a baby! It wouldn't be fair to marry you, Josh, just to get myself out of trouble! I'm still ashamed, lad.'

Josh blamed Mecca more than Hester for her predicament. She'd been inexperienced, very young for her age, when he got his hold over her. As her employers, the Metcalfes should have looked after their maid. But he had to be content with her reply.

Josh went back to Leeds in a happier frame of mind about Hester, although he was still not sure whether they'd ever have a future together. But the lass herself was well and safe. And she was less rough, much less awkward than she had been. Hester must be learning a few things from Meg . . . and she hadn't sworn once!

The Ackroyds were pleased to have their lodger back, and for a few days Josh was content to get back into the work routine, and to push away the problem of Sarah Jane. But it refused to go away, and he realized that he'd have to come out honestly and tell her about Hester. It might mean that he had to find new lodgings, but he'd face that later.

About a week after his return Sarah Jane said that she was going to the library, if he'd like to come. The evenings were light now, so there was less danger in the streets. As they walked along together, Josh was wondering how to start the conversation, when Sarah Jane turned to him with an earnest face.

'Josh . . . I have to tell you something. While you were away I had a letter from Africa. My friend . . . James Seymour, he's a missionary at the moment, has asked me to marry him!' She blushed.

It felt as though a load was lifted from Josh's shoulders. But he looked at her with concern as he said: 'He doesn't expect you to join him in Africa? It's no place for a little thing like you!' This James must be a selfish sort of chap.

Sarah Jane drew herself up to her full five feet and tried to look haughty. 'I would be quite capable!' Then she relaxed. 'But no, I'm a teacher, not a missionary. James is coming back next year, so we'll stay here in Leeds.'

Josh couldn't decide which was the worse fate, to face the wilds of Africa or to stay in Leeds for ever. But he only smiled and said heartily: 'I hope you'll be happy, Sarah Jane!'

The girl explained that she and James had worked in the same school, and she'd fallen in love with him. They'd been writing to each other, but for months she had heard nothing. 'And I didn't know about you, Josh . . . you've never mentioned a young lady. . . .' She'd evidently had the same worries as he'd had about their friend-ship.

'Well, yes. I do have a lass in mind, though I'm not sure how it will all work out. Happen it will, in the end. I saw her while I was back home.' Then a thought struck him. 'So that's why you cried when I mentioned the dangers in Africa!'

Sarah Jane nodded, and they went on down the street, happy that they could be friends.

# CHAPTER FOURTEEN

Reuben sighed deeply into his tankard of beer, and considered his options.

Coming back from Pateley on an errand for the boss, Reuben had planned to be in Kirkby before dusk. But the sky had darkened alarmingly, and flashes of lightning over the moor had suggested to him that a pint of beer at the Moorcock would be a good idea. The storm was long in coming – should he risk it? He could drink up quickly, and be off before the rain started, or he could sit tight and wait until it passed over. Dolly and the trap were under cover, and they weren't expected for duty before the morning.

The groom looked round. There was a game of dominoes going on in one corner, and several sheepdogs lay under the table. A group of men was playing cards beneath a paraffin-lamp, quiet for the most part, but with occasional mutterings. The stakes must be high; there was tension at the card-table.

The fire burned brightly, and outside the wind howled round the old grey buildings. It should have been a cosy scene, but the atmosphere at the Moorcock Inn was uneasy tonight. The patrons were on edge, and even Reuben was not enjoying his beer as much as usual. For one thing, the unpredictable Roger Kettlewell was playing cards, and if he lost, there would be hell to pay for somebody. And for another, the best seats by the fire were taken up by the Kings.

A gamekeeper in tweeds looked round and scraped his chair back on the slate floor. 'I'm off! There's bad weather brewing.' The Moorcock bore the brunt of all the winds, perched on top of the pass that led to Pateley. As he opened the door a gust of wind brought the bad weather into the room, a flurry of rain and a peal of thunder. There was a lurid sunset, with black clouds over the hills.

115

Reuben didn't want to be out on the moor in a thunderstorm, and he'd reckoned it would all be over in another hour. But he didn't care for the company tonight; he knew too much about them. He looked over from his bar-stool at Roger's dark, brooding face as he hunched over the cards. The last time he'd seen Roger, he was chasing the medical team with a shotgun. How unlucky Hester was, to have him for a father! The lass was right to keep quiet. She'd be in trouble, right enough, if he ever caught up with her. But how long could she stay in hiding with Meg?

Reuben watched from behind his pint as Letty King put down her glass of gin, and clenched her teeth round the clay pipe. She looked with calculated menace round the company, while everybody else looked away hurriedly. Toby King, one of her three scruffy sons, lounged at the other side of the hearth, grinning. He didn't mind that everybody kept well away from them. He drove the carrier's cart, and they were on the way home, like a couple of black crows, no doubt from having made a profitable deal – illicit, of course. Everybody knew that the King lads were criminals, but they got away with it by sheer intimidation – and by having Letty for a mother. She was the brains of the organization.

Tim Cooper, the landlord of the Moorcock, was used to mixed company. The pub was used as a meeting-place for shooting-parties in the grouse season. As he said to Reuben as he polished glasses, you could easily find yourself serving a glass to a bishop or a lord, not to mention a poacher or two.

The thunder grew louder and Tim Cooper said hopefully: 'Maybe you'd best get home before rainstorm, Roger.' He was smaller than Kettlewell, and always extremely polite to him. Most people thought it best, when they couldn't keep right out of his way.

The dealer glared at him, and turned back to the cards.

In a few more minutes he sprang up, laughing, and collected all the money on the table. Roger had won, and that was the end of the game. He hiccuped, stowed the money in a pocket and lurched to the door. Being Kettlewell, he left the door open and Reuben, walking over to close it, saw what happened next.

Toby had been waiting for Letty to give the word to go home. And as Roger went out, she finished her gin and stood up. In the windy twilight outside the inn, Toby untied the pony from the rail and Letty went round to get into the cart.

Kettlewell untied his horse with difficulty. He was much better-mounted since he'd come into Horner's money, and tonight he rode a big Cleveland Bay. Reuben admired the horse, and felt sorry for it. He'd seen Kettlewell's spurs.

Reuben watched to see whether the man could mount. He scrambled up, and Reuben was about to shut the door when Kettlewell suddenly rode straight at the carriers, aggressively and with whip raised. His horse tried to avoid Letty, as horses will usually do, but brushed past and knocked her down. Kettlewell laughed and cut at her with his whip, catching her across the face.

The carrier's pony reared and squealed, Toby King started to shout and swear and the noise brought everybody else out in front of the pub. Letty struggled to her feet as the thunder rolled round louder than ever, and forked lightning played over the moorland, lighting it to a strange beauty.

'Damn you, Kettlewell!' she yelled above the storm. 'May you rot in hell! Curses on you!' She went on for some time; Letty had also been primed with much gin. Reuben was glad he usually stuck to beer.

This was very good drama for the patrons of the Moorcock, but they kept well back from Letty's line of fire. They had no wish to be cursed, and at the moment, she was like a loose cannon, shouting to all points of the compass. Maybe the curses didn't work, but you never knew.

They were about to find out.

Roger Kettlewell rode off, taking his route to Hagstones directly over the ridge. It was one of the most exposed places on the moor, visible for miles around. The man was heading straight across country instead of sticking to the track – a dangerous thing to do, at any time. But it was often Roger's way home from the pub, and the horse knew it well.

'Damn you, Kettlewell. . . !'

The watchers in the pub yard could see the big horse climbing in the failing light. The rain was over towards Kirkby now, sweeping down the valley, leaving the moorland clear.

A bolt of lightning played over the ridge, looking for somewhere to earth itself. It found the horse and rider, just as they reached the top.

Before the horrified onlookers, Roger and his horse were outlined against the flash of light, then fell, struck and killed.

117

There was an awful hush in the pub yard.

It was a shock, seeing a man killed before his eyes. Reuben was awed by the deadly force of nature, so dangerous and unpredictable.

Afterwards, Reuben thought of Hester and the rest of Kettlewell's family, and all his neighbours, and there was a great feeling of relief that the storm had removed a dangerous force from the community. As he'd heard the vicar say many times: 'The Lord moves in a mysterious way. . . .'

Many people said afterwards that the dealer was asking for trouble, out on the moors in a thunderstorm, and that folks had been killed that way before. There was iron along that ridge. The more credulous said that Letty had cursed him and after that, he was a dead man. The story enhanced her reputation for trouble, among the cottagers.

'So you have more choices now,' Meg White reminded Hester, who had been to see her mother after the funeral. She had made her peace with Lizzie, and she was happy that little Susan would be safe, but she had no intention of making a home with her family, who now lived in Ripon.

The summer had been wet and cold, but Hester had been happy, working with Meg and watching her baby grow. She didn't want choices, and said so. 'I know it's coming up to my second winter with you – but I'd like to stay as we are, if it suits you as well. And Tommy is happy here.'

Meg laughed. 'Nay, lass, that's not what I meant. But you've been a bit hermitlike, staying about Larton here and never going out . . . except to pick berries and such. And now you can go to Kirkby – and Ripon even, without looking over your shoulder. Folks know you're with me, and that you're a respectable lass.'

She was leading up to something. Hester thought. 'So . . . where do you want me to go?'

'Well, you could both come with me to the harvest festival, you and Tommy. That's Sunday night. And it would save my old legs,' she said artfully, 'if you'd take round some of these salves and herbs to folks, at times.'

Hester shook the water from her cape in the porch and went into church with Meg. Sounds from within were drowned by the

battering rain. The north wind, fierce and predatory, howled round
the Norman doorway, and flung itself on the glistening stones of
the tower in an endless buffeting. What a night!

Everybody was there, the Methodists joining for one night of the
year with the Church of England supporters. Hester and Tommy
sat down demurely beside Meg, about half-way down the aisle. She
felt quite composed, part of the scene. It didn't matter that the
Metcalfes were among the Methodists. She was going to face up to
everybody.

The doctor rushed in a little later, wet, and looking tired. He was
often late for church when duty intervened; only Hester noticed as
he slid quietly into a pew beside Mary.

The vicar was pallid above his cassock, more uneasy than usual,
and the farmers were not in good voice. In fact, they sounded
almost mutinous.

> 'All good things around us
> Are sent from heaven above. . . .'

Hester looked demure, but she was cynical. She glanced round
the church at the evidence of God's bounty, and felt that it was a
poor show. There was no golden sheaf upon the altar steps, the
apples suggested stomach-ache, and the flowers were windblown
and pathetic. She'd never seen such small marrows before, nor such
mediocre cabbages. Kirkby's vegetables were usually splendid. But
then, she never expected heaven to be bountiful. Why should God
worry about little cabbages at Kirkby, when he didn't look after
their Billy?

Tonight's downpour was the splashy finale to a disastrously wet
summer. Kirkby depended upon the land, the farmers kept the
community going, and in spite of this official thanksgiving, the
harvest was not all safely gathered in.

Hester understood that the date for the service had been set
months ago, and that the vicar could hardly call it off. But there
were glum faces everywhere, and even Meg's crops of herbs had
been of poor quality and tending to mould.

What would folks do on the High Side without hay this winter,
to keep the cattle alive until the spring? Hester knew that there
would be some hardship on the moor this season. Meg had better

make plenty of cough-syrup, for that would be needed. And there was no corn. 'Not one dry sheaf has been harvested in this parish,' a neighbour had told them as they went into church.

Hester looked around. Some of the farmers had lost heart, and stopped singing. She could only hear two voices, Mrs Bishop's determined soprano, and the semi-trained baritone of Richard Sayers, the large and prosperous landlord of the Shoulder of Mutton Inn just down the street. He hadn't toiled in the fields, but he probably felt sorry for the vicar, and he liked to sing. Even though, this winter, the pub would have fewer customers with the local shortage of money.

With creaks from joints and boots, the congregation sank to its knees. Along the walls the candles guttered and the paraffin lamps swayed in the draught down the central aisle, casting weird shadows over the vicar's face. Hester felt almost sorry for Grimshaw, so out of place on this moorland. But he didn't feel the bad harvest in his aching bones like the farmers did.

Reuben was scowling over his stiff collar, making his annual appearance at church with damp hair plastered over his brow. But he had winked at Hester earlier; he was another friend to be thankful for.

The vicar rose. 'Hymn number 382 in Hymns Ancient and Modern.' He had a beautiful voice, but he talked too posh to be quite human.

The farmers knew that hymn: 'Come, ye thankful people, come.' The farmers were not thankful. A clatter in the porch, as another latecomer straggled in, was lost in the first notes of the organ.

It was an organ solo; the farmers' lips were closed and grim. Why should they sing? The organist tried to compensate by making more noise, and it was not until the end of the first verse that anybody noticed the newcomer. He announced his presence quite easily, by shooting the glass out of the nearest lamp.

The shot was deafening in the enclosed space, and people were stunned at first. Little Tommy began to cry and adults cowered as the glass tinkled to the floor. The organ gave a wail, and died. There was a frightened silence.

'Keep on singing!' said the man with the gun in a deep, strong voice. 'Sing, I tell you!' Hester ventured a sideways look; he was quite near her. The gun was still in his hands, a double-barrelled shotgun, with only one cartridge used.

The people of Kirkby knew that gun, and they opened their mouths and sang. The vicar obviously had powerful support, though perhaps not of his choosing. Maybe they were to be punished for their lack of thankfulness. . . .

> 'All is safely gathered in
> Ere the winter storms begin.'

It seemed that the storm itself had come among them, sweeping into the village something from violent and ancient times. Yes, they knew the tall figure, but that was no consolation. He was over six feet, well over the local average, and a top-hat make him look taller. The huge shoulders were draped in a red shawl, and under the hat was a fair Viking complexion, a reddish moustache and piercing blue eyes.

'Sing! You don't sing loud enough!' he roared.

Hester gently passed Tommy over to Meg.

The hymn came to an end, the intruder uttered a loud AMEN! The vicar knelt and prayed for their deliverance, and the red shawl sank as the man kneeled in prayer in the middle of the aisle.

The smell of paraffin from the seeping lamp was strong, mingling with the acrid smoke of gunpowder.

Hester was used to dangerous men with guns. She moved quickly out of the pew, and the man opened his eyes and saw her coming towards him. He raised the gun, but by then she was past the long barrel, and into the safe area at short range. Before he knew it, the girl had grabbed the gun out of his hands.

Reuben came up behind her, took it, sprinted into the vestry and locked it in. Nobody else had moved. The kneeling figure paralysed them – it seemed like sacrilege to touch him.

An audible sigh went up from the congregation. The man stayed where he was in prayer, and it seemed wrong to remove him. Reuben stood by his side in case of further trouble, Hester went back to the pew, and Grimshaw went on with the service.

At some point in the prayers, vicar and people were reconciled. Their differences were forgotten as the vicar prayed in a firm voice for deliverance from the perils of the night, and for those in trouble . . . and those with a harvest still to win. Even the kneeling figure in the aisle was included. He surely needed help.

The intruder shook his head, stumbled to his feet and then went quietly past Reuben, out into the dark night. Reuben shut the big door after him and heard him singing a hymn as he rode away.

The vicar went into the pulpit for the sermon, his notes shaking only slightly in his hand. The moorlanders admired anyone who stuck to his duty. Rustling, they settled down with strong peppermints to hear what he had to say.

# CHAPTER FIFTEEN

'She should've been sent away, that's what I say,' insisted a purple-faced woman in a large hat. 'Women like that set a bad example to young girls. She should be made to pay for her sins, the brazen hussy!'

'No young lad in Kirkby'll be safe with her about,' agreed another plump farmer's wife. 'Lily Metcalfe says she was taken with her at first, but she soon realized what a trollop she was. They turned her off without a character, because they didn't want her near the bairns.'

Lily herself was not present. Being a Methodist, she wasn't a member of the Mothers' Union. But she'd made sure that they were fully informed with her version of events.

'Ay,' agreed Mrs Robinson. 'She was right enough at cheese-making, and I thought she was steady, but all the time she was . . . ahem . . . too friendly by half with some lad, you have to say. They reckon it might have been Josh Bell. He went away about that time.'

There had been many mutterings about Hester when the news got out, and the Mothers' Union seethed with righteous indigna-tion. It boiled over at a church bazaar, which was opened graciously by Miss Bramley of Kirkby Hall. The lady stayed to take tea, and was there when the talk about Hester started.

'What can you expect, from a Kettlewell?' The self-appointed critics ran on about brazen women and how they led good lads astray.

Miss Bramley had heard enough. 'And how many of you,' she enquired in her ringing, opening-a-bazaar voice, 'can honestly say that you were a virgin on your wedding day?'

There was a horrified silence and Mary Bishop, doing her best to hide a smile, tactfully steered the lady over to inspect some lace tablecloths. They all knew that sometimes the banns were called only just in time, before a baby made its appearance.

Hester was aware of the hostility, and she had been pointedly ignored by several good Christian ladies. It had been hard to leave the safe haven of Meg's cottage and come face to face with the High Side folks, to try to live it down. But fortunately the main talking-point at the moment, on the popular topic of Kettlewells, was Roger's dramatic death. There was talk of the shameful way he had treated the Horner sisters, now rescued, and indeed, his own family. Hester came in for a bit of discreet sympathy on that score. To more charitable folk, Tommy's obscure parentage was . . . well, the lass had made a mistake, but she was respectable enough now. Nobody connected the dark-haired little lad with the Metcalfes, but quite a few thought he might be Josh Bell's bastard. So that was why he went away to Leeds, some said.

In the end Meg had eventually got her own way, and sometimes stayed with little Thomas at home while Hester delivered the wise woman's healing salves and lotions, although she didn't presume to give advice. Didn't say much at all, because Hester was not sure of her ground. But it was good to be out in the moor wind again after her long imprisonment, even though the familiar landmarks reminded her of the past.

There it still stood, the boulder where she had talked to poor Kit Horner, so long ago. Hester shed a few tears for Kit when she passed it. The road down to Metcalfes' farm, where she had been so thoughtless and learned so much. And the sight of Josh Bell's family farm in the distance made her sigh. It was too late to think about Josh now.

Josh wrote to her sometimes, in rather precise police style, but she hadn't seen him since the night of the concert. Josh, too, belonged to the past, and Hester had decided to concentrate on the future.

In the basket she carried the last order of the day, some cough-syrup made from elderberries for Rose Balderstone. Hester remembered Rose at school as a fragile, dark-haired child, a little younger than herself. They'd always got on well, but Hester had lost touch with her school friends when she left school. Roger had actively discouraged any social activities.

Rose had survived a bad bout of pneumonia, thanks to Dr Bishop. And he had suggested that Meg's syrup might be good for the invalid.

It was a drizzly day, a few weeks after the harvest festival, and the weather had still not improved. As Hester crossed the farmyard she was surprised to see, marching down from the top of the yard, a large stook of oats. The normally golden sheaves were brownish and wet and the grain looked dull.

The stook stopped in front of her and it bowed slightly. 'Good day to ye!' it said rather shortly and marched off to the kitchen door.

Following into the kitchen, Hester watched in fascination as three or four sheaves slid to the floor to reveal the red and sweaty face of Fred Balderstone. He was not smiling.

'This is bloody harvest,' he said grimly, arranging the sheaves in a row by the fire. Fred was a solid, thickset man and in normal times he was sociable, but this harvest had soured him.

'I've never seen corn drying like that before,' Hester admitted.

'And I hope you'll never see the like again, lass. Another season like this would ruin us.' Fred's sensible wife had come into the kitchen, followed by daughter Rose. They smiled kindly at Hester.

'And cattle prices are down because corn's dear. Ye see,' Fred was pleased to see her interest, 'we must dry corn, and this is the only way we can think on.'

'I hope you don't have to sit by the fire among this wet stuff,' said Hester quietly to Rose, who was coughing. Meg said that dust and damp were the enemies of lungs. And Rose was far too thin.

'Nay, Hester, Mother and me have a fire in parlour these days. We're right happy in there, come through and see.' She still had a transparent look, but she seemed glad to see the visitor.

Hester followed them with interest. The cheerful firelight in the parlour was reflected in the mirror of the huge mahogany sideboard at the back of the room. There was a decent piano against one wall, Hester noted enviously. She'd always fancied a piano.

'Folks round here don't use their parlours much.' Hester thought that the only home where all the rooms were used was Meg's cottage.

Martha Balderstone, Rose's mother, agreed. 'My mother only used best room for weddings and funerals, or when vicar called,' she remembered. 'And we've been the same. I suppose we've been too busy to be in here much. But when Rose was on the mend it was better for her to be away from the kitchen. Sit yourself down, Hester. Have you time for a cup of tea?'

The simple, conventional welcome, the kindliness of the two women, marked a turning point to Hester. It might take time, but she could live a normal life, for the first time ever. It was an amazing thought. Invited to take tea in the parlour, just like a normal guest!

Rose went off to make the tea, and Hester relaxed with a sigh. It was pleasant after a long walk to sit by a good fire, and let a gentle flow of talk wash over the room.

'Fred's a good farmer, mind,' Rose's mother was saying. 'He does rotations of crops and everything scientific when he can. Only one weakness, has Fred.' She looked at Hester and then closed her mouth firmly as if she had said too much.

Hester thought she knew what Fred's weakness was; she had seen him coming home from Ripon on market-days, swaying with the cart, letting the horse take him home. She hoped he wasn't violent when he was drunk, like Roger. But this was a far happier household than the one at Hagstones had been.

Then Rose brought in the tea, and the talk turned to her ginger biscuits, made to a local recipe. They were exceedingly hot and very hard, and Rose was proud of them. As Queen Victoria frowned down from her portrait on the wall, fan half-raised as if to rap her knuckles, Hester swallowed the hot tea and ginger biscuits and felt the tears come to her eyes.

The main thing on their minds was, naturally, the event at church. Hester had acted quickly, and had probably saved someone's life. The Balderstones had been there, they'd seen the whole thing. 'But how did you do it, Hester?' asked Rose, her eyes wide.

Hester took a deep breath and decided to be honest. 'Had a bit of practice, being a Kettlewell,' she confessed.

She said nothing about the times she'd taken guns and knives from Roger when he was drunk. There was a way of doing it; you didn't look at him first, you came out of nowhere, grabbed and hung on, and aimed a kick where it hurt if you could. Hester was beginning to learn that honesty does not mean that you have to tell all.

Lance Wood, the villain in this case, was discussed in detail.

Sometimes, especially at the full moon, he went about armed and dangerous, on a big black horse.

'Lance is prosperous enough, owns his own farm at Uplands. Educated above his station, they say . . . half the village can't understand the words he uses.' Martha sighed. 'He was reasonable-like, until his wife died . . . then he took queer, which is why the two sons went to Australia. Even housekeeper won't stay with him now. We were that frightened when he started shooting!'

'Doctor said he told the constable the next day. So now it's up to the police.' Rose was on familiar terms with Dr Bishop after her illness. 'And doctor said, why can't High Siders be more normal?' They all laughed, including Hester, who could see that to an outsider many of them were eccentric or worse. Kettlewells, Kings, Horners, Woods . . . was it the climate, the isolation or the drink? The doctor had once told Hester of his private theory: that it was all of the above, plus inbreeding.

'There's both choice and chance in life, and maybe that was a bit of both.' Meg White, with Tommy on her knee, was drinking tea with Dr Bishop. He had seen her in the garden on his way back from the rounds, and accepted her invitation to take a cup of herb tea, at the same time as Hester sat down in the parlour at Balderstones'. Four o'clock, time for a cup and he could still get home before it got dark.

Bishop agreed. 'Hester had a choice, indeed. As a woman and a mother, nobody would expect her to disarm Lance Wood.'

But Hester had told Meg, as they slipped out quietly at the end of the service, that she just did it, without thinking. There was no time to think.

'Either way, she was cool and effective. And this has made me wonder . . . do you think that Hester would make a good nurse?'

Bishop told Meg of the neat way she helped him with the ether, that sunny day at Garth. And he was impressed by her robust good health, and ability to lift weights. 'But you know her better than I do, Meg. . . .'

Meg put Tommy back in the cradle and smoothed her skirt. 'I do know her very well, by now. And I think you're right, but she wouldn't go to do the hospital training, you know. She wouldn't fit in!' The thought of Hester in a nurses' home, being supervised by a dragon of a matron, made them both smile. 'Hester's a wee bit . . . independent. . . .'

'They wouldn't let her in!' The moral standards in the Ripon nurses' home were those of a nunnery, with rather less forgiveness for sinners, the doctor thought. No, Hester wouldn't find a place there.

Bishop had other ideas for Hester, and he outlined them now to Meg, while Tommy slept. 'Nursing isn't regulated by law, you know, as my job is.' He thought that between them Meg and the Bishops could teach Hester enough to make her a competent private nurse, someone he could recommend to local families in need of extra help. And maybe even an extra pair of hands for himself, in an emergency. She would need training in scientific cleanliness. That was the main thing in modern times.

'Money isn't a problem, bairn,' Meg offered, in case that was his motive; some way of helping them financially. She thought of him as a young lad, and sometimes it just slipped out.

Bishop grinned. 'Never thought of it. It's the girl's future career I'm interested in – that, and finding a useful woman in Kirkby when someone falls sick. We're not likely to get a trained nurse.'

'But I can't. I'm a fa—' Hester began, but was cut short by Meg, who was unusually agitated.

'If you call yourself a fallen woman once more, Hester Kettlewell, I shall . . . spank you!' They both laughed, which eased the tension. 'Really, lass, if you respect yourself, other folks will show you respect. And of course, all this will have taught you a lot about how to treat other people . . . they all have their point of view, and it doesn't do to judge.'

Over time, as Meg talked to her, Hester realized that it would be useful to learn home nursing, and interesting. By the winter fire they sat making the besoms, while Meg talked about what she knew: soothing minor ailments, caring for sick children, even laying out the dead. The women who had been local nurses were all retired, and there was certainly a niche in Kirkby. But not yet, whispered Hester, frightened by the thought of so much responsibility.

The doctor spent several afternoons with the trainee at the surgery. Apart from rolling bandages and practising bandaging, she learned about germs. Hester was dismayed to learn that she lived surrounded by countless millions of invisible living creatures, some good, some bad. She learned to scrub and to disinfect, to keep the risk of infection down. So it was even more important to keep things clean in a sick room.

Hester would have been terrified if she'd known where her first nursing assignment would turn out to be.

The trainee had suggested to Bishop that he call her a helper, rather than a nurse. She was someone who could clean, prepare meals and help to nurse the sick. And, of course, faithfully carry out the doctor's orders. Hester had a good memory, and could be relied upon to do as she was told. She made two new light dresses and pinafores, and a neat little cap, all ready for the fray.

But when Reuben came for her one night Hester nearly fainted. 'Vicar's took bad. Boss wants you there right away, lass.'

The vicarage was damp and cold, and the housekeeper was away. Bishop said he'd been shocked to find Grimshaw, just returned from a visit to relations, struggling with a sermon in his gloomy study, and shivering with a feverish cold. His temperature was dangerously high.

'Quick, light a fire in the bedroom,' the doctor said to Hester as she came in, shivering with fright. 'And warm some bricks – we'll put him to bed.'

The patient might have been surprised to see the nurse, but he was in no condition to argue. 'The young pagan . . .' he murmured to the doctor, who ignored the remark.

'Soon get you right, Vicar,' said Hester, quite convincingly. She felt so sorry for him that she wanted to cheer him up, and forgot about her own fears in the process.

In an hour or two the patient was feeling very much more comfortable, wrapped in a shawl, in a warm bed, sipping chicken soup. Bishop came back to see him about ten o'clock and found Hester making up the fire.

'Well done!' He smiled, and she glowed with pride. 'The vicar may be difficult . . . parsons often are. But you will follow my instructions, for his own good.'

Hester had to visit the vicarage each day until the housekeeper returned, four days later. The vicar was by then full of praise for the 'helper'. He had evidently decided to exercise Christian forgiveness for her moral lapse. It was the only position he could take, since the girl was there, doing a good job. He couldn't have managed without her.

The housekeeper was pleased to find fresh bread in the house, made by Hester, and all the rooms dusted, clean and neat. Hester went home with money in her pocket, and a new idea of her own capabilities. Her first patient had actually recovered! And no mention had been made of fa— of bad women.

# CHAPTER SIXTEEN

'Come in, lass, we need help! Little Jimmy's in trouble again!'

One winter afternoon Hester called at the Peacocks' farm with some dried herbs, to find a crisis. Jimmy's father was away at Pateley, and his mother could not cope. The noise of his screams was such that she could do nothing but wring her hands.

Jimmy had his head stuck between the bars of a kitchen chair, and his face was crimson. Hester sized up the situation quickly. She went into the pantry, found a crock of lard, and applied plenty of grease to the child and the chair, shutting her mind against the noise. Then she moved him this way and that, until finally he wriggled free, and the screams subsided into a quiet sobbing. 'She hurt me,' he said accusingly, pointing at Hester.

Sally Peacock was so grateful that Hester had to stay for a cup of tea, and some scones and jam, while all the time the dark of night was creeping over the moor. And there were two more deliveries yet before she could go home to Meg and little Tommy.

The frost was setting in as Hester left the Peacocks and strode along the Pateley road to the next call, to Mrs Brown, a great talker. She had to listen to a saga of family troubles, but she could tell that it did the old lady good to tell someone about her worries.

An hour later, she came to the last call: the widow Little's cottage, with some urgently needed elder-syrup. This was another of Bishop's cases, now recovering. Sam Little, pale and thin, needed some heart putting into him.

Hester remembered, as she turned off the highway and on to the track, that Tom Sutton's coffin had rested here on its way to burial, and that Jenny Little had known the old form of blessing.

It was a lonely place on that windswept stretch of moor, but not very far from the road. Pausing before she approached the cottage,

Hester could hear the distant creak of the carrier's cart on the Pateley road. Bound to be one of those scruffy Kings.

'Hester, I'm glad to see you!' Jenny Little's thin face was lit with pleasure as she opened the door. 'Sammy's much better, but doctor said he needs fruit – and it's winter, so there's not much about. Elder-syrup might do him good, though.'

Peering through the smoke of the peat fire, Hester almost collided with the low lintel of the kitchen door. Straightening up inside, she saw young Sam in a small chair by the fire, with a book on his knee. The fire was pulled together, and soon the kettle was boiling, to make a hot elderberry drink.

And then of course the women had a cup of tea, and Jenny wanted to talk. Hester knew that Meg wouldn't worry if she was late, and Tommy would be put to bed as usual. 'Stop and talk where you like, lass, help folks if you can, and never worry about getting home late!' she'd said cheerfully, knowing how hard it was to get away from moorlanders in a talking mood.

At first the talk was of the weather, and rug-making. Dr Bishop had brought a big bag of old clothes for her to cut up to make rugs – wasn't that kind? Then Sam went to bed, and Hester thought she should go home, but Jenny made another cup of tea.

'Aren't you frightened of walking in the dark?' Jenny asked, pouring hot water into the teapot.

The candle flickered as she spoke, and a chilly draught blew down Hester's neck. She repressed a shudder, and smiled reassuringly. 'Nay, Jenny. The wolves and bears have all gone and there's nothing dangerous out on the moor.' Nothing except a few crazy people, she added to herself.

Jenny Little was not convinced. 'Well . . . I live here alone with the bairns, and I'm used to it. But I sometimes wonder!' She sipped her tea. 'I do know as there's many a one who still believes in fairies, that make butter for farmers o'nights . . . and ghosties and all manner of things. More on the moor than down in village. Did you . . .' she lowered her voice again. 'Did you ever see Will-o'-the-wisp, dancing over the marsh?' Her eyes were young and round as Sammy's as she looked at Hester over the edge of the cup. She really wanted to know what a bold lass like Hester, and a clever one too, would make of her deepest fears.

'Will-o'-the-wisp?' Hester drank her tea with composure. Part of her training, which still went on, was about attitude; always be calm, cheerful and composed with frightened people. It had worked with poor little Jimmy, caught fast in the chair.

Hester had often seen the eerie lights dancing over moor water. She'd asked teachers at school about them. 'It's a gas, that's all! Just coming off old rotten plants, in the water. Nothing ghostly!'

'And the fairy rings?' Now she had started, there was no stopping Jenny Little. 'What about those rings in the grass where fairies dance? We used to run round 'em – when we were bairns, that was, of course.'

'Somebody told me they were a sort of mould,' said the expert thoughtfully. 'But I'm not sure. Well . . .' she stood up rather wearily and went to the door.

The woman opened the door, and whirling snowflakes powdered her hair. 'It's snowing . . . you must take care, Hester. Not to miss your road.'

A laugh was her answer, as the girl wrapped her warm shawl round her shoulders. Hester could see in the dark, and she knew many of the tracks over the moor. She was not going to think about that night when she ran away from Hagstones in the snow.

Confidently Hester struck out for Larton, supper and bed. It was so still that she could hear the Kirkby church clock striking ten. Late! Meg would be in bed by now.

The snow tonight was only light. Soon it ceased, and the clouds parted slowly, blown by breezes, so that the stars came out again. Then the moon appeared, ringed by a halo of silver. It was very cold. Hester set herself a brisk pace back to Meg's cottage.

The wind had died down, and Hester's footsteps rang firmly on the frosty ground. Although she was tired, she looked round with pleasure at the rolling lines of the moors, spangled with white drifts of snow, shining back to the luminescent moon. It was an enchanted night, with a cold, hard beauty.

Hester paused to listen. Nothing disturbed the stillness except the far-off tinkle of a beck running over stones, and the muffled cough of an old sheep. She smiled to herself; the moors belonged to her. Lord Bagley, who held the deeds and occasionally shot a grouse, didn't know the high places half so well as she did.

The road down to the villages and civilization was pale in the moonlight, and easy to find tonight. But when the snow covered it, the only way a traveller could keep to the road was to aim from one to the next of the standing stones, monoliths which guarded the way at intervals over the bleakest stretch of moor. How long they had been there, nobody knew. Some said they were fairy stones.

From habit, Hester was looking along the way to the next stone when she heard a thin, high sound, rather like a wail. Then it stopped, and there was just the silence of the night.

Hester stood still, and listened again. It was only a small sound, but she couldn't account for it. For a moment she could only hear the beating of her own heart, a little faster for the brisk walk. A small breeze moaned round her, and died. Then she heard the sound again, and she thought it must be music.

In later years, Hester never forgot that moment. In the white and frozen waste of the moor and under a cold moon, she stood under the spell of music. It was a magic sound, a wild and lovely lament, and it held the aching sadness of the Celt, the sorrow of lost causes. She had heard such tunes played by Scottish pipers in Ripon. But this was the pure sound of a violin, carrying sadness deep into her heart.

Then suddenly the music changed. The sorrow died away, and a dancing rhythm took over; the music seemed to leap and twirl in a mad pattern of gaiety. And Hester, as if enchanted, was drawn towards the violin.

It was so unexpected that the girl rubbed her eyes to clear them, and shook her head. The music seemed to lie in front of her. Then it sank so that it came from under the ground . . . didn't the fairies live in caves under the earth? Had Jenny Little's fairies come to haunt her? On such a night it was half-believable!

Music was rarely heard in Kirkby, but Hester loved it – she even enjoyed singing the old folk songs. She went forward. She was almost at the stone by now, the fairy stone, and the music was coming from the ground at her feet! She broke into a sweat in spite of the cold air, and shivered as a cloud passed over the moon. Then she gritted her teeth, and remembered that she was a cynic when it came to fairies.

In the shadow of the stone, Hester found the explanation. With his back comfortably lodged against it sat a fiddler, totally absorbed in his music. He was slender, but quite human, and about her own age. She had never seen him before.

The tune came to an end, and the musician drew the bow across the strings with a final flourish. And then he looked up, and saw Hester looking down at him. His face altered, but he didn't get up.

'Good evening, mistress! His voice was soft. 'I knew you would come.'

'Nay, lad, it's sheer chance that I'm here . . . and what may you be doing, out of your bed at this hour?' The shock had made her more aggressive than usual. 'Folks out of bed at this time of night are usually up to no good.' That was the accepted village judgement.

The young man was not put out by the stern reply. He looked dreamily up at her and smiled faintly. 'I need help, mistress. My leg's broken.'

Now she could see that he was thin and haggard. The trainee nurse went down on her knees on the frosty ground and gently examined the leg in the poor light. 'What happened?' She looked carefully at the young face, and could see that the lad was in pain.

The fiddler passed a hand over his eyes. The energy of the music was gone now, leaving him drained. Perhaps he'd relaxed, knowing the worst danger was over. 'I . . . fell on it.' An odd answer.

'We'll get you down to the village, there's a doctor. I'll go down and fetch him, we'll come back for you with the trap. But . . . why? Why were you sitting there, playing the fiddle?' And frightening me half to death, she thought.

The bent head looked up again. 'What else could I do? I couldn't walk. It was sweeter than calling for help . . . and it brought you to me.' He had a sweet, rather impish smile.

Hester looked down at the youth in exasperation. On a night like this he could have died, easily enough, frozen to death. He was brave, though, and he'd played so well . . . too well, perhaps. If some of the moorland folk had heard that unearthly music they might well have run away very fast, gone home and hidden under the bed. Especially if they'd been talking to Jenny Little.

But how on earth had the lad come to be in that dangerous situation? Perhaps this was not the time to ask. Hester took off her shawl and wrapped it round the slight form. She noticed how thin his clothes were for such a night: indoor clothes. Standing up, she looked down at him. 'Don't worry – we'll be back as soon as we can.' She set off quickly down the road to Kirkby.

'Mebbe it's tinker lad.' Reuben, roused from his bed, was soon yoking up the trap. He was instantly awake, as soon as the doctor called him. They were both used to emergencies, and quite soon the team turned out into the night, Hester in an old coat of Reuben's. She was thrilled to be part of the medical team, rushing off and saving people's lives.

The tinker lad, Reuben volunteered as they trotted up the road, was a new one. The folk of Pateley seemed disposed to like him. Where he came from, nobody seemed to know. He'd heard a rumour of fiddle-playing, which had given him the clue.

When they got back to the stone on the moor, the frost had tightened its grip. The stars were inscrutable, and the world seemed a huge and unfriendly place to Hester's now weary mind. The young man was barely conscious and very cold, but he had managed to put the violin back in its padded case. A small bundle lay beside him on the ground.

Carefully the men lifted the lad, and found that he was light enough, but the trap was high, and the job was made awkward by his broken leg. Bishop bound the injured limb to the sound one, to keep it straight. The pain brought him round again and he tried to sit up.

'Please take care of the violin. . . .'

Hester handed it carefully into the trap. The lad was polite, she noticed, and his accent was funny – it wasn't local.

As smoothly as possible, but all too often painfully jolted by the deep ruts in the road, the team clopped back to Kirkby.

Gilbert, the lad said his name was. 'You are a very lucky young man,' said Bishop, quite severely, when they got him into the surgery and the lamps had been lit. Reuben went off to see to the horse, and Hester stayed behind to help, or perhaps to learn.

To take the patient's mind off the procedure of setting the limb, Bishop talked as he worked. 'What were you doing up there, anyway? How long had you been there when Hester found you? Was there an accident – or was it foul play?' But Gilbert had fainted. Bishop let it go, and concentrated on the plaster of Paris, which could be tricky.

Once the leg was attended to and a hot drink administered by Hester, who had boiled a kettle on the kitchen fire, the young man was given a bed in the clean straw of an empty stable.

Hester called in at the doctor's the next day, after her errand in the village was done. She'd expected that by daylight they would find a dirty and ignorant itinerant. So she was surprised to find that here was a clean, pale and rather handsome young man, quiet but articulate.

The lad was politely grateful for all they had done for him. He thanked Hester, taking her hand, for saving him from death on the moor, in the soft voice that was so unlike the rasping accent of the High Side. But his eyes belied the humility, as though it was an act, a well-used act but not his true self. He had the clearest green eyes Hester had ever seen.

'It would have been death for me sure, out in the snow and the frost. It was a beautiful night . . . not a bad way to go, maybe. But I'm thankful to be alive and . . . er . . . Reuben seems to think you can spare the stable for a while, master.'

Trust Reuben to arrange matters as though he were the master. Looking down at the young tinker, Bishop asked: 'Where are you going?'

The lad looked at his leg. 'Not very far at all, just now, master, I'm thinking. I was working my way to . . . to Scarborough, mending pots and pans in the villages. I could mend a few here, if the folks will bring them, and if you don't mind.' He shot Bishop another glance of those green eyes. 'I'll heal quickly, never fear.' He seemed to have the gypsy's aversion to revealing too much.

'And have you no home?' The question came from Hester. The lad's life was his own affair, but he seemed very young. How strange to be a vagrant. She remembered the night when she left Hagstones, with nowhere to go. Tears for the tinker lad came into her eyes.

A flicker passed over the pale face, and was gone. 'I have no home,' said the tinker evenly.

# CHAPTER SEVENTEEN

'This nursing and helping folks is all very well, but it leaves you with extra work, looking after Tommy.' Hester looked up worriedly from her task of rubbing up dried herbs for storage. Leaves of sage were spread on paper across the table, and were being crumbled into powder. The strong, spicy scent of sage reminded her of the warm summer days, the buzzing of bees in the sunshine. . . .

'And what is this herb good for?' Meg was testing her pupil's knowledge.

'Cooking rabbits!' Hester was mischievous. 'And . . . sage-tea: one ounce of dried sage to a pint of boiling water. A little sugar and juice of a lemon if you have one. There.'

'And for what would you use sage-tea?' Meg persisted.

Hester folded her hands and pretended to recite. 'For indigestion, for a mouthwash . . . oh, yes, as a tonic for the stomach, for liver complaints and-fevers-and-sore throats-but-see-Dr Bishop-if-symptoms-persist.'

'Well done. And, of course, it's one of the things we put into embrocation for rheumatism. Yes, Hester, about the nursing – it will do Tommy good to manage without you sometimes. Let me enjoy his company while I can, lass!' Tommy was on the verge of walking and talking, being nearly a year old. He was very mobile, with a fast crawl, and he could talk in his own way.

Hester looked at the older woman in alarm. 'You're not thinking of . . . dying, or anything, are you?'

Meg White looked reproving. 'Nay, lass, the other thing about sage, which you forgot, is that if you eat sage in May you'll live for ever! No, I was only thinking that young Thomas will be growing up before long, and his baby days will be over. Don't be so anxious, lass! I'm looking forward to teaching Tommy his letters, and nursery rhymes and all the things that little children should enjoy!'

Hester looked at Meg, and remembered that she had lost her own child. It was good that she could enjoy Tommy's company.

The next nursing assignment had just come up, and Hester was booked for a week, at Kirkby. A whole week without Tommy! Reuben came for her that afternoon in the trap, on boss's orders, and took up Hester and her bag of clothes. She was crying a little as she kissed Tommy and told him to be a good boy.

Reuben said quickly: 'Why, lass, Meg can come down with Tommy on Sunday to see you. Come to my house, it's handy enough for you to pop out for a minute or two.' And Meg nodded, smiling.

Susan Benson lay in bed, weak after much loss of blood, hovering in the balance between collapse and recovery. She'd been prescribed iron tonic, complete rest and no, absolutely no visitors at all. Not even young James, Susan's fiancé. The Bensons lived in Church Street, only a few doors from the Bishops, in a rather noisy position opposite the church.

The nurse soon realized that Susan had something on her mind: weak tears rolled down her cheeks as Hester washed her.

Eventually Hester decided to act naturally. To hell with all this meekness, that kept people at arm's length. 'What's up, love?' she asked cheerfully as she patted the patient dry. 'Cheer up, you'll be better soon. Dr Bishop never fails!'

Susan looked up at the healthy, smiling helper, and shook her head. 'The vicar came . . .' she whispered. 'He told me to prepare for death and . . . he said the church bells had a message!' Her head turned uneasily on the pillow.

> 'All ye that hear my doleful sound
> Repent before death ye confound!

'That's what the biggest bell has inscribed on the side. Mr Grimshaw said so! And he said . . . he said . . . I'll be in the church-yard soon!' She sobbed again.

'Never you mind about parson. He knows nowt. All you need is a nice rest and good food, and with Dr Bishop of course, you'll be right in no time. Trust me. I know.' Hester grinned, mocking herself – who was she to talk so? 'Now, when are you getting married to that nice lad? Architect, isn't he? Tell me about him.' Bugger the parson, she muttered to herself.

It was a black rage that Hester carried downstairs and afterwards, down to the doctor's, carefully controlled now, but very strong, against that black crow of a parson. Hester realized that she would always have strong feelings: a curse and a blessing. She urgently needed to tell Bishop that a patient's body was in danger, because of her immortal soul.

Hester flew down the street as fast as her long skirt allowed. Taking the steps two at a time, she bounded into the doctor's house, using up her anger in movement. She found Bishop putting on his coat.

'Doctor, you've got to do summat – something. Miss Benson's being killed by parson!' Hester's eyes were flashing as she faced him, and her voice was shaky with anger. 'Talking a young girl into her grave!' She was still wearing the nursing-apron.

Bishop smiled. 'You never do things by halves, young Hester! And what particular form of murder is the vicar bent upon?' But when he heard the story, he grew serious immediately. 'I'll speak to him. It can't be allowed.'

They talked for a few minutes about the effect of mind on body, until Hester calmed down. She realized that Bishop agreed with her.

'I'm going to the stable, come with me,' suggested the doctor, and opened the door for her.

Reuben was measuring out oats for the evening feed. He looked up as Hester went in, with a slight twitch of a smile. 'Now, lass.'

Bishop sat on a feed-bin as Reuben said to him quietly: 'I've put tinker lad in my spare room . . . it's ower cold in stables of a night.'

Bishop raised his eyebrows. 'Should you have asked me first?'

Gilbert appeared, and Reuben said quickly, 'It's nowt. Er, boss, folks asked me to tell you that Lance Wood is on the warpath again, him as took a gun to church. Lost his memory, they say. Should be locked up, and doctor is the man to do it.' Gilbert stirred uneasily.

Hester smiled as the doctor adroitly turned the tables. 'Since you offer me medical advice, how about this sample of oats?' He picked up a handful and ran it through his fingers. 'Smells musty to me . . . and it's very light. Not good, at the price.'

Reuben shrugged. 'Got them from Tanfield. Maize is cheaper this year, but I don't hold with it.'

As the discussion on feed continued, Gilbert hopped over to where Hester stood in the doorway.

The last remnants of Hester's anger evaporated as she looked at the slim lad on crutches, the pure profile, the green eyes. He looked very thin, almost fragile, and pale – certainly not robust enough to sleep rough. Not, in fact, a seasoned vagrant. The accident must have given him a lot of pain, she thought.

'Who are you?' The question came out of its own accord.

'I'm Gilbert.' There was a pause. 'And I'm staying here, in Reuben's house for a while ... people are so kind!' He paused. 'Reuben tells me that you are a nurse. I'll never forget you finding me on the moor. I looked up at this beautiful vision, a young lady in a shawl, so graceful!' He smiled at her, so foreign and so charming. Hester blushed.

Reuben pulled hay into the racks. 'That Lance Wood ... what are ye going to do about him? He should be certified and locked up.' Hester nodded; she agreed.

Bishop laughed grimly. 'Half the High Side should be certified, in my opinion. When people have brain damage, can't remember how to behave, we should put them in care for their own safety and that of others. I'd better go to the vicarage now, catch him before evensong.' He went out, dusting off his jacket.

Gilbert suddenly sat down on a barrel, looking shaky. 'What's matter, lad?' asked Reuben, concerned.

'Nothing, Reuben, nothing ... just my leg gave a twinge, that's all.'

Meg and Tommy came into the yard, Tommy in a pram that Reuben had found for him. Meg had been able to wheel him down the village street from Larton, and Hester was so pleased to see him that there was no polite conversation for a while.

Reuben took them all into his cottage, where a kettle was boiling on a bright wood-fire. Gilbert, who seemed a handy lad, got out cups and saucers, and Meg produced a cake. Looking round the neat little room, Meg smiled and said, 'You're very comfortable here, Reuben.' Especially for a single man, Hester thought. There was a neat home-made rug on the red-tiled floor and some gleaming brasses on the mantelpiece. The walls were hung with

141

various prints of horses, and a big clock ticked majestically on the wall.

Tommy sat on his mother's knee, but the new surroundings were too much for him, and he began to cry. Large tears rolled down his baby face, as he clutched at Hester convulsively.

'I'll have to sing to him . . . sorry!' she said to the others, and rocking him gently she sang a few nursery rhymes, until he was quiet again. She put him back in the pram, but as soon as the singing stopped, Tommy howled again.

Hester told him to be quiet, but Gilbert got out the violin. 'If Tommy likes music, let's all sing!'

So they sang all the nursery rhymes they could think of, and a few folk songs, and Gilbert seemed to know them all. Gilbert played and Hester sang, Meg and even Tommy joined in with a few notes of his own, and Reuben formed the audience. Hester had a sweet voice, and she'd sung to Tommy since he was born.

Gilbert looked happy with his violin on his shoulder and the fire-light playing on his face. Reuben seemed at ease; he must have been lonely, Hester thought, since Marjorie died. She wished the party could go on, but Meg needed to get home before dark. They had another cup of tea, and Hester noticed that the tinker had quite good manners and didn't drink tea from his saucer.

Hester had to get back to Bensons'. Bugger that parson! Susan would have to improve in health before the nurse could go home. Gilbert took her hand again at the cottage door.

'Thank you,' he said quietly. 'Music is precious, and but for you, I wouldn't be here at all to enjoy it!'

'Nay lad, anybody would have done the same.' Hester was embarrassed, but pleased to be appreciated. How attractive this lad was, with his soft voice . . . a bit younger than herself, she judged.

Time went on, the days got shorter, and Christmas drew nearer. Susan Benson recovered, thanks to Bishop, and to careful nursing. Hester, pleased with their success, went thankfully back to Meg and Tommy.

Then one night snow fell and they woke to a fresh new world. The Bishops were at breakfast with a bright fire burning when the maid looked into the breakfast room rather hesitantly, having been told that they liked a quiet breakfast. 'The vicar's here, mum.'

'Show him in, Lizzie, and bring another cup.' Mary Bishop was quite equal to the vicar, even at this time of day.

'Good morning, Grimshaw.' The doctor stood up as the vicar bustled in, bringing large quantities of cold air with him. 'Come to the fire. Will you take a cup of coffee?' The matter of Susan Benson was over, but they hadn't spoken since.

Grimshaw looked more uneasy than usual, as he rubbed his cold hands together. 'No, thank you, I have just breakfasted,' he said precisely. 'To tell the truth, Bishop, I wanted a word with you. On a rather delicate matter.' He looked at Mary, and Mary stayed where she was.

' Please don't worry about me.' The doctor's wife was placid.

The vicar cleared his throat and looked out of the window at the church opposite, as if for support. 'The truth is, I wonder whether we ought to encourage . . . vagrants?'

Bishop looked puzzled, but Mary saw the point. 'You mean the tinker?' She smiled.

'Well, er, yes.' The vicar shuffled. 'I hear that he has visited the – ah, school, and conversed with our . . . young people.' He was gaining confidence. 'I ask, you, Bishop, as a medical man and a leader in this village, do you not think that the man could be a bad influence?'

Silence, except for the crackling of the fire.

'We know absolutely nothing about him, I gather, except that he is a vagrant. With no possessions. Who wanders about in the middle of the night.'

There was another silence, broken by the silvery chime of a clock.

In response to Mary's gesture, the vicar accepted a cup of coffee, and subsided into a chair.

Bishop looked into the fire for a while. Then he looked up, having decided to toe the conventional line.

'Well, Grimshaw, I see your point. We must safeguard the children, and our property. We must not encourage in the lower orders any tendency to vagabondage or loose living.' He looked stern. 'However, I must insist on being allowed to exercise my own judgement. In my opinion, my man acted in a Christian spirit in giving the fellow a bed when he was injured and couldn't travel on. He is still not able to travel. But he is clean and decent, and healthy, apart from a broken leg.'

Grimshaw's jaw set more deliberately. 'As usual, Bishop, you think only of the body, while my concern is my flock's immortal souls. What if they are corrupted by his influence?'

Bishop took a deep breath and counted up to ten. Then he chuckled. 'It's Christmas, Vicar. Use your own influence. Why don't you invite the vagrant to join the carol-singers on their rounds this year? Might even increase the donations, to have a fiddle as well.'

Grimshaw put down his cup rather shakily. 'Does he – ah – use foul language?' The pale blue eyes were apprehensive.

'Not in the least,' said Bishop cheerily, overlooking the insult to his judgement. 'He is soft-spoken and polite. But come and meet him.' Mary poured herself more coffee, to hide her smile.

Grimshaw hesitated. 'He will probably not know any hymntunes, Bishop. Is he – Irish? He could even be . . . a Roman Catholic!'

By this time Bishop was at the door. 'Come along, Grimshaw. And visit him as a temporary member of your flock. What about *his* immortal soul?'

With a look at Mary, Grimshaw took up his hat and followed to the stable yard. Flurries of snow danced on the cobbles at their feet.

The slender young man must have been a shock to the vicar. He stood slim and straight, apart from the crutch, in the kitchen with a broom in his hand, not put out by the pale-blue stare.

When catechized, Gilbert admitted to knowing all the old carols. He got out the violin to play over a few, since the parson seemed unconvinced.

'I can see that his technique is quite good, but of course a vagrant will not be able to read music,' Grimshaw whispered to the doctor.

'And how many singers have you?' the tinker asked politely.

'About ten, but we could do with a few more, especially female voices.'

Gilbert looked at Bishop. 'Well now, I was thinking, there's a young lady called Hester who sings very well . . . she maybe could be invited, if she isn't a singer already.'

Lady? The doctor and the parson both nearly choked. The vicar tried to be vague. But Bishop said he would send a message to invite Hester, and when was the next rehearsal?

Grimshaw decided to give in gracefully. The man must have had a decent Christian upbringing, even though he was now a hardened vagabond. 'I will look out an old coat to give to the boy,' he said to Bishop in his charitable voice. 'Then he might pass for a respectable villager.'

# CHAPTER EIGHTEEN

' 'Course I know all the carols. "Hark the herald", all that lot, we used to sing 'em at school.'

The Reverend Grimshaw was seen to repress a comment on this casual approach to choir-practice. A Kettlewell and a tinker ... poor man, thought Hester, he was still not quite sure about this year's collection of carol-singers.

Hester herself had grave reservations, thinking they'd be a churchy lot, but was pleasantly surprised to find that the chief singer and conductor was Richard Sayers from the Shoulder of Mutton, who was quite human. She knew a couple of the others, too, and she enjoyed the rehearsals, enlivened by Gilbert's violin music. And his polite admiration of her; it was nice to be admired, for a change, even if he was a tinker. Hester was beginning to realize how lonely she had been, shut away at Larton all those months. Gilbert said how pleased he was that she'd joined the singers, the sort of remark that a High Sider wouldn't have thought of.

The snow was just enough to be seasonal, but not enough to hamper people's movements and keep everybody indoors. The first night out, the singers went round Kirkby village and were very well received. Word got around and they were invited further afield. On these evenings Tommy was in bed well before Hester set out, and Meg was pleased to keep an eye on him.

One night Hester came home rather excited. 'We've been asked to sing at Holly Hall!' That was at Masham, miles off over Nutwith Common, and they would get the carrier to take them there. Sir Marmaduke was having a dinner-party, and wanted music for the guests.

Hester had never been inside a really big house, but the others told her tales of huge, gilded mirrors, great crystal chandeliers and enormous libraries. The vicar rubbed his hands and told them that Sir Marmaduke was generous when it came to donations, as a rule.

Mary Bishop was talking about the poorhouse again, since Scott-Jones, the parson from Kexmoor, had defected to Dr Johnson, who was skilfully collecting the better class of patients. He was smoother, less rugged than Bishop. But people like Meg White could easily see that he was ambitious above all, and less concerned about his patients.

'What with Johnson in the big houses, and Meg White among the cottagers, Robert, you have quite a lot of competition!'

Robert replied that Johnson could keep the big houses. Those patients were often overfed and under-excercised, and too critical altogether. And then his wife handed him a note on heavy, embossed paper, with a crest on the top.

'Oh dear, the county again,' the doctor groaned. 'Wish I could stick to the farmers! Sir Marmaduke invites us to dinner. The last time we were there I had to give free consultations.'

Bishop got up and put more wood on the fire, then looked across at Mary. 'I suppose Sir Marmaduke has been good to us. Quite a few useful introductions to people who pay their bills.' Rich patients helped to subsidize the poorer ones. But when the Bishops heard the rest of the guest-list, they wondered what sort of an evening it would be. Dr Johnson and his wife were also invited, and the Kirkby singers would perform.

The full moon shone from a clear sky when the guests set out for Holly Hall. Hester sat by Gilbert in the big carrier's cart from Thorpe, hired for the night to take the carol-singers to the party. She was warmly wrapped in a dark cloak they had bought with some of her nursing wages. Gilbert was resplendent in the vicar's old coat, which fitted him quite well, since it had belonged to a younger, slimmer edition of the vicar of Kirkby.

Hester felt like a young lass when she was with Gilbert, as though she were having some of the youthful fun she'd missed. But Gilbert, although so friendly, was also detached, mysterious. He was from a different world. One day he would go away again, and that would be that. Meanwhile, she loved to look at him, to hear his soft voice. It was an enchantment, a sort of spell. It was a new feeling for Hester, not in the least like her passion for Ned.

Under the winter moon, the Ure valley was benign, softened by centuries of human occupation. Scattered farms hid among clumps of trees, and from the roofs of the little town rose the graceful spire of Masham church. It was a different world from the moorland.

'How beautiful!' said Gilbert, as they looked down over Masham. 'I've never been here before.'

Before a huge log fire, Sir Marmaduke West and his lady greeted their guests, graciously including the singers in their greetings. Johnson was there already, his dark head bent attentively towards Lady West as he agreed fervently with what she was saying. Mrs Johnson's fragile beauty was directed like a dazzling beam at Sir Marmaduke. The baronet was a patient of Bishop's, Hester knew. Were the Johnsons trying to replace him?

There were a dozen other guests, including the portly Reverend Scott-Jones and his high-bred wife – Bishop called him a Squarson, a squire-parson – and Miss Bramley, the gentle benefactress of Kirkby.

The carol singers were taken to the servants' hall, which was less frightening than 'upstairs', where they were to appear during dinner. In the housekeeper's room, a similar ritual was taking place. The Hall servants were out to show their paces to the visitors, the carol-singers and assorted grooms. The log fire burned just as brightly as the one upstairs, and there was hot punch to warm them once they'd seen to the horses.

Hester looked round with wide eyes, taking everything in. Mrs Bain the housekeeper presided, since the butler was on duty upstairs, and she looked round with satisfaction at her guests. 'That's right, John, give everybody a glass before you go to wait at table. I'm sure that Holly Hall is very pleased to see you all.'

It wasn't often the servants got together like this, but they nearly all knew each other. Lloyd, the Johnsons' groom, had been brought by his employer from Wales and was obviously the outsider, so they did their best to make him feel welcome. 'Have some punch, Mr Lloyd,' said young John politely.

'I'm not allowed to drink,' replied Lloyd in the high tenor of Anglesey, with great emphasis on the consonants.

Reuben looked him over. He didn't reckon much to Lloyd's way with horses, having seen him in the stable. He fingered his tight collar uneasily, ready for any opposition from the Johnson camp.

The supper that followed was lavish by High Side standards, a real feast. 'We won't be able to sing after all this, Mrs Bain,' joked Richard Sayers.

Hester and Gilbert were quite relaxed, anonymous in the singers' group. They talked to each other about Kirkby, Masham and the local area; Gilbert wanted to know as much as she could tell him, and he really listened to what she said.

Reuben looked over the piles of food and winked at Gilbert. He allowed John to refill his glass with small beer. That punch was too strong for a working groom.

The footman went on down the table, and Hester noticed that Lloyd had taken to the punch, after all. He was drinking it down like water. Maybe they'd put salt in his food . . . an old moorlander's trick, that was, and not quite fair.

Bishop, as he'd predicted, was not having so easy a time. The company upstairs hadn't been long at the big polished table with its row of silver candlesticks before a colonel, visiting for the hunting, brought up the subject of medicine. 'As we have two physicians here tonight, I believe, we may get a little free advice – eh?' He laughed, and his yellow teeth made him look like a horse.

Across the silver, Johnson's sleek head was lowered over his soup. He looked up suddenly at Bishop. 'It depends,' said Johnson smoothly, wiping his mouth on his napkin, 'on what the topic might be. We wouldn't wish to offend the ladies. Medicine isn't always suitable for mixed company.' He looked meaningfully at Lady West, who smiled graciously back.

Colonel Gray could have taken the hint, but he didn't. As the soup-plates were removed he went on: 'My doctor tells me to take the waters at Harrogate.' He puffed.' Now . . . do you think it's a good idea? Or would another spa be better – Knaresborough maybe, or Cheltenham?'

Sir Marmaduke brightened up considerably. 'Cheltenham they say is very good. I'd go there if I were you.' Cheltenham was a nice long way from Holly Hall.

Miss Bramley's pleasant voice carried down the table. 'What do you think, Dr Bishop?'

'I can't disagree with Dr Johnson,' Bishop began, one eye on Mary. She'd told him to agree with the man. 'Because I've never sent anybody to Harrogate.'

There was a little buzz round the table. 'So you don't believe in the water-cure?' Gray was persistent.

Mrs Johnson gave a tinkling laugh. 'Oh Dr Bishop, but would you deny us the social benefits of Harrogate? Think of the people one meets at a spa!'

'Precisely. This I think is the chief benefit of the spa. No doubt the spirits are raised by seeing new faces, if the patient is not too ill. I am so glad you agree with me.'

Johnson's heavy brows drew together over his dark eyes as Miss Bramley smiled across at him.

To Bishop's relief, the carol singers trooped in at this moment, and though the dinner went on, conversation was not possible.

They sang well, Bishop thought, and the tinker lad played very well indeed. Hester's bright eager face, singing in the back row, heartened him. That girl had come a long way.

The Bishops were not sorry when it was time to go, and they could call for Reuben to take them home. The groom Lloyd was called by Dr Johnson at the same time and Reuben, watching him fumbling with the straps, decided to give him a hand. He was surprised by the powerful smell of drink in that stall. 'It can't be the horse,' he said grimly.

Lloyd hiccuped, but said he could manage. 'Daren't keep the doctor waiting,' he muttered.

Reuben got away first, and sighed with relief as they moved down the drive, just ahead of the Johnsons. Lloyd would have to look out for himself now. The moon was still bright, it was a lovely night. . . .

The next minute there was the sound of fast hoof-beats behind them and Johnsons' trap came careering down the drive, the young horse quite out of control. It attempted to overtake Reuben and the Bishops, but they had reached the gateposts just as it drew level, and with a splintering crash the two traps collided and both horses fell.

A woman's scream sounded above the squeal of the horses. Johnson and his wife were still in their partly overturned vehicle. Bishop jumped out just as the carrier, with the carol-singers aboard, came trotting round the bend. He managed to stop the vehicle before it reached the scene of the crash.

Hester was out of the cart almost before it stopped, and Gilbert hopped out awkwardly after her. 'You can't help!' she said in exasperation, looking at his plaster cast.

'I can calm the horses . . . tinkers are good with horses.' Gilbert limped over to where Reuben was carefully getting Dolly up from her knees, and took charge of her so that the groom could see to the other horse. Dolly had grazed knees, but she was more indignant than afraid. Gilbert ran his hand down her legs, feeling for cuts, and whispered in her ear.

The Johnsons' horse was foaming at the mouth, squealing and rearing. Reuben waded in, cut it loose from the trap, and walked it down the road. In ten minutes or so he was back, and the horse had settled down.

Gilbert then held both horses while Reuben sorted out the tangle of harness. 'Thanks, lad,' said Reuben briefly, with one of his rare smiles.

Lloyd, the cause of the accident, was sitting among the wreckage, singing in Welsh, in a high tenor.

Hester was aware of the others working around her as she carefully bandaged Dr Johnson's head. Johnson was shouting loudly. He was injured, and worse, he was being used to teach a peasant girl how to bandage. His trap was ruined, his horse was cut. Dr Johnson was not a happy man.

'What's the matter now?' he said irritably to his wife, when she leaned over and tapped him on the arm.

'Sorry, dear . . . but I have some glass in my arm, from the carriage lamp, and it's bleeding rather badly.'

Hester was appalled. The man hadn't even glanced at his wife after the crash! She saw Gilbert looking at him. 'Would you believe it?' he whispered to Hester.

It took some time to clear the drive, so that the other guests could leave. The Johnsons were invited to stay the night at Holly Hall, and Lloyd was to be given a bed in the stables, although his master wanted him thrown into the lake. Reuben found that the Bishops' trap was drivable, and Dolly was anxious to get home.

The singers jogged home in the carrier's cart. Hester was weary, her head full of the accident, and the calm and competent way that Gilbert had done what he could. She was trembling now, a reaction after the event. Gilbert talked quietly to her about the splendours of Holly Hall; the glitter of candles, lamps, silver, polished antique furniture, and the gilded portraits of Sir Marmaduke's ancestors,

151

gazing down their noses from the panelled walls.

'I could never live there!' Hester said to Gilbert. 'You'd be afraid to sit down on those chairs!'

The tinker smiled at her dreamily. He too was tired, having for much of the evening leaned on the wall so that he could play. 'You could get used to it. You can get used to anything.'

# CHAPTER NINETEEN

'I wonder where Reuben and the lad are having their Christmas dinner? They could come and join us, if they liked.' Meg had often invited lonely people in to share her dinner at Christmas, she said.

This year Hester had made puddings, big puddings boiled for hours in a cloth. And there was a goose in the shed, waiting to be plucked. They would have plenty to share.

The women worked on at their knitting in silence for a while. It was Hester who thought of the difficulty. 'But Gilbert couldn't walk this far, he's still in plaster. And Reuben stays at home, just in case there's an emergency.'

'Well . . .' Meg looked across at her helper. 'Maybe we should offer to take our dinner down to Reuben's, and share it. I think his side-oven will be plenty big enough. And we all fitted into his kitchen the other day.'

The next day Meg made it her business to see Reuben in Kirkby.

The groom almost smiled. 'Ay, Meg, that's a right good idea.' He pushed the cap back on his head, and gave her a hard blue stare. 'Are you sure, now? We'll have to cook it in my oven, if you can trust me!'

Meg looked back at him peaceably. 'I'd trust you with my life, lad, let alone the Christmas goose.'

On Christmas Eve Hester trundled Tommy, who was sharing his pram with the portable Christmas dinner, down to Kirkby. There were the dressed goose ready for the oven, the sage-and-onion stuffing, the potatoes, turnips and Brussels sprouts from Meg's vegetable garden, the puddings and a few mysterious parcels. At the last minute Meg had added a bottle.

There was a bright fire in the cottage, beside which Gilbert was looking at a big book. 'You can read!' said Hester, and her hand went to her mouth. 'Sorry, I shouldn't have said that!' She hid her confusion, brushing the mud from her skirt.

Gilbert appeared not to have heard. 'Hester and Tommy! How good to see you.' He stood up politely, and offered her a chair. 'We are taking this cookery seriously,' he confessed, with a comical-serious look. 'It's a big responsibility for a tinker and a groom. We're not sure we are equal to it, at all!' Gilbert consulted the big book again. 'Roast goose!' he said happily. 'Mrs Beeton says two hours, but Reuben thinks more.'

Reuben had taken on himself the responsibility of making frumenty, an ancient Christmas ritual. Hester had never tasted it before.

'Well,' said Reuben, 'with all due respect, I shouldn't think ye had much of a Christmas at Hagstones, now?' Hester nodded; it was true. She was happier now than she'd ever been at home.

Frumenty was for Christmas Eve, so they each had a dish, right there and then, a mixture of whole corn and dried fruit, baked in the oven, and with spice and a hint of rum or brandy.

Reuben went out to feed the horses, Tommy went to sleep, and Hester relaxed in her chair, resting before the long walk home. From the other side of the hearth, Gilbert put another log on the fire, then sat down and looked at her.

'Why didn't you have much of a Christmas at your home, as Reuben said?' The voice was gentle and the eyes were kind. Gilbert really wanted to know how she felt. But she didn't know how to explain.

Looking across at the clear, green eyes, Hester remembered that she'd decided to be honest for the rest of her life. 'My father – he's dead now – was a terror, he beat us, we just lived in fear of him. I've had to learn so much since I left home! About manners, and not swearing, and such!' She felt suddenly shy at all this attention. They looked at the fire for a while, in a friendly silence. 'But what about you, Gilbert? Were you happy, when you were little?'

The lad looked away, and there was a sad expression on his face. 'I hope so.'

Then Reuben came back, with a whiff of cold outside air.

'I'd best be off with the bairn!' Hester stood up. 'It's Tommy's bedtime.'

Gilbert limped to the corner with Hester when she left, saying he had to keep his legs moving. He looked at her with a hint of mischief. 'Shall I tell you a secret? Hester, I've got a job!' But that was all he would say. He smiled, mysterious as ever.

When the plaster comes off, he'll be able to leave. He hasn't mentioned that. Hester realized that she would hate him to leave. She enjoyed his company, more than she could say.

'I'd better let you go home before dark.' With a brief kiss on the cheek, the tinker abruptly left her. Hester stood in the middle of the village, her hand to her burning cheek. High Side folks rarely did things like that.

The next day Hester was up well before daylight, feeding the animals and lighting the kitchen fire. Tommy was dressed in his new sailor-suit, and they all had a bowl of porridge before they set out, warmly shawled against the cold wind.

By the time they arrived at Kirkby, rosy with the walk, Reuben's kitchen was festive.

They'd decorated the room with holly and ivy, bringing into the kitchen the fresh, mysterious smell of the woods. Gilbert had prepared the vegetables. They had not forgotten to put the puddings on to boil, good and early. And the goose was in the oven; they could tell by the scent of it cooking.

It was Tommy's first Christmas, and he was naturally the centre of it for a while. Hester had wondered how she could buy presents for her little boy, but she needn't have worried. She knitted him a pair of little gloves and a woolly hat, and he looked so sweet in them that Meg nearly cried. And Tommy had his first big, important present. Gilbert had been busy with his gypsy arts, and had been carving bits of wood for weeks. Reuben had asked to help, and together they created a wonderful farmyard, with all the animals a farmer could possibly imagine. It was amazing, and Tommy was to remember it with pleasure for the rest of his life. He was too young to play with it yet, but by next Christmas he'd really appreciate it.

Where would Gilbert be, next Christmas? Hester wondered.

The dinner was perfect, and even the rhubarb wine tasted sweeter than usual. The pudding was served with white sauce, laced with a little rum donated by the Bishops.

Reuben brought in a yule log, while Gilbert was busy drying the dishes, his big scarf still round his neck in spite of the heat of the fire. Hester had knitted him a scarf with love, a green scarf. And she had also knitted one for Reuben, but he had managed to tear himself away from it by now.

The two men had both been touched by Hester's efforts, but Reuben was his usual grim self. Gilbert seemed to be under a spell. He is being bound to me with a green chain, Hester thought, and smiled at the romantic notion.

Hester could almost read his thoughts. They smiled at each other, but spoke little and the others didn't notice the golden haze that wrapped around them that day. Hester was almost afraid. It was a deep, deep feeling she had for Gilbert.

Just as the church clock struck four, Meg thought that they should walk back to Larton before it was quite dark. Dusk was falling gently on the village when they said goodbye and turned into the main street of Kirkby, Tommy carried on Hester's back. Gilbert watched them out of sight.

More snow came to the High Side after Christmas, and the villages were divided by the winter. Three feet of snow kept most people at home, and the villagers to themselves, thrown back on their own resources. It was only a mile or so from Larton to Kirkby, but it might as well have been a hundred. Hester wondered very much about Gilbert, but she saw only Meg and Tommy.

The three of them were snug enough in their own little world, with plenty of food and plenty of firewood. A few months ago, Hester would have loved the peace of the snowy landscapes, and would have watched the birds come in for scraps with a quiet mind. But now there was Gilbert, and she missed him: his mystery, his quiet smile and the way he pushed his fair hair out of his eyes.

Meanwhile, in Kirkby things were much the same. Reuben hoped fervently that those unwise females about to have babies would hang on to them until the thaw. He worried about the doctor's journeys through deep snow to go to emergencies, and fussed like an old hen until Bishop protested. 'Don't want to have to find another place!' was his excuse.

Gilbert felt as free as a bird, having finally got rid of the plaster cast on his leg so that he was able to move about more normally. Bishop said the break had healed well, but the muscles needed building up. There was no question of Gilbert's leaving just yet. No chance at all, said Reuben happily, looking at the depth of snow.

After a few weeks of enforced isolation a warm west wind brought the thaw, and people could move about again. Hester had to go to Kirkby every day to help out with old Mrs Simpson. But she didn't see Gilbert on her travels, and she hesitated to go looking for him. He was a vagrant, a young lad passing through, and she was a staid mother who shouldn't go chasing after lads; it wasn't right.

The doctor told Hester that he'd stopped wondering about Gilbert. His tactful enquiries, as he removed the plaster, had met with a blank wall. The lad was polite, but evasive. A gypsy habit, it had to be. Best to leave him alone, and let him go when the weather improved. He could have been hiding a criminal record, but Bishop didn't agree that he was a threat to the village, even though Grimshaw had told him that the lad crept about at dead of night!

Bishop mentioned the creeping habit to Hester, who was puzzled. Gilbert was certainly reticent and had volunteered no information about himself. But she didn't think he was dishonest.

Then, one night, Hester saw Gilbert flitting about the village.

It happened to be late when Hester set off for home that night. The old lady had taken a fit of indigestion, and had kept Hester with her until an enormous belch relieved the situation. Bicarbonate had done the trick, and she wasn't going to die tonight, after all.

Turning into the main street of Kirkby, walking between the piles of shovelled snow, Hester saw a slight figure ahead. Was it the vagrant? There was a click as the man slid through a side gate into a little paddock belonging to Village Farm.

A faint light gleamed from a shed, as the figure opened the door and slipped inside. Without stopping to think, Hester followed. But, going over the uneven trampled snow, she had time to wonder whether some illegal activity was going on in there, when decent folk were in their beds.

'Well! So this is what you're at!' Hester nearly fell over a lamb just inside the door. There was Gilbert among the sheep, looking like a very good imitation of a shepherd. A lantern on a nail shed its light on the lad's fair hair, and on the placid eyes of the ewes, some of which had lambs at their side.

The tinker's eyes lit up as she came in. 'Hester! It's good to see you. Yes, Mr Potter asked me to stay with the sheep at nights. I help them with lambing if they need it. He's with them during the day, and he needs his rest.'

'So during the day you're sleeping . . . I see. Well, that's good – this is the job you told me about. But why are you . . . creeping? Why so . . . sort of secret?' The girl was relieved; it could have been a gambling-den, although there were not too many of them in Kirkby.

Gilbert reached out, picked up a straying lamb and hooked it back on the mother's teat. 'I try to be as quiet as possible, to avoid waking people.' He looked guileless, the green eyes clear and honest.

'I spent some days with Mr Potter at the start,' the new shepherd explained. 'He's taught me a lot. And he couldn't find anybody else to help – not with this weather.'

She should be off home, but Hester sat down on the straw with Gilbert and they talked for a long time. He asked her all about sheep – what a lad for asking questions! And he listened earnestly to the answers, seeming to file away the information in his memory.

It was warm in the shed with the heat of the animals, and clean and tidy, just as Hester liked a farm to be. It was hard to drag herself away, to go out into the cold night and back to her lonely bed. What a way to think, for a respectable woman!

Gilbert walked with her to the door, moving easily now without his plaster, slim and straight as ever. He put his hands on her shoulders, and the green eyes looked straight down into hers. 'Come and see me again, if you can!' he said lightly, and touched her cheek gently with one finger. For a moment, Hester felt the world spinning round. Gilbert the tinker was having an effect on her. Was it just because they were both lonely and in need of affection, or was it . . . something else?

Hester, thinking about it afterwards, was slightly ashamed of her feelings for Gilbert. A mother should not take any interest in lads, especially a younger lad. She felt that Gilbert was younger than she was, if not in age, then certainly in experience of women. He was tentative where Ned had been assured. But he seemed much more sincere than Ned; looking back, she should have guessed that Ned didn't love her, only himself. But a dedicated nurse should not take any interest in men, except as patients.

Hester tried to immerse herself in work, but she was quieter as the days went by. She longed to pay another visit to Gilbert's shed.

Then came a week of night duty at Kirkby, to sit with a patient from ten o'clock, so that the family could get some sleep. On the first night Hester knocked quietly on the door of Gilbert's shed about nine: she had an hour to spare. And the lad was so pleased to see her, she felt giddy again, as she stepped into the light and warmth.

They sat and talked, and then Hester promised to come again the next night. And the next . . . by the end of the week, Hester couldn't stop thinking about Gilbert, although she tried. He scarcely touched her, and he talked about shepherding, about Reuben and the doctor, everyday things. Gilbert never mentioned feelings, but she sometimes caught him looking at her rather sadly. And Hester was deep in a feeling she recognized from long ago . . . but it was different from her love for Ned. More protective, gentler.

Gilbert looked at her on the last night. 'You know I have to leave, one day soon? I was on my way . . . to Scarborough.'

Hester's heart gave a lurch. Yes, she knew he would leave. And that a woman with a baby couldn't go off with a vagrant. It shouldn't have been such a shock.

'I shall miss you, Hester.' And he kissed her gently on the lips.

She choked back tears. Would he come back to Kirkby? Why did love cause such pain? The ache was physical, a feeling round her heart.

There was a nursing job at Larton after this, at the manor, and that kept her very busy for a while. The dairymaid had become, in Bishop's opinion, a very good nurse. She was more graceful and quiet in her movements than before, and kept her voice low, although she'd always had a pleasant voice.

Hester had learned from the doctor a great deal about scientific hygiene, and other medical mysteries. She knew about lying-in and laying-out. She was getting paid for her work, and was able to give Meg money for her keep. Her heroine was Florence Nightingale, now an old lady, advising governments on how to run medical services. Bishop had told her about Miss Nightingale, and read some of her letters to the trainee nurse.

From Meg White, Hester had learned many herbal remedies,

tolerance and forbearance, and the value of common sense. 'It's not so common!' Meg often said. But she had not learned yet the cure for a bruised heart, although she wished for one. Why should a tinker lad cause her to lose any sleep?

# CHAPTER TWENTY

Rose Balderstone, white-faced, was crying as she called to Hester. 'Father's all swollen up – I think he's dying! I'm going for Dr Bishop! Can you come?'

It was a warm spring evening and Hester was weeding in the garden when the rattle of a cart driven at speed made her look up. It arrived in a flurry of dust, and stopped dead at the garden gate. And there was Rose, in trouble.

Quickly Hester hitched up her skirt and, with a word to Meg, hopped into the cart. 'I'll drive to Kirkby, if you like.' Rose nodded and moved aside, and Hester took the reins.

As she drove, Hester thought about the possibilities. A swelling with acute discomfort sounded like a stomach upset, which was nothing to get alarmed about. But Rose was very frightened, and she was a sensible lass.

'What happened?' asked Hester, pushing the horse along as fast as she could.

'He was late home from market,' Rose sobbed, hanging on to the sides of the cart. Of course, it was Thursday – and Fred sometimes drank too much at the market. 'Mother heard the horse and cart coming in. I was in the byre.' She shuddered. 'And cart was empty!'

Hester looked into the warm night, which was darkening by now. There was a smell of growing things from the moist earth, a sweetness of spring flowers. 'You found him, then.'

'Mother and little Bobby – he's only ten, you know – walked back down the farm lane. All the gates were open except the last one – on to the road. And there he was, lying in gateway ... he'd been crushed against stone gatepost as cart went though. Horse maybe moved before he told it to.' Rose wiped her eyes with a handkerchief. 'A couple of lads from next door – they carried him home on a door. He's all smashed up. . . .'

The doctor was at home, thank goodness, and responded imme-diately. He drove Dolly fast along the lanes, and got there before Hester and Rose. Bishop took the stairs two at a time, nodding to the farmer's wife as he went by.

Hester followed soon after, leaving Rose downstairs.

Hester had some experience by now of medical conditions, but she was horrified when she looked down at the figure on the bed. It was nearly unrecognizable. Fred was like a blue balloon, as if some-body had inflated him with a pump. He was only just conscious, and not aware that Bishop had arrived. He could see nothing. The man was a bluish purple from lack of oxygen in the blood, and this was also making him gasp for breath.

'The instruments! Thinking to treat indigestion, I've got no surgical instruments with me. Someone will have to go back to Kirkby – Hester, will you do it?' He told her what he wanted, and where to find them. 'Take Dolly – I know you can drive like the devil! And get Reuben to drive you back.'

Hester turned Dolly round in the yard and raced off again. As the doctor talked quietly to the patient, trying to reassure him, Hester raced through the night, at seventeen steady miles an hour, with the mare's racing blood well and truly up by now. It was a matter of life and death; nobody could take that pressure for long. And if she were too late, she'd never forgive herself. . . .

To Hester's relief the moon rose, helping her to see the track.

Already in her life, Hester had spent a good few anxious moments. But she never forgot that drive. The night was very quiet, with not a breath of wind, unusual for the moorland. Dolly's hoofs sounded loud on the road. Rushing towards her, Hester saw the huge bloated figure on the bed, and knew that she had to race to save him.

There was no time to wonder whether the harness would hold. The trap was swaying and creaking, but there was no thought for safety. Reuben was a careful groom, and all the leather was supple and well-cleaned. Weak parts were renewed at once, because Reuben knew that a gallop like this could happen at any time.

Hester had not stopped to light the candles in the carriage lamps that hung at either side of the vehicle. Although most people carried lamps these days, they were not always used in the country.

Up here, folks had always been used to finding their way about in the dark. But lights were about warning others. Just as she came into Kirkby, at the crossroads the girl nearly crashed into a man riding sideways on a big Clydesdale carthorse, going home late from work. The Clydesdale reared and threw the man off into the lane, where he sat and shook his fist at the whirling trap. 'I'll have the law on you. . . .'

Hester raced into the surgery, grabbed the instruments and came out to find the mare blowing gently, getting her breath back. She knew that the job was not over yet.

The lights in Reuben's cottage were out; he was in bed, and she wouldn't disturb him. He had to catch up sometimes, after a series of night calls.

Hester decided to drive back on her own, as fast as she could. Thank goodness she knew her way round these lanes, just as she'd known where the doctor kept his instruments.

Martha Balderstone met Hester at the door as she jumped down. 'It's too late – he's gone!' She spoke in utter hopelessness. All they could do now was to lay him out decently.

The doctor had failed and once more death had won. Hester subsided, feeling suddenly very tired indeed.

Martha had gone upstairs, against orders, and had hysterics when she saw Fred. Bishop cursed, furious with himself. If only he'd brought the trocar with him. . . .

With a beating heart, Hester went upstairs again. Fred lay blue and lifeless, hardly recognizable as a human being. It seemed impossible to her, quietly watching, that even if Bishop had brought him round, he would ever have been normal again. She too thought he was gone.

As he watched, the doctor pointed to what Hester thought was a slight movement. It might just be the air in the body, but there was nothing to lose; it was worth a try. Bishop took out the sharp hollow trocar from its sterile case and plunged it into the patient, at the side and slightly below the ribs. There was a loud hiss, and a great deal of air escaped. The body decreased slightly in size.

Walking round the bed, Bishop held the trocar poised again when Martha screamed. 'Have ye no respect for a dead body? Let him be!'

Hester gently moved her aside and held her off, while Bishop concentrated and plunged again. Another loud hiss. The balloon was going down.

Then slowly, Fred started to breathe again visibly, falteringly at first. He was still alive – for the moment. Bishop didn't dare to massage his chest, to get the lungs going, for fear of broken ribs. The pain of breathing must have been great – and only heaven knew what damage was done to internal organs.

Martha couldn't believe her eyes at first, when she realized that Fred was breathing. By the time Bobby came up to see what was happening, the farmer was conscious again. He was still blue and inflated enough to upset the little boy, but the child insisted on staying, and was standing by his father's head when Fred opened his eyes. 'Are you there, Bobby? I can hardly see.'

Martha and Rose cried quietly, and Hester almost cried with relief. The doctor tried to be bracing. 'Don't worry,' he said cheerfully. 'Your ribs will be mighty uncomfortable and I'll give you some laudanum to deaden the pain. The rest of the air will go by degrees. Your sight might take a few days to come back, but you'll be back to normal ... I hope!' he added in French, as he dabbed the stab wounds with antiseptic.

Hester knew that Fred's survival would depend on how much internal damage had been done. But if the patient believed he would recover, he'd have a better chance, she'd learned.

'What happened, Doctor? Did you ever see the like before?' Hester asked, her eyes on the patient.

'He broke some ribs of course, when the cart crushed him. He'll need careful nursing; young Rose can perhaps manage that. There isn't much I can do to strap him up.'

Bishop looked at the patient, who was still a horrible colour. 'When they carried him upstairs – and round the turn in the staircase, too – the sharp edges of one or two ribs must have gone through into his lungs. That opened up the lungs to the rest of the body. Every time he breathed in, the air went into the pleural cavity, and then into the space under the skin. A most unusual case.' He sounded not so much detached and clinical, as rather shaky. 'I've read about it – Erichson, I believe.' He seemed to feel the need to talk, and Hester was an attentive listener. 'But I've never actually seen it before.'

Hester made some notes in her mental file, storing it for future reference. But it wasn't likely they'd get another case on the High Side.

'My!' Martha Balderstone found her voice. 'Doctor's grand mare were a clipper to go!' They all looked at Bishop with awe. This was powerful drama, and would do his reputation much good.

'And Hester did well!' said Bishop. 'It's the first time I've let anyone apart from Reuben drive my outfit. I knew she could drive at speed, having seen her in action with the Robinsons' cart . . . nerve and skill, you need both to drive at speed.'

Hester was beginning to feel the strain, and when Bishop smiled at her she wiped away tears. Thank goodness they had been in time. Fred now had a chance of recovery, but he must have been dangerously close to death. It was harrowing work, this nursing. She hadn't realized until now how much it involved you in the patients' lives, their hopes and fears, how much of their stress and strain you carried.

'I wouldn't have missed it for anything!' Hester admitted. She'd been able to help to save Fred, and that was something special.

Sensible Rose produced a cup of tea, some of those ferocious ginger biscuits, and a special smile for Hester. She was pale with strain, and looked more fragile than ever, a delicate little dark rose.

'You're going to have to manage without Father for a week or two, possibly longer. How will you get on?' Bishop asked, as he took the cup.

Her mother answered. 'We'd have managed better if there wasn't so many ewes still to lamb. We're later this year; first tup wasn't up to the job. In fact, we could do with a good shepherd, for shearing and all. Do you know of a shepherd wanting a place, Doctor? There's too much for Rose and me to manage, with cows as well.' She was already coming to terms with the situation.

The doctor smiled. 'Well, you could do worse than the tinker lad – remember him playing for the carols at Christmas? He's done some lambing for Potter . . . he stays with Reuben. Maybe he would like the job.'

Across the kitchen table, Hester felt herself blushing, and hoped that nobody noticed.

Mrs Balderstone was dubious. 'What do you think, Hester?'

'I know the lad, went carol singing with him. He's clean and quiet enough . . . don't know how he'd be with sheep, but I think he'd frame, right enough. He was grand with the horses, the night we had an accident at Holly Hall.' She spoke quietly, sounding quite detached. That was medical training for you.

Gilbert was very good with sheep, she happened to know, although she couldn't say so. Those hours in the lambing-shed with him – at dead of night, too – would ruin any reputation she had left, if anyone found out!

Hester had watched the lad handling the animals, and had answered his many questions. If he remembered half she'd told him, he'd know quite a bit about sheep.

The memory of that shed made her smile slightly. He'd been so young, so innocent, and so unlike Ned Mecca. She loved his youth and innocence, treasured the memory of his one gentle kiss.

And of course, the job might keep Gilbert in the district for a while. Might even make him want to settle down? Steady, Hester, don't get your hopes up. She drank more tea, to hide her burning face.

'Well . . .' Martha looked at Bishop. 'He could sleep in stable loft. I'll come down to Kirkby myself, Doctor, and see him.'

Bishop took his nurse back to Larton on the way home to Kirkby. They were all tired, including the gallant little horse, and not much was said. As the girl jumped down at Meg's gate the doctor looked at her. 'Well done, young Hester. You were quite cool. I can trust you in an emergency!'

'I did nowt.' The girl shrugged, just as Reuben might have done. Then she looked up, with her new-found politeness. 'Thanks, Doctor. Pleased to be of some use.'

# CHAPTER TWENTY-ONE

The local nurse went through the wrought-iron gate, up the garden path and knocked on the neat front door. She was dressed for work in clean cotton, under a dark cloak. Her hair was tied back, and she carried her bag of medical bits and pieces: her measuring-glass for accurate doses of medicine, and her much-prized thermometer. She felt most professional as she stood there on the scrubbed step on a bright sunny morning in May, a few days after Fred's accident.

The door opened, and a housemaid peered out. 'G'day, Hester. What do you want?' was the cool greeting.

'Morning, Gertie, I've been sent by Dr Bishop as a day nurse to Mr Hodgson.' This was another moorland lass whom Hester had known at school. Hester took a step forward, but Gertie half-closed the door in her face. 'Just a minute.' She vanished inside the house.

Hester looked round at the manicured gardens, the clipped hedges, the greenhouses and the orchard. Well, they could certainly afford a nurse, there was plenty of money here. It might be a pleasant job for a few days, and she could go home to Tommy at night.

A few minutes later an elderly woman came to the door. Hester's heart sank when she saw the sour expression, even before the woman spoke. 'I'm sorry, there's been a mistake. We have no use for your services, thank you.' She turned away.

'What's wrong? Dr Bishop arranged it!' Hester had walked all the way from Larton, just to be dismissed. It was cruel!

Mrs Hodgson turned back to the girl. 'Well, if you must know, we do not wish to encourage immorality in the village. We will not employ a fallen woman. My maid tells me that you are Hester Kettlewell!' It sounded as though the devil himself had knocked at her door.

167

It was hard to be professional, but Hester tried. 'The doctor said I was the best person for the job. I have a little son, but I'm not immoral.' She didn't want to work there anyway by now, but she was burning to set the record straight.

Mrs Hodgson snorted. 'I am surprised that Dr Bishop would recommend an unmarried mother for a position of trust, or any other position in a decent Christian household. You should realize, woman, that you have forfeited your right to be received in any decent house. Many people in this village believe that you should have left the neighbourhood. You are not welcome in Kirkby.'

Hester seethed. Who was this old prune to sit in judgment? She'd only lived in the village for a few years! She could stick her job, so could all the righteous old biddies. The sight of Gertie smirking in the hall was hard to bear. But maybe this was another test of a good nurse; she wouldn't tell them where to go, after all. She went back down the path without another word.

Anger carried Hester back to Larton very quickly, but at the sight of Meg's pleasant, surprised face, she broke down and cried. She cried for an hour, all the sadness coming out for her ruined life, for the death of poor Kit Horner. She cried for the waste of her father's life, a clever man ruined by drink. Hester wept for her bleak future, the feeling that Gilbert would have misgivings about her past . . . even a vagrant would think she wasn't good enough for him.

Meg left her for a while, and took Tommy out into the garden. Tommy was uneasy. He was beginning to talk, and he clung to Meg's skirt as he quavered: 'Mama crying!'

The day went on, time passing, in spite of the fact that Hester's bright new life had fallen apart. They had a meal, and planted the beans in the vegetable patch – a different spot every year, Meg insisted. The tea she gave Hester was a soothing mixture of sage and mint, and it calmed the girl, although nothing would take away the physical feeling of a lump of lead in her chest. Hester made a great effort to work, but she had no energy left. All her vitality was gone.

By afternoon, the clouds had come in and there was a shower of rain. Meg thought it was time to encourage Hester to talk. They put Tommy to bed for his afternoon nap, and settled down to making besoms in the shed. But the girl was silent except for a sigh now and then. Now that the anger over her rejection in the village had burned itself out, her thoughts were with Gilbert.

Gilbert was young, probably a year or two younger than Hester, and inexperienced in love. He was elusive, he liked women, but Gilbert had his different ways, like kissing her on the cheek and taking her hand; they were maybe just the way he'd been brought up. Odd for a tinker, though!

The problem was, he was most lovable. Perhaps he was worth fighting for. Her jaw set with determination. But then, what future would they have? The feeling of lead came back, worse than ever.

They went back to the broom-making, Tommy woke up and then it was play hour with the little boy. Tommy was learning new words almost every day, and he could stagger round the kitchen, holding on to table legs. He was a little character, and Hester felt guilty that she was unhappy when she had Tommy to be thankful for.

From her place on the floor, kneeling beside Tommy's farmyard toys, Hester suddenly looked up at Meg. 'How I wish I could have a quiet, happy life like you!' She sighed.

Meg said nothing for a moment. She moved to put more wood on the fire, then came over to Hester with a strange expression. 'Maybe it's time I told you a bit of my story.' She hesitated. 'Hester, I lost my husband and my bairn, all in the same week. I've had a share of trouble.'

The girl jumped up, looking guilty. 'I'm sorry, I was selfish!' She sat with Meg at the table. 'You've never said . . .' There were tears in both their eyes.

Meg told her story simply and briefly, and Hester listened in appalled silence. If I lost Tommy I would have something to cry about, she thought.

'And now, I have to put up with age. So have we all, in time . . . it's another fight in front of you, Hester. You needn't worry about it yet.'

'Age doesn't worry you, Meg, surely? You're very strong!'

Meg smiled, and it was a tired smile. 'Ay, well, that's so. But it gets hard to remember things . . . and very hard to be patronized by the young folks, as a daft old woman. Not you, lass – I didn't mean you. But those that don't know me . . . and the work, it does get harder, y'know.'

They sat quiet for a while, then Meg said; 'But I don't intend to

169

die slowly. I won't think too much about being old while I can do anything at all. Some women give up when they get to forty, you know!' She laughed, a clear happy laugh, and some peace came stealing back into the room.

The fire flamed up, Tommy laughed too, and things were more cheerful. 'Cow, Mama!' he chirruped, holding it up.

Hester bent down and ruffled his hair. 'Clever boy! He's very good for his age, isn't he, Meg!'

They sat quietly for a while.

'When I was shut up at Hagstones, and things were very bad, I nearly lost hope,' Hester remembered. 'Then I looked out of the window one night, at sunset it was, there were all these little pink clouds, so pretty. I called them hope clouds. There was something free and pretty in the world; I might get out there one day, things might get better. So I started to tidy the place up, and make baby-clothes, and cheer me mother up a bit.'

Things got worse after that, but then they did get better, thought Hester, until today. She wiped away a tear. If only she didn't feel so worthless! Just as she'd felt when Roger beat her. Defeated.

Meg led her out into the garden. The showers had cleared away. A pale evening sun was shining in the west, and there in the sky were some little pink clouds. 'There's your hope clouds, Hester,' said the older woman gently. 'There's always hope, you just have to start again. Never give up! I'll say no more. I don't like sermons!'

After this, Hester found herself busier than ever, though the feeling of lead persisted. Meg took care to give her plenty of work and errands to set her walking for miles through the lanes between the villages.

Meg suggested once that she should go over to see Rose and ask how Fred Balderstone was getting on. Hester thought of Rose as a friend, but she didn't want to go there while Gilbert was their shepherd. He might think that she was chasing him, especially after the nights when she had gone to see him in the lambing-shed.

The spring ailments were rife, and watercress was one of Meg's favourite remedies for people who were short of greens. So Hester picked watercress in the Crimple beck, baskets at a time, and sour dock, dandelion, nettles and chickweed from wherever she could find them.

Dr Bishop told Hester that the Hodgsons had gone over to Dr Johnson, and had announced their decision in a stiff note handed in at the surgery. They didn't want a doctor who encouraged immorality. They had apparently heard all about Hester's wicked ways from Mrs Metcalfe.

Hester was at the surgery that day, helping Mary to spring-clean. She felt miserable. To think that her past was now affecting the doctor! The ripples were still spreading.

Mary Bishop frowned worriedly, but her husband laughed. 'Another rich patient defects to the enemy.' But there were plenty of other households needing a competent young nurse, were there not? 'It's a lot of humbug, this high moral tone!' he said briskly. 'But I suppose it might be hard to find Hester a place after this. We might have a fight on our hands, just as I had a fight to get any patients at all. The High Side knows its own mind, especially when it's informed by Lily Metcalfe!'

Once it was clear that Hester Kettlewell was going to brazen it out, as she put it, Lily Metcalfe got busy. She would make sure that every woman in the community was aware of Hester's sinful ways, and the threat she posed to society. Hester would have to pay for the rest of her life.

As she went about her work, busy as ever, Lily pondered. She didn't know what to think about Ned. He hadn't seemed very surprised when Hester left them so suddenly, and he wasn't really indignant like Lily was. 'We'll find another lass, love,' he'd said calmly.

If Hester's child had been fair, Ned would have been in deep trouble, Lily decided as she assaulted a carpet with the beater, out on the line. But the bastard was dark, like its mother . . . or maybe like Josh Bell?

So in the end Lily decided to give Ned the benefit of the doubt over Hester. She didn't really want to know what his relationship with the girl had been. But she realized, now, that she had left them alone together a great deal. That wouldn't happen again with a dairymaid, however plain and lumpy she might be.

Just in case Hester had seduced Ned, Lily was bent on punishment. The slut should be left out of any village events and any chance of work. If the bastard were put to school in Kirkby, Lily

171

would petition against it.

As for Dr Bishop, who brought all this on them in the first place, she would tell everyone that Dr Johnson was a far better doctor and had decent moral standards, too.

The doctor also came in for some criticism about his vagrant, living openly in the Bishops' stable yard. A threat to the village, some said, and Lily Metcalfe agreed with them. If anybody lost valuables, they'd know where to look. Everybody knew that gypsies were thieves.

Lily didn't know what the village was coming to. She decided to turn as many people as possible against the doctor, in the hope that he'd have to leave. Then they could get the High Side back to some sort of decency.

It was late May before Fred Balderstone was back on his feet again. The farmer had aged, and he seemed stiff and awkward to Hester. She noticed that he was thinner after his suffering, but she could see that the wounds had healed up very well. Bishop was busy with a spate of children's ailments; he sent Hester to have a look at Fred, and perhaps bathe his scars if they needed it. It was one place where he knew she'd be welcome, and she agreed to go.

Fred grinned at Hester. He could dimly remember how she had stood by him that night, when everybody else was having hysterics. 'We're tough up here, lass. You can't kill us off that easy,' he boasted, as they all did once they knew the doctor had won. He looked round the sunny farmyard. 'Have you time for a look round farm?'

Hester looked suitably severe. 'You shouldn't walk too far yet, you know. All right, a few minutes then. Take my arm.'

Fred laughed scornfully, but he picked up a stick at the door, and leaned heavily on it as they crossed the yard.

The hedges were dazzling with may-blossom in the lower fields, and they walked in the sun, Hester sniffing the scented air. They went though the cow pasture, where the cows were snatching at the spring grass, and the air was filled with the sound of munching. It was good to get back among cows again. Hester felt it, as well as Fred. 'Short horns give best milk of any!' he remarked.

Hester made admiring noises as they stood surrounded by the herd, tame cattle that liked human company. This was another farmer who took a great interest in his animals and their welfare. 'Grand bunch,' she agreed.

At the far side they went through a gate and came out into a green lane, one of the ancient droving roads that led up to the sheep pastures. Fred's farm was on the edge of the moor and had both lowland and moor grazing. Bees buzzed in the sunshine, and far away they could hear a lark spiralling upwards, singing for joy in the perfect day against the quiet bleating of sheep.

'This would be a grand short cut for me,' said the girl, thinking of her herb deliveries for Meg.

'You're welcome to come this way, any time you like. See over there? Gilbert and the lass are gathering ewes. That lad makes a rare shepherd. Seems to understand sheep.'

Hester said she was glad to hear it.

They came to a gate and leaned on it, because Hester could see that the farmer was tired. In the big rolling sea of the hill grazing, they could see two dots on the skyline, each with a smaller dot at heel. They could hear a faint barking. 'Bringing them down to pen in bottom corner.' The sheep started to pour down the hill like a woolly fountain.

'How did you get on with Gilbert?' asked Fred suddenly, chopping off the head of a thistle with his stick. 'I dunno what to make of him.'

Hester decided to be honest. 'Neither do I,' she confessed.

'He won't talk about himself!' The farmer smacked his fist on the top of the gate in exasperation. 'Seems a decent enough lad, he'll talk for politeness, always talk about sheep and farming, always ask questions . . . which means that we talk more than he does.'

Hester considered. 'Sounds like how an apprentice should be.'

Fred passed a hand over his face. 'But he never talks about his home, or where he comes from, or what he's done before. It's as if he dropped out of the sky, that night you found him. Did he ever tell you owt?'

Hester shivered. 'Never.' It was her own feeling, exactly. Gilbert was a man with no past.

The flock was drawing nearer. Gilbert covered one side, and Rose the other, and between them they cut off all retreat. The gathering-pen had high walls of stone, so that no sheep could jump out of it.

'Don't know what we'd have done without the lad, all the same,' Fred admitted. 'Not after my accident. Young Bobby's too small, although he does well, poor bairn. But Gilbert, he frames well.'

One lamb was left outside when the pen gate was closed, and it set up a dismal wailing. Gilbert extended an arm sideways, collared the lamb gently with his crook, and hauled it in without effort. He was indeed framing well.

Rose now lived up to her name, rosy with the healthy clear skin that comes from working in the fresh air. She waved to the watchers by the gate, and they carried on with their work, trimming a hoof here and there.

'Time I was off!' Hester pulled her eyes away from Gilbert with an effort. But when they got back to the farmhouse, the kettle was boiling, and it was time for tea.

Hester sat at the kitchen table with Fred and Martha, comfortable and accepted.

Martha poured her tea, then sighed as she put down the teapot. 'I just hope as our Rose doesn't get too fond o' that lad. He's very clean and decent, but it wouldn't do.'

Hester's heart seemed to miss a beat. That was something she hadn't thought about. Why ever hadn't she? Rose was smaller, more fragile than she was, more appealing . . . and Rose was quite clever, too. Gilbert and Rose would get on so well together!

'Of course not!' said Fred. 'A farmer's daughter should look higher than a tinker, useful though he may be. Our Rose'll know that.'

Martha took another piece of tea-cake, and motioned to Hester to do the same. 'Well,' she said, 'we never intended the hired man to come into the parlour! But that's where he is, most nights!'

This was surprising. The vagrant, Hester knew, had good manners. He wasn't likely to go in uninvited.

Martha saw her look, and explained. 'It started the very week he came. Our Rose was playing the piano.'

Hester could now imagine the scene. Gilbert loved music, he'd be drawn to the piano.

'Next thing we know, Rose has invited him in, because he wants to show her how that piece should really be played. Lass has been playing so Fred could hear a bit of music, while he was lying upstairs.'

So now Rose and Gilbert were playing together, piano and violin. 'How a tinker lad comes to play the piano, I can't imagine! Fiddle, yes, but a piano!' Martha shook her head. 'He's so good, it's uncanny!'

'They are good, I grant you.' Fred was almost grudging in his praise. 'But it's too friendly-like, for me, and too airy-fairy. It's time our Rose thought of settling down with a decent farmer. If it gets out that she's spending time with a tinker . . .' He stopped, as the pair in question came into the kitchen.

Gilbert and Rose were bright, both extremely pleased to see Hester, most friendly. It was good to see them . . . except that they had a sort of glow about them that Hester suspected very much. It made her feel awkward with them, almost shy.

They could be falling in love.

# CHAPTER TWENTY-TWO

It was quiet down by the river. After a warm day, the evening breeze with its cooling touch was refreshing, and the scents of blossom and growing herbage were more insistent as the sun went down. It was one of Rose's favourite places on the farm, and she was glad that Gilbert loved it, too.

Gilbert, restless in the house, went out into the golden evening. He went to check the boundary fence in the hay meadow, and Rose went quietly out after him.

They talked about the cows as they walked, and about the small happenings of the day. At a gate that faced west, they came to a stop, awed by the loveliness of the sunset over the blue hills of Nidderdale.

It was a perfect evening, solemn in its perfection, fleeting, gone before you could grasp it . . . the sky was a backdrop of gold, fading to green and then blue as the sun went down. It seemed natural just then, for Gilbert and Rose's hands to be clasped, with no words said.

They moved on down to the river, where something entered the water with a silver ripple. 'Look! An otter!' Rose whispered. 'See his nose?' Gilbert strained his eyes to see the creature.

Quietly they wandered on, hand in hand along the riverbank, where the shadows were falling softly among the alder and willow. There was a cool smell from the water, and a quiet splashing over the stones. Gilbert looked down at Rose, and smiled. 'I like being here,' he said gently, 'and with you, especially. I wish this spring could go on for ever. Is spring always as beautiful as this?'

The girl looked into his green eyes. 'Meg White says that everyone should have a spring to remember. Maybe this is yours, Gilbert.' Rose was feeling more emotion than ever before in her life, and she was trying to contain it.

'Are you happy, Rose?' This was said more urgently. His face above her was full of tenderness and concern for her.

There was a pause. Rose was wildly happy and sad at the same time. She knew now that she loved him, but why couldn't he tell her anything?

'Look, a star has come out. . . .' They looked together at the evening sky, where faint stars were appearing against the velvet blue.

Rose turned to Gilbert, and her smile was sad. 'I'm happy in your company, lad. I'll be sorry when you go.' She felt as though she would die when Gilbert went away. But what could she do?

The tinker's arm went round her waist then, almost reverently. He was very gentle for a tinker. And Rose's head seemed to fit into his shoulder, quite naturally.

'How I love you!' The voice was soft as ever as he stroked her hair. 'I'd like to stay with you for ever. Your parents . . .' He looked serious. 'They'd never approve of a tinker lad.'

Rose reached up and kissed him gently. 'I know. Let's leave it for now, and enjoy your spring. But, Gilbert,' she turned and walked on, slipping her arm though his, 'one day – will you tell me about your life before you came here?'

A cloud passed over the thin young face, and Gilbert turned to look at the river. 'One day . . . I will.' He turned back to Rose impishly. 'I'll teach you gypsy tricks, how to roast a hedgehog. I have talents – you don't know the half of them!'

Fred Balderstone and his wife persevered in their efforts to persuade Rose to get out more, to see other young people. She could drive the trap, and it was only about five miles to Kirkby.

'There's a quoits match in Kirkby tonight, love,' Martha reminded her, one bright evening. 'You might see Mabel and some of the other lasses there.'

Rose smiled, and said she would change her dress. Ten minutes later, she and Gilbert were laughing as they yoked up the pony, and off they went together, towards the village.

'That's not what I intended,' said Fred heavily.

Kirkby Green was busy, with the quoits game in full swing, and a gleaming copper kettle on view, the first prize. Kirkby folk were pleased to see their vagrant back among them. Reuben clapped Gilbert on the back, as they watched the heavy rings being thrown. With the usual poker face, he growled: 'How's farming life, lad?'

And to Rose: 'Does he frame at farming, then?'

'Of course he does!' said the girl, with a rosy blush.

Nellie Wilson observed that blush, and said to Ella Watson, 'Seems as Rose Balderstone has taken up with tinker. Thought she would look higher than that.'

'Wonder what her folks think. She's too good for him, o' course.' Ella looked sideways at the couple as she spoke. 'Young Bobby'll get the farm ... but I hear as Rose has a field or two left her, by old Jonah Balderstone, as never married.'

'Ay, she could farm, if she wanted to. But she'll need a farmer for that, not a gypsy boy!' was Nellie's verdict.

'She'll mek herself cheap if she doesn't watch out.' Ella nodded as a look of pure love passed between Gilbert and Rose.

Hester had stopped in Kirkby on her way home, and decided to see who was winning on the green. She was standing near the women, and heard their verdict on Rose. She, too, saw that look, and the touch of hands. Gilbert and Rose ... so she'd been right, it had happened. Martha's fears had come true!

Wonder if I could get him off her, if I really tried? The black eyes flashed, and Hester breathed fast. She watched them for five minutes more, and was convinced that they were in love. Then she walked quickly back to Larton, scheming like Roger Kettlewell used to scheme, about getting her own way. I want that lad. I want him for mine, she thought, slamming her boots hard down on the dusty lane.

Hester schemed for half the night, and then the tears came.

He was hers, rescued from the cold moor. It had seemed to bind him to her. Oh, Gilbert, she sobbed, why did you come to disturb our peace? He was so sweet-natured, so very dear and so mysterious, unlike anyone else. He must be clever too, to learn new things so quickly.

The scheming went on for days, and although she tried to hide it from Meg, the older woman knew that Hester was disturbed. She made up large quantities of chamomile tea; Meg's answer to a hurt was always herbs. Hester drank the tea, and thought and thought.

Then she had an idea. If she told the Balderstones what she knew, that there was talk in the village which might harm Rose's reputation, they would get rid of Gilbert immediately.

They could manage without a shepherd now, he would go away,

and Hester would follow him somehow. She'd have to leave Tommy with Meg for a while, and come back for him later, when she'd persuaded Gilbert to settle down. He could get a job as a shepherd on a big sheep-run, with a house, and then they could get married! Rose would get over him; she was young for her age and had probably never been so close to a man before.

Another thing: Rose was a dutiful daughter, who had never been away from home. She would do as her parents told her.

Hester decided to walk over to Balderstones' that Sunday, when Meg would be less busy, get Rose's parents on their own, and paint a black picture of their only daughter's future. They would be most alarmed. She could even hint that Gilbert was experienced with women, and that Rose's virtue was in danger. After all, what did she, Hester, know of him? That piano-playing was most suspicious. His past had been very well concealed.

On Saturday night Hester went to bed early, planning to walk to Balderstones' the next day. But sleep did not come, and instead she rehearsed over and over what she would say to get Gilbert away from Rose. She tossed and turned. Well, it was true, wasn't it?

About two in the morning, the schemer sat up in her narrow little bed with its patchwork quilt, and realized that it wouldn't work. She could not interfere. She wasn't bitch enough, in the end, to come between Gilbert and Rose. They were both her friends.

It was quite possible that a young man like Gilbert might want a gentler, more feminine sort of lass than Hester Kettlewell. She could imagine how she might appear to somebody like Gilbert; a rough, uncouth female, using bad language, too quick and impetuous. It wasn't a pretty picture, and she didn't like it. Come to think of it, she'd never heard him swear.

And then there was poor little Tommy! How could she think of leaving him? He deserved a better mother than Hester Kettlewell. In the end, her loyalty was to Tommy, not to a handsome stranger she'd taken a fancy for. 'Get a grip on yourself, woman!' she muttered savagely. Then she got up and went over to Tommy's cradle, and touched his cheek. 'I won't leave you, not ever, honey!' Tommy stirred in his sleep, and smiled.

Well, that was it. She'd best forget about the tinker. Let them be happy if they could, and Hester would be the best nurse in Yorkshire. And the best mother that Tommy could have. She would be like Florence Nightingale, giving up her chance of happiness to help other people. She wondered whether the ache would ever go away.

Meg White could see that Hester was miserable; even Tommy thought that something was different. She wondered a little about Gilbert, but she also knew that Hester's confidence had been badly shaken by her rejection in Kirkby. The lass needed more work.

As Hester worked silently at her tasks, Meg in her turn did some scheming.

One afternoon Meg went over into Dallagill, a pretty village in a hollow near Larton. She carried her basket of cordials and remedies, delivering orders, and one of her calls was at the Slaters, a young farming family.

Meg was touched by the obvious struggle that the Slaters were quietly working through. They were trying to keep their heads above water, but David and Alice were having a tough time. Their new baby was sickly, and Alice had not yet recovered from the birth.

That night as they ate supper, Meg introduced the subject of the Slaters, whose tale of troubles might bring Hester out of her gloom. The shearing was over, but haytime was still to come. Cows were calved and there was plenty of milk, which poor David was trying to make into butter and cheese for sale, as well as coping with all his other work. Alice was sad and silent, and the baby cried all the time.

But their story brought no response from the girl. She sat at the table, looking intently at the blue-and-white crockery. She was trying to concentrate on the plates, the cups, solid things with no feelings. She wanted to blot out the misery of thinking of Gilbert.

'I think poor Alice might be low in spirits, as well,' Meg finished. 'New mothers can suffer like that.'

'Happen so,' said Hester absently, still gazing at the cups.

This was not going very well. After a while Meg sighed, got up and cleared the table. Hester washed the dishes mechanically, while Meg went out into the soft summer evening, trying not to feel miserable herself. She weeded the garden for a while, until she felt the serenity of growing things coming back to her. Slowly, she gathered the strength to try again.

Meg made two cups of herb tea, took them to the seat under the apple-tree, and asked Hester to join her. 'Come and have a cup of tea, love,' she said, sounding more kindly than she actually felt.

They sat in silence for a while, and then Meg looked at her. 'Is it a lad that's bothering you, Hester? It's only natural, for a lass your age. You can't live like a nun for ever.'

'Well, I don't want to talk about it.' Hester's mouth set obstinately.

It was time to change the subject.

'The Slaters could make a bit of money, this summer, with just a bit of help. They take in paying guests – you know, visitors – but the place isn't ready. First folks due the end of this week, and nowt done.'

Hester finished her tea and set down the cup. 'Visitors? Ay, I've seen town folks tramping over the moor in summer, watching birds and such. We never saw no visitors at Hagstones.' She was slipping back into the rough, unspirited tone of voice again.

'That baby needs careful watching. I'm not sure what's wrong with him. And there's a sight of cleaning, washing and baking to do.' Meg persevered. 'Poor lass has no milk, and bairn's getting cows' milk. Their best cow, of course, but it's not digesting well. Can you remember any remedies for sickly bairns?'

There was a glimmer of interest. 'I think you told me once,' the girl said slowly. 'You said some bairns thrive better on goats' milk. It might be worth a try.'

'That's a right good idea, lass!' Another silence.

Hester sighed. 'Oh, well, I suppose I could bottle some of ours tomorrow, and take it over.'

The next morning Meg packed two bottles of goats' milk in a basket of useful tonics, including her famous elderberry-syrup. 'Don't forget the sage tea!' Hester had a ghost of her usual smile.

Hester strode out with something of her old determination, covering the ground as fast as possible in order to get there quickly. But it was an effort; she had lost the will.

It was only about an hour's walk from Larton, but Dallagill was a separate little valley and a different community, not of the moorland, or of the villages. It had its own school and little church. While Hester knew the Slaters slightly, she had never had much to do with them.

181

# CHAPTER TWENTY-THREE

'I'll take a few days off, if it's all same to you,' Reuben suddenly informed Bishop one day. 'Got to see our Sarah in Thirsk.'

'Of course I can manage without you. Stay as long as you like, Reuben.' Attached as he was to the recalcitrant groom, as the boss called him, it would be pleasant to live without that eagle eye upon him. Just for a change, he'd be able to come and go without comment.

Reuben's sister was a widow, and every year Reuben tried to spend some time with her, partly to keep an eye on her two young boys.

'It should be a quiet time for the practice.' Shearing was over, and hay had not yet started on the farms. Quiet farms usually meant a slack time for the medical team, but not always.

So Bishop groomed and fed the two horses, whistling between his teeth to imitate Reuben. He enjoyed the work, but found it harder as the days went by. Trust the High Side to discover a spate of urgent medical problems during their quiet period.

It was rather too much for a busy doctor, who wondered if there were anyone in the village who could be trusted to help with the work. Reuben did quite a lot of work, he was discovering.

On a grey and drizzly day Bishop was driving himself back to Kirkby when he decided to pay another visit to Fred Balderstone. 'We'll just take another look at those ribs,' he muttered to Dolly the mare, and the little horse twitched her ears in reply, as though she knew the case.

Hitching Dolly to a post in the yard, Bishop could see through the window that the family was gathered round the table. It looked homely and comfortable, a proper farmhouse scene. Young Bobby opened the door to him.

As he stepped into the kitchen Bishop could sense that all was not well. Instead of the cheerful atmosphere he had known here, there was a cloud on every brow. 'Cup of tea, doctor?' asked Martha kindly, but without her usual smile.

On the table was a crusty home-made loaf, a pat of deep yellow butter and a pot of bramble jam. But nobody was eating very much. 'Thank you, I will.' The visitor slipped into a vacant chair.

Fred coughed and shot Bishop a glance from under his heavy brows. 'We may as well tell you, Doctor,' he said deliberately, 'and this is a mite painful for us, you understand. But Gilbert here, as was recommended by you, and as was a good shepherd and a great help when needed, it must be said – Gilbert has decided he must be going. He's leaving tonight.'

There was a short silence, while Bobby fiddled with his crust of bread.

Bishop looked round. 'I don't know what to say. I know you're fit now, Fred, and shearing's over, but I'd hoped you might find a place for Gilbert on another farm, if he was worth recommending.'

Mrs Balderstone passed over a china cup to the doctor. Gilbert looked at Bishop as he handed on the cup. The lad was thin, the prominent cheekbones under the tan like those of the waif he had been when Hester found him on the moor.

'Is anything wrong?' the doctor asked gently, looking from Gilbert to Rose, who kept her eyes on her plate.

'Well, yes. You might say so.' Fred sighed. 'Gilbert and Rose have got friendly, which is not to my liking. I suppose it was only natural, a lad and a lass with time together. But we don't feel she's right for a tinker, nor him for her. She needs to look higher than young Gilbert, and I don't mind saying it to his face. He agrees with me. And it's not lad's fault if he were born under a hedge. But that's not all . . .' The farmer looked at Gilbert, and Rose wiped away a tear.

'I'm sorry, but I can't say anything about . . . my past, or even my full name. That's the problem.' His voice was low and pleasant. 'So I'd better go away, and not cause you any more trouble. Thank you for all your kindness to me.' The lad looked at Mrs Balderstone. 'Can I come back for Rose, if I do well – in the future?'

Rose's mother smiled at him and it was a smile of real motherly love. 'I'm sure I hope you do well, Gilbert.'

Fred frowned, and his voice grew rougher. 'Nay, lass isn't going to waste her life waiting … youth is soon overed with. She'll happen wed somebody else.'

Rose looked up then. 'I'll wait for you, Gilbert, however long it takes.'

'A pity it's an unsuitable match.' Bishop felt a lump in his throat. 'Ahem. Well, I can take the lad back with me to Kirkby now, if you like. I will just take a look at Fred's ribs first.' He was glad he'd called in; at least he could take Gilbert back with him.

The tinker protested quietly. 'No, master. You have been kind to me, but I won't be a burden to you again—'

'You're needed, as it happens.' Bishop was curt. 'Reuben's away, and you can look after the horses tonight. Save me a job.'

Fred was duly inspected, and found to be healed. 'The Lord takes all the credit for this one,' Bishop told him. He hadn't been able to do much to help the healing.

'And your mare, they tell me she takes a bit of credit as well!'

As Dolly was turning round in the yard Gilbert came down from the stable loft with his pack and the violin. Rose was not there to see him go.

'Do you play the violin still?' the doctor enquired, to try to minimize the pain of departure.

Gilbert looked at his hands, now work-worn and brown. 'Don't get much time for that when you're a shepherd, Master. But Rose and I played in the evenings, sometimes. I liked working with the sheep. These folks have been good to me.' He relapsed into silence and Bishop drove home thoughtfully, his collar turned up against the steady drip of the rain.

Back at the stables, it was a relief to the tired doctor to have the young man there to unyoke Dolly, and take her away for the evening feed. 'Here's Reuben's cottage key. Make a fire and be comfortable, and if you can stay at least until Reuben comes back, I'll be grateful. I miss my groom.'

The lad managed a smile. 'It's a grand thing to be able to help you, sir,' he said in his quiet way.

Gilbert knew the stable routine and slipped back into it easily. Bishop, walking across the yard later, heard him talking to the horses as he worked.

That night Bishop ate his evening meal in a subdued frame of mind that was not entirely due to the weather. He told Mary about

Gilbert. 'I won't speculate on what will happen to him next. Common sense says that the Balderstones are right. Mixed marriages hardly ever work. And he is too secretive, has been right from the start. It's a grave fault in him.'

Mary heard his sigh as he laid down his knife and fork. 'This is very good mutton, Robert, better than usual!'

Her husband looked up. 'All right, I won't brood over him all evening. He's not a medical case any more.' But it was hard not to feel for the boy. He was well-mannered, and a good worker – what a pity he couldn't marry Rose. They would have made a handsome couple ... but after all, they'd only known each other for a few weeks.

For dessert, Lizzie brought in some excellent Wensleydale cheese, fresh and pale, crumbling to the knife. But the doctor had little appetite. After coffee, Mary looked at him again. 'Would you take some soup across the yard for Gilbert, dear? There's plenty in the kitchen.'

So Bishop crossed the yard with a steaming bowl of Mary's chicken soup, and pushed open the cottage door. The room was full of shadows, except for a small fire. The tinker sat hunched in Reuben's wooden armchair, staring at the fire. He looked surprised to see the boss, and stood up politely.

'Here you are, get this down you.' The doctor tried his famous High Side bracing manner, used to get patients out of bed. It had been known to make strong lads quail.

From a drawer in the dresser he produced a spoon, then he busied himself putting a log on the fire. Eventually, he sat down opposite, produced a hunk of bread from a pocket and quietly insisted, until Gilbert took the soup to please him. A little colour began to come back into the thin face.

'Now, my lad.' Even though this was not a Yorkshire lad, the dialect seemed friendlier than standard English. He'd found it cut through a few barriers. 'Why,' said the doctor, looking into the flames, 'could you not tell Rose of your past life? Surely you can talk to her – if not to me?' He looked carefully at Gilbert, and the lad looked back with eyes that were clear of guilt, but held a deep sadness.

The crackling of the fire in the silence was comforting, and the room was getting warmer. Bishop tried again. 'Why don't you tell me what's the trouble, Gilbert? I think you should be more open with us all.'

The tinker made an effort. He passed a weary hand over his brow, and took a deep breath. 'Well now,' he said in the quiet voice that was so different from the accents of Yorkshire, 'would you be reporting me? Or betray me, or tell another soul . . . if I tell you my trouble?'

'A doctor gets to know more about other folks than most men. But he doesn't tell their secrets, Gilbert, he is sworn not to do so. Secrets are safe with me.'

There was a huge sigh from the chair opposite, where Gilbert's face was now in shadow. 'The whole trouble is . . . I can't remember anything.' He was very still. 'I've no memory of a time before I came here.'

'So that's it . . . amnesia.' Bishop jumped up, feeling the need to move about. 'I am very relieved, you know . . . that there's no crime, or anything like that.' He must take it gently. 'Why does it worry you so? It must be difficult, I know . . . but you could have told me this at any time.'

Gilbert moved then, indignantly. 'Yes, and get myself arrested like Lance Wood! The same thing happened to him; I heard you say it. He couldn't remember what he'd done, and everybody said lock him up, and they did, too. And he was a respectable farmer, not . . . a vagrant like me. Vagrants don't have many rights, Doctor.' A deep shudder shook him. 'And those ladies, two Miss Horners . . . certi-fied insane. Could've been locked up in a madhouse, for life. That was loss of memory!' He lay back in the chair.

For a moment Bishop saw the world from a vagrant's point of view, a hostile world, full of traps. No wonder he was defensive: no property, money, friends or place in the world – and at the mercy of charity, once he broke his leg.

'What a good job you came back here.' The doctor let out a sigh. 'Well, you know, Lance Wood had alcohol poisoning. There was a family history of mental instability, and then he had drinking-bouts which caused his loss of memory . . . and he did some violent things. Certainly nothing like your case, my boy. From the whites of your eyes I should say that you drink very little alcohol.' The green eyes were opening wider now.

After a pause the doctor thought he would probe a little deeper.

'Let's see ... tell me what you do remember. How do you know you're a tinker? I promise you, it's not likely to be the effect of insanity – more likely an accident. Perhaps when your leg was broken?'

Gilbert still had a troubled look. 'But what about all the time that is a blank to me? I could have done anything, been anything. I don't know! Just imagine how it feels – to have no past.'

It was Bishop's turn to shudder, as a black pit opened at his feet. 'Horrible. But tell me, what you do remember?'

The tinker thought for a moment. 'I am remembering ... finding myself on the moor with a broken leg on a frosty night, with a few bits of things in a bag. I played the violin – it was natural to do it. And then Hester found me. I wasn't worried then – sort of happy. She was like an angel, I thought. The headaches came later.'

'And that's all?'

'That is all.' The tinker inclined his head gravely. 'I had some of the skill of mending pans and kettles, and the gear to do it, and folks from Pateley said I was a travelling tinker. There was no money, no papers, nothing – apart from the name, Gilbert. I lay there saying to myself, "I am Gilbert". Oh ... and there was a big lump on the back of my head.'

Bishop cursed himself for missing that lump, hidden no doubt by the long, fair hair. 'A blow or a fall could have caused you to lose your memory. It might come back. Odd, that whoever was on that road didn't stay to look after you. . . .'

'I keep hoping that memory will come back, one day. I thought maybe when the lump went down ... I didn't want to deceive anyone, least of all Rose. But it would be nice to know my place in the world ... no doubt it's a humble one. I know how to cook a hedgehog.' He smiled bitterly. 'That will not impress the Balderstones.'

Bishop frowned. 'That's a gypsy trick. But I don't think you are a real vagrant, Gilbert. You speak very well, for one thing. I can't place you in a social class, to be honest.'

'I've thought about it. Sometimes folks think I'm sounding Irish, and I know the folk tunes, and ghost stories and fairy tales ...' He shook his fair head.

They looked at each other. Then the doctor smiled. 'Look here, lad. You have a slight Irish brogue, but you talk more like an educated man than anything else. You can play very well, classical as well as folk tunes and carols – I've heard snatches of Beethoven at times!'

'And I can snare a pheasant, nobody in Kirkby taught me.' The impish grin was back.

'I should think not, indeed! Poaching is a serious offence! But worry won't help. Relax if you can, it will help the brain more than anything else.'

The doctor got up to go, then turned to look down at the young man. 'You've had a difficult time. Emotion, long hours of hard work in a harsh climate . . . no wonder the brain took time to recover.' He thought for a moment. 'How did you get to where Hester found you? Only the carrier's cart goes that way at night. We must find the carrier.'

'Thank you, sir. I feel so much better for talking to you!'

'Let me check that head.' Bishop ran his fingers lightly round Gilbert's head, under the hair. 'Nothing to show for it now, that's just as well. Good night – try to sleep. You have plenty to do in the morning! I want the trap for eight o'clock, please.'

# CHAPTER TWENTY-FOUR

The Slaters' yard was quiet. Too quiet. Where were they? Hester glanced at the sun, now climbing above the green slopes of the gill. Cuckoos were calling across the hay-meadow as she paused to look round.

Maybe it was breakfast time, after morning milking and before the chores of the day.

The little stone-walled garden looked prosperous, but nobody had picked the rows of ripe gooseberries. The grass edging the paths needed cutting, and there were a few weeds in the cobblestones of the yard. Not exactly neglect – nothing near as bad as Hagstones, but not as neat as Hester and Meg liked, either.

Never sure of her reception these days, Hester knocked loudly on the closed kitchen door, with more confidence than she felt. Nothing happened for a minute or two.

There was the quiet sound of a big key turning in the lock. Then silence.

'If you don't want to see me, I'll go away!' she shouted, exasperated. 'It's only Hester Kettlewell, with a basket of stuff from Meg White, and good day to you, too!' If they were too toffee-nosed to let her in because she was a – an unmarried mother, good luck to them!

After a while, a quavering voice asked, 'Anybody with you?'

' 'Course not. Just me and my basket, and if it's all the same to you, I'll get off back to Larton. Haven't got all day.' She turned to go.

At that, the door opened a crack and David Slater peered out. 'Come in, Hester. It's that Lance Wood, he came here last night. We thought he was back for more.'

In the kitchen the baby was crying fretfully. Alice Slater sat at the table, staring down at the pattern on the cloth. The place was untidy, with dirty dishes piled in the sink.

'Come now, Alice, it's Hester,' her husband coaxed.

Alice looked up briefly. 'Good-day.'

Hester looked round. She wasn't afraid of Lance Wood, having deprived him of one of his guns at the harvest festival. Since then there had been tales of strange behaviour, and then Lance had been locked up in the prison at Ripon for some months.

Dried out, Lance was sober and charming, and so they'd let him go. And now, it seemed he was at his tricks again.

Alice Slater sat in silence as David told their tale of woe: how Lance had demanded whisky, let off several shots, and at last, to their relief, ridden off on the big black horse with a fresh loaf and a bag of potatoes. Alice had been feeling low since little Richard was born, and now she was frightened as well. The shotgun pellets had pattered on the privy door, and had just missed David.

'Well!' Hester set down the basket and pulled out a bottle of milk. 'No wonder you were worried! They say he never does the same thing twice, so you mightn't see him again. Now, Alice, this is goats' milk, which Meg says might be better for the bairn. Why not give it a try?'

It was time for a feed, so David warmed the milk over the fire, put it into the baby's bottle, picked up the squalling Richard, and gave them both to his wife. Listlessly, she fed the teat into the hungry little mouth. The baby tried to suck and cry at the same time.

Meanwhile, the struggling farmer started on his next chore. 'Put kettle on for a cup of tea, Hester, will you?' He poured cream into the churn in the adjoining scullery, and started to turn the handle. Both the Slaters took no further notice of Hester; she might as well go home.

The basket was soon emptied on the table, and Hester started for the door. Then she caught sight of David's red face as he forced the churn faster and faster, whirling the cream round and himself into a frenzy. The barrel flew off the stand and crashed to the floor.

Hester couldn't leave him like that. 'You'll never get butter if you go too fast!' She helped him to pick up the churn, which luckily had not burst open. 'Here, let me show you. It's not speed, it's . . . impact that does it,' she explained.

The farmer mopped his face and sat on a stool to watch. 'I must say I never tried it before, being women's work, but we need to sell some butter and cheese . . . and milk is piling up.

Hester rolled up her sleeves and finished the butter-making. 'Leave it to me,' she said bossily. 'Go and do your farming jobs, I'll stay for a bit, and give Alice a hand.'

That was easier said than done; Alice took no interest. So the girl pitched in. She washed the dishes, swept the floor and shook the mats. Then she made a hot elderberry-drink and gave it to the woman, while the baby went to sleep in his cradle. So far, so good.

After a while Alice lifted her head and looked at Hester. 'Why are you here?'

Why, indeed? Hester felt impatient with the woman's apathy, even though she had been in a similar state herself. The butter-making had energized Hester, and now she felt ready for anything.

Alice stood up, went over to the cradle and touched the sleeping baby's cheek. For the first time she showed some slight animation. 'Poor mite, he's hardly slept . . . and neither have we. What did you say that milk was?'

'Goats' milk. They say some bairns take it better than cows'.' Hester showed her the second bottle. 'It might pay to get yourselves a goat, if he does improve.'

When David Slater came in, he was amazed at the changes. The baby was quiet, the room was in order, and his wife was actually talking to Hester, who by now was back in the nurse's role again: quiet, competent and firm. Dr Bishop would be proud of me, she thought. She advised Alice about drinking plenty of liquids, and trying to relax, to get her own milk flowing if possible. And Alice was coming round a little.

The urgent problem, they explained, was the guests, due on Friday. Mr Bogg, who wrote books about Yorkshire, was a regular visitor. He walked in the area, talked to the locals and took notes. This year, he was bringing a companion, and they would visit places of interest together.

Folks from the towns paid well, said David, but they expected good farmhouse food, a nice clean bedroom apiece . . . and quiet nights. No crying babies.

How was it to be done? The money was desperately needed. 'But I can't see as how we can be ready by Friday.' The young man was despairing, his fair complexion flushed with worry.

Hester took this as a challenge. She'd forgotten by now about going home. 'If I gave you some time this week I think we could get you ready!' she said with confidence. 'But you, Alice, you'll have to help.'

The Slaters looked at each other. 'I . . . I can't think, these days,' said Alice weakly. 'What with having no sleep at nights. . . .'

They all looked at little Richard. But the baby was still asleep; with only one feed of goats' milk he seemed to be settling.

Hester rolled up her sleeves again. 'Right. I'll do some of the thinking. Help me with the list. It looks as though we need to make some cheese to sell, and maybe some cream-cheese for visitors. Talking of food, I see you have a good ham there, and a bag of flour . . . we could make some gooseberry pies, most folks like them. Then we'll clean and polish the bedrooms, and the parlour where they take their meals. Have you any silver to clean?'

The Slaters helped her with the list, and she sent Alice off to pick some gooseberries. By late afternoon the farmhouse was fragrant with polish and Alice seemed to have improved a little. 'We'll bring in some nice spring flowers, just before they come.'

'I'm off to Thorpe with trap. My cousin keeps goats – I'll likely borrow one.' David Slater was now much less agitated. 'And Hester . . . thanks to you, girl. We can't afford to pay you, but there's a young pony there you can borrow, if you can ride.'

When Hester reached home in time for tea, Tommy ran out to meet her, and she swung him up on to the little Dales pony with a laugh. Meg heard the laugh, and smiled a quiet smile.

'I'll go back tomorrow, Meg, if it's all right.'

Over tea Hester told of what had been done and what was still to do. She seemed absorbed in the Slaters' problems and their solution. To her own surprise, she was looking forward to the job. She might even get to meet these posh visitors of whom the Slaters seemed so much in awe. It would be so much easier to get about, now she had a pony for a while. Tomorrow, they would wash all the sheets and towels and turn out the parlour.

'And this is my friend, Professor Jameson. We were educated together,' and Edmund Bogg looked up at his tall companion. Both men were dressed in rather shabby tweeds, and wore stout walking-boots. Bogg came from Leeds, Jameson was down from Newcastle, and they'd been picked up from Ripon station by 'my friend Reuben', said Bogg. David carried their bags in from the trap.

Hester, neat in her cotton work-dress, looked at the men with interest as she served their midday meal, a light one of home-made bread and cheese, followed by gooseberry-pie. Tonight their dinner would be a leg of lamb, since David had killed a sheep. The parlour furniture gleamed as only old oak can, the windows sparkled and the men looked very contented.

'I knew you'd like it here,' said Bogg to Jameson. 'Might get you out of yourself a bit.'

Jameson smiled rather sadly. 'It's kind of you, Bogg.'

Oh bugger, not another case of feeling low, thought the demure-looking Hester, handing round cups of coffee. Alice was improving, but still had a long way to go, and that was why Hester was serving the meal.

'June is the loveliest time of year on the High Side,' Bogg went on, sounding like a man intent on cheering up. 'The spring flowers are later here than in the lowlands, of course, but the ferny dells are exquisite!'

Sounds just like a writer, Hester said to herself. She passed the sugar.

'Yes, I'm sure you are right. It all looks very beautiful. I can only stay until the twenty-first, of course ... the solstice, you know.' Jameson nodded. Hester couldn't remember what exactly a solstice was, although they'd had one at school, she was sure. She decided to ask Meg.

They lingered over the coffee, and Hester was included in the conversation because Mr Bogg always talked to everybody in the hope of finding out something new. 'And what have you to tell us about Thorpe, my dear?' He twinkled at her.

'Thorpe?' Hester thought hard about what would appeal to a visitor. 'Well, there's a church to look at, not very old, though. And Hack Fall, but you'll know about that, a lot of oak-trees and the River Ure, all done up with paths for walking and little ruins and that. Oh, and Thorpe cheese.'

'Do you like the cheese?' asked the Professor.

'Never tried it. It's sent off for rich folks to eat,' said the serving-maid casually. 'They wrap it in cabbage leaves. Don't see why, though.'

*Ann Cliff*

Later, Hester helped Alice to wash up in the kitchen, and they ate their own meal. Little Richard slept peacefully, catching up on the sleep he'd missed since birth. He had never looked back since his diet had been changed to goats' milk, and the rash on his arms and legs had almost disappeared.

David, leaning back in his chair and more relaxed than Hester had seen him, told them the news of Kirkby, collected at the shop. 'Reuben's gone to see his sister at Thirsk. Young tinker lad seems to be working for doctor.'

Gilbert! The pain came back, but Hester was surprised to find it a little easier. She hadn't thought too much about Gilbert since the beginning of the week. Well, she'd better keep on working hard and forget him. Even though he was now parted from Rose she wouldn't look for him. Gilbert had made his choice. She wondered why he'd left the Balderstones. Was it because of Rose?

'And the other bit of news,' David was saying, 'is bad news. There's some folks worse off than we are, Alice lass – much worse.'

Alice was looking better, and Hester hoped that any bad news wouldn't send her back down again. 'Do we have to hear your bad news?' she asked lightly.

'Well, it affects none of us, of course. It's just that . . . they say Josh Bell's been sent home to die.'

194

# CHAPTER TWENTY-FIVE

Reuben was back with Doctor Bishop after a couple of weeks.

The Bishops had thought he would stay away longer, but he said that ten days was long enough for anybody in Thirsk, where there was nowt much to do. Walking round a town was not the same when you didn't know anybody, and the indispensable groom said he was very happy to be back in Kirkby.

It was good that the boss had needed a replacement. Proved he was indispensable, didn't it?

It was good, too, to find Gilbert there, but he was a very subdued vagrant, with a lot on his mind. Reuben told the boss he had worked out what the trouble was: woman trouble, but he couldn't think of a remedy. When all was said and done, a gypsy lad couldn't marry into a farming family.

As they clattered into the little greystone village of Thorpe Bishop agreed with his groom. 'Well, Reuben, it can't be helped. Let's get on with the job. Stop at the cheesemaker's, will you? He's in pain, by all accounts.'

There was nobody in the dairy, which had the fresh, clean smell of a well-scrubbed milk pail. The doctor went through a door into the house, and there in the spotless kitchen was Smithson, the cheesemaker, sitting awkwardly on a chair. As soon as the man stood up, Bishop could see that his shoulder was dislocated. He felt it gently and the man winced.

'Grit your teeth, and we'll soon have it back.' It was all the better for being quickly done, and Bishop didn't give the patient time to think about it.

As he checked the result, he noticed an ugly red weal on top of the man's shoulder. 'Hello. What caused this?' the doctor asked.

The man was still gasping a little. 'T'other one's same.' And he moved away the shirt at the other side.

'Well?'

'Doctor, if you walked from Thorpe to Kirkby every day, half an hour it takes as you will know, and back again, with a yoke on your shoulders and two heavy buckets, your shoulders would be a sight worse than mine. I'm used to it.'

'Well, I should take a rest if I were you, and pay a lad to do it. Then, you could pad the yokes when you use them. You'll have an ulcer if you don't watch out.' But Smithson was not listening.

'Would ye like a pat of cheese, Doctor?' Proudly he led the way into the inner room of the dairy, where muslin bags of thick cream were hanging, gradually turning sour and dripping whey into buckets.

'There you are, Doctor. Best cheese in Yorkshire. . . .'

'And known all over the world!' said a jovial voice, as Edmund Bogg walked in. 'How are you, Doctor? I've brought Jameson to try the famous cheese.'

Out on the green Jameson was chatting to Reuben like an old friend. Professor Jameson, holding the chair of mathematics at Newcastle University, might by his title have awed some people, but not Reuben.

Looking at the neat grey beard and old tweed suit, Bishop got the impression of sadness. The doctor was impatient to be off, having more patients waiting. 'You must come to dinner, both of you, before you leave. How about the twentieth?'

Bogg had been to dinner with the Bishops several times, and accepted with obvious pleasure. 'It's the last evening we spend here.' Jameson smiled. 'You are very kind. We will look forward to it.'

The trap was soon rolling swiftly through Thorpe, back up the Bramley lane, taking the medical team to a call they did not want to make: the Bells, at Bramley.

Josh Bell was sitting on a chair in the old farmhouse, dressed and, at first sight, almost normal. His hands and neck were heavily bandaged. His voice was a hoarse croak, produced with difficulty.

He appeared to recognize the doctor, but without much interest. Josh had been washed and dressed, made presentable. But he seemed not to be present – not the real Josh, that was. The body was there, but where was the spirit of the man? Bishop decided to tread softly.

At the other end of the long, low room, Josh's mother went to a mahogany desk. She opened it with difficulty, her hands twisted with rheumatism, and drew out an envelope. Bishop meanwhile looked round at the antique furniture, the old beams of the ceiling. This was a family with long tradition. The Bells had been here, yeoman farmers, for hundreds of years. Josh was back in the place where he belonged.

'Here you are, Doctor. Read this. It's a letter from the doctors in Leeds . . . and here's another, from the police.'

The doctors were detached, describing the damage Josh had suffered: smoke inhalation, severe burns, the lungs were damaged. The patient had not responded to treatment, and they were not optimistic about his recovery. They gave him a few weeks to live.

The police letter told the poor mother what she really wanted to know: the story of what had happened. Showing great bravery, the young constable had rescued five people from a burning house. He had sustained severe injuries and, what was worse, had suffered something like a mental breakdown when he was not able to rescue the last old man from the ruins. Josh had raved for days, which had not helped them to treat his injuries, and they feared for his sanity.

'Constable Bell was a very capable and conscientious officer,' the chief constable had written. 'But he was never happy in Leeds, and sometimes had appeared to be low in spirits. We understand from the doctors that he has little hope of recovery. Therefore, we are sending him back to his home, to live his last days in peace.'

The constable was to be awarded a medal, which would be sent as quickly as possible in the circumstances.

'I'm sure I don't know where to turn, Doctor.' Josh's mother was leaning heavily on a stick. 'I can't look after him myself – it takes me all my time to keep the house straight, with the rheumatism so bad. Young Elijah's getting married to Mabel soon, but the lass is too busy helping her sister with a new baby. And Elijah's all out running the farm, with haytime coming on.'

Bishop led Mrs Bell to a chair and helped her into it, noting how the rheumatism and the shock of Josh's condition had aged her since his last visit. Then he sat opposite her.

'I'm not sure what really ails Josh, but he obviously needs some-body to dress the burns and so on. To make him comfortable . . . and to do anything we can to raise his spirits, should that be possible.' He paused for a while, wondering whether to say it. . . .

Then the doctor took a deep breath. 'Hester Kettlewell is now a capable nurse, and she would be able to do all that is necessary. How do you think Josh would take it?' He didn't need to spell out the problem.

Mrs Bell smiled, a sad smile. 'All that – his fancy for Hester – was over, long ago. Before that they were bairns together, and that might still mean something to him. But it would be sad for the lass, watching him die. It's terrible for us all.'

They talked it over quietly together, and Mrs Bell said that of course they could pay for a nurse, Josh had insurance. And Bishop offered to call in to see Hester. He would ask her to come over and help Josh Bell to die with dignity. That was all anyone could do.

'Comfrey tea, made from the root.' Meg White was quite firm. 'That will help the lungs, you know.' Hester and Meg were plan-ning a fight for Josh's life, against the odds.

Hester had already heard about Josh Bell when Bishop called in at Meg's cottage. He was pleased that he didn't have to break the news.

'It won't be easy, Hester,' the doctor reminded her gently.

Hester felt that she had changed, even since she last saw the doctor. She was more determined to make the best of things, and to stay cheerful, even if only for the sake of Meg and little Tommy. Gilbert no longer kept her awake at night; she thought of him with only a small pang, and the intense feelings had given way to a gentle affection. This was strange. She couldn't imagine how you could fall in and out of love like that, but it was a relief.

Hearing about Josh might have had something to do with it; imminent death made you work out what mattered, Hester decided. The news of Josh had shaken her, as it had shocked all his friends.

Hester realized that Josh had been her best friend. If he needed her, she would help him all she could. It would help to make her conscience easier. Hester now knew what Josh had gone through; she knew what it was to love someone who, in the end, did not love her. She'd been very unsympathetic to Josh. Quite cruel, when she thought about it.

David Slater had said that a young lady had brought him home to his mother, a Leeds friend of his, travelling with him in the police vehicle.

To Hester, Josh was now doubly out of reach. She felt sorry for his young woman, and wondered what their relationship had been. Josh would have been kind to her, and behaved honourably, that was certain.

'Nursing isn't easy, Doctor,' she said now. 'It's hard to see other folks suffer, and sometimes they can be hard to help!' She was thinking of Alice Slater.

Bishop agreed. 'You've hit the nail on the head, as far as this practice goes!'

They told him about the pony lent by the Slaters, which made Hester able to travel more easily. She could be with the Bells during the day, and come home to Tommy at night.

Hester went out into the garden, to dig comfrey-root and to hide her tears for Josh Bell. She remembered his honest brown eyes, his obvious sincerity, and his kindness to a scruffy little farm girl when they'd been at school together . . . then she thought about the task in hand . . . comfrey was smooth, like a jelly, and it healed like nothing else did. At least, it should ease the pain.

When Hester arrived to take up her duties the next day, breathing fast and feeling nervous, Josh seemed to have taken a turn for the worse. He had stayed in bed, asked for more laudanum to ease the pain, and was now sleeping.

The nurse busied herself with tidying his bedroom. She talked to Mrs Bell and was given a free hand, so then she got down to dusting and polishing. She brought in a bowl of roses from the garden, and their fragrance cheered her.

The sight of Josh's pale, thin face, with livid scars, and his ravaged body made her want to cry, but that was no help to a patient. Hester knew she had to find reserves of strength, somewhere, to help her through. Meg White had been her support in the dark days when she was hiding from Roger. It was her turn now to be a support, and she tried to find something of Meg's serenity in herself.

For an hour or so, while the patient slept, Hester willed herself into a calm frame of mind. She wondered again about the young lady from Leeds; if she loved Josh she would be most unhappy now.

When Josh woke there was Hester, sitting at the table in a shaft of sunlight, hemming dusters out of old sheets. 'There's always a job to do,' she said to the patient cheerfully. 'Would you like a drink of herb-tea?'

Josh's mind was confused, and he thought they were back in the old schoolroom at Kirkby.

'Why, Hester lass, have you finished your sums already?' Obediently he drank the cold comfrey-tea; Meg had thought that a hot liquid would not be good for him. Humouring him, Hester talked about their schooldays. She could tell that, in his mind, he had gone back in time. It made things easier for them both. She changed his bandages and made him comfortable, and persuaded him to take a little bread and milk.

The early summer weather was perfect that year: blue skies and a gentle breeze every day. Folks on the moorland felt a little lightening of the heart in the brief spell between shearing and haytime. Hester cantered gently back to Larton on the pony that first evening, feeling the joy of summer but, much more strongly, the pain of seeing Josh in such a state. The lovely sunset, such a beautiful world, and Josh had to leave it soon!

The next week Josh seemed a little stronger and more lucid. He thanked Hester for coming to nurse him and said he was sorry to be a burden to everybody. But he talked in a hoarse monotone. He was still in shock, she decided, and his feelings were closed down. And of course, the laudanum would be affecting him.

Hester persuaded him to go outside, into the garden in the sunshine. Because of the burns she would make sure he stayed in the shade.

Into the shade of a huge old elm-tree Hester carefully pushed the patient in a Bath chair, lent by Dr Bishop.

Josh wasn't in the schoolroom by this time, but he still seemed to be in a world of his own. He told her that there was to be compensation for his injuries, a tidy sum of money that would buy a little farm. So together they planned what sort of sheep he would buy, and how the house was to be organized, and what they would plant in the garden. Josh seemed happy, making these plans, and Hester thought it would do him no harm.

'It's true enough, he could buy a farm.' Josh's mother had overheard the talk. 'But he won't live to see it. . . .'

The next day, Josh showed her an advertisement in the Ripon *Gazette*. 'There's a nice little place at Thorpe for sale; some of the fields are good enough to plough for oats. Hundred and fifty acres. Would you like to farm with me, Hester?' he croaked.

Another challenge for the nurse.

She didn't want to hurt him again, after all the damage she'd done in the past. In fact, it looked as though Josh's plight could be laid at her door, another ripple caused by her affair with Ned. Mrs Bell said that she was almost sure he'd gone off to Leeds because Hester didn't want him. If he hadn't gone to Leeds, he wouldn't have been injured. It was a burden for her to bear. But Josh wasn't blaming her, not at all.

Hester smiled at the patient. 'Why, what sort of a farmer do you think I'd make? I'm a nurse, you know, these days!'

'And a good one. But you always were good with stock, lass, and you're at home, here on the High Side. City lasses wouldn't live up here!' He paused to cough.

Maybe he was thinking of his young woman in Leeds? Hester wondered whether he missed her.

'So, Hester, how about it? Do you reckon you'd come with me to Thorpe?'

Before she could think about it any more, the words came out. 'I'd do anything with you, Josh. You're the best man I know!'

Was it true? Yes, it was. Gilbert was charming, but he wasn't the same reliable, downright person. She wasn't giddily in love with Josh, she just . . . liked him. Was that it?

No, she loved him. And, too, Hester understood him now. She'd never understood Gilbert, although she'd wished to, many times. She'd completely misunderstood Ned Mecca.

Then Josh's pain increased, and he asked to go to bed.

That night Hester cried tears of rage at a cruel fate that was killing Josh before his time. And for the first time, she talked about him to Meg White, after Tommy had gone to bed. They sat with a cup of herb-tea, under the apple tree in the garden. It was Hester's favourite place.

'I've been stupid,' the girl confessed, looking at Meg with a wry expression. 'There was Josh, all the time, just the lad for me. He likes the same things . . . just think, Meg, he wants a little farm at Thorpe, and a garden and all that. We'd have suited, very well. And it's only now that I can see it – when it's too late!'

'Don't you think he shows any improvement at all?' Meg asked quietly, putting down her cup.

'It's hard to say. I don't think so – and neither does he. He's in more pain, now. And in any case, he's got a young lady in Leeds, I think. His mother says that a little lass, a teacher, came home with him, to see him safely home.' Hester shook her head. It looked as though Josh would soon be beyond anyone's reach.

'Can you get me some more stuff – the one that deadens pain – from the doctor, lass?' Joshua asked a few days later, as they sat together looking out over the garden wall to the rolling moors beyond.

'Well, Josh, it's not good for you, you know. Dr Bishop said that folks get add-addicted to it, and you should take as little as possible.'

The young man turned stiffly and looked at her. 'You do know that it's all over with me? Only a few days left; they said in Leeds. I'll be gone by the end of June. So I'm not going to have time to get addicted!'

Nurses were supposed to know what to say, but Hester watched a butterfly for a few minutes, feeling at a loss. Oh Josh, she thought, only a few days left!

Then her usual energy took over, and she said just what she ought. You could be honest, and positive at the same time. 'Well, I heard the same tale, but there's no use in dying just to prove them right!'

Josh smiled and shook his head. 'I'm going to die, Hester. But I've right enjoyed these past few days.'

The nurse blinked away tears. 'I'll tell thee what Meg said, my lad. She has seen comfrey work wonders! It healed up a horse with lungs so bad, it fell down when it walked! The horse got better, and it could even gallop again. And – and she believes it could heal your insides up real fast.' She paused to see the effect.

Josh was laughing. 'You think I'm a horse?'

'And another thing. Meg says she has seen folks die just because they believed they would. She says you've got to make up your own mind.'

Josh shook his head.

Dr Bishop said something on the same lines when he visited Josh and doled out some more of the precious drug. But Hester could see that Josh's own nature, steadfast and unchangeable, was working against him now. 'Nay, doctor,' said the patient with great composure, 'my time's up, and we've got to face the truth.'

The doctor was honest enough to agree; he never lied to his patients. But he couldn't resist saying, with a look at Hester: 'While there's life there's hope, Joshua.'

Meg White heard all this, and decided to see for herself. She offered to take Hester's place for a day, to give her some time with Tommy and relief from the stress of nursing Josh.

Meg was very pleased with the way the external burns were healing. But Josh complained of great internal pain. Not just in the lungs, but round his heart, and indigestion after meals.

'It could be just the healing up,' Meg suggested. 'Mending can hurt a fair bit at times.'

'I've only got a few days to go,' Josh told her firmly. 'Hester's been so good. Everybody has, I feel bad at leaving you all.'

'Hester loves you, lad. Think on, that might be worth a fight. Get yourself better, for heaven's sake, and less talk about dying!'

But Josh had drifted off again, into the strange world where pain went away and there was no feeling. Meg went away in the evening, feeling quite hopeless.

# CHAPTER TWENTY-SIX

'But you can't begin to realize the beauty of Hack Fall woods in winter!'

Mr Bogg leaned forward earnestly over the dinner table, his floppy tie dangerously near the onion-soup. 'Nature in her sternest mood . . . the mist spreading up from the river like a phantom. . . .'

Bishop laughed, and passed him another roll. 'Better write it all down, hadn't you? That bit of prose should be captured before you lose it. One of these days it might be needed for a book about Thorpe.'

'What about the Druid's temple?' Mary Bishop asked Jameson. 'Robert told me that you're going there at dawn!'

Professor Jameson smiled at Mary. 'It's not really scientific research, of course . . . the temple is a folly, as I'm sure you will know. But I would like to know whether the creator, Mr Danby, had any calculations in mind when he drew up the plan.'

The Bishops looked interested.

'It's thought that the ancient Britons may have used the stones for some kind of calendar, to mark the seasons. To observe the solstices and equinoxes, for a start. We shall see,' said the professor. 'I'm going to watch the sun rise up there at the temple, and see what's in line. I keep wandering about in the vacations, trying to take an interest in things. I have to keep occupied, since – since Bertie left.'

Mary looked sympathetic, as she handed him a tureen. 'Are you alone at home, Professor?'

'You're never alone in a university.' Jameson's eyes were sad. 'But yes . . . it can be lonely. My wife died two years ago, and my son is . . . away.'

The maid cleared the plates.

'And then I must leave immediately,' the professor finished. 'University business calls. I will walk to Masham and catch the train. I'll be sorry to leave Yorkshire, Bogg has shown me some beautiful countryside.' Mr Bogg beamed.

Lizzie brought in the cheese, and Bogg eyed it with delight. 'You've got a Stilton, Bishop!'

The doctor smiled. 'It's a blue Wensleydale. Quite rare, they only happen by chance. I think you'll enjoy it.'

A good old port was brought in, and Bishop sat back to enjoy his party. It was not often he had the company of men like this.

The evening passed quickly, and at length Jameson stood up. 'I must catch a few hours of sleep before the dawn watch at the temple. We're both staying at the Crown Inn at Thorpe tonight – off home tomorrow.'

Bishop went to the door. 'I'll get my man to drive you there. He must be back by now.' He brushed aside their polite protests; it was nearly a two-mile walk to Thorpe.

Reuben was available for duty, but not in the best frame of mind. Bishop's loud knock on his door produced his head. 'Aw heck, boss, what now?'

'Take the professor and Mr Bogg to Thorpe in the trap, that's what, and look sharp about it. Really, Reuben, you are impossible.'

The only reply was a sniff as the groom shrugged himself into his jacket.

The evening of Bishop's dinner had been a sad one for Reuben.

The night had started well, with a ritual clock-boiling. After their supper of cold meat and mashed potatoes with pickled onions, the groom sat in the kitchen looking at the old wall clock, which had stopped and left an empty silence in the room. 'I feel lost without old clock.'

'Boil it,' suggested Gilbert, dishcloth in hand at the sink. He put the kettle on the fire for their cup of tea.

'Boil it?' Reuben echoed, and looked so astonished that Gilbert laughed. When questioned further, the tinker said that everybody knew you could boil old clocks to make them go.

Gilbert filled a large pan with water and as he watched it fill he said, without turning, 'It's Barnaby Fair tomorrow at Boroughbridge, isn't it?'

'Ay.' Reuben was busy with cogs and wheels.

The pan was lowered carefully on to the fire. 'And the tinkers and gypsies and horse traders will all be there, they tell me. It's a big horse-fair.'

'Ay,' said Reuben miserably. 'I know what's coming next.'

Gilbert picked up some of the clock mechanism. 'So maybe I should go to Barnaby Fair to see if my old mates are there . . . and then make tracks for Scarborough.'

The voice was so soft that Reuben had to listen hard to catch the words. The groom heaved a deep sigh into the silence. 'Well . . . you've been like a son to me, lad. I mislike to see thee go.'

'See, it's dirty.' The vagrant bent over the clock. 'Barnaby's the biggest horse-fair in the North . . . if I have friends among the travellers, that's where I'll find them. Pass me soda.' The pan started to boil.

'Timepiece stew,' said Gilbert, and they both laughed. Then their eyes met, full of pain. 'I'll have to leave tonight, Reuben. A warm night's perfect for walking.'

'What's up, lad? Tell me what's up.' Reuben had never asked Gilbert anything before.

So the story came out. Gilbert explained that he could wait no longer for memory to come back. It might never come back. So he must go out to look for it, to find someone who knew him, who could help him to fit the small things he remembered back into a pattern. 'I was going to Scarborough for some reason, that's all I know. So maybe I should go on there, unless somebody at Barnaby knows me.'

Twenty minutes later the clock was ticking away on the wall. 'Let's go down to the Shoulder of Mutton for a pint.' Fancy Gilbert worrying away all this time about his memory, and never saying owt! 'Boss is tied up with folks tonight, and we need cheering up.'

'It's not just that you've got to go,' Reuben continued, as they walked up the yard, 'but to what? It's not knowing . . . that's what gets me. You'll likely be sleeping rough, going hungry . . .' Reuben shook his head.

As they passed the doctor's house they heard piano music. 'Chopin,' murmured Gilbert dreamily, and stood listening for a while. 'It reminds me of something . . . I can't catch it, though.' They walked on down to the inn, the music followed them down the street.

In the Shoulder of Mutton there was the usual swirl of tobacco-smoke and the odour of various types of livestock. Dogs sat quietly under the tables, as their owners exchanged information on sheep prices. 'Hey lad – you'll be off to Barnaby!' cried the landlord, serving them beer. Gilbert nodded.

They drank in silence, neither knowing what to say.

The green eyes looked up briefly. 'Will you give . . . give my love to Hester when you see her? She's been like a sister to me. I'll miss her, and you, and – of course, Rose most of all. I hope to marry Rose, one day.'

'Young Hester thinks a lot of you, lad,' said Reuben briefly.

Back at the cottage again, the tinker's few belongings were soon packed. Last of all, he shouldered the violin on a new leather strap that Reuben had made for him. 'I'll be back, never fear. Thanks for everything, Reuben.' A quick handshake, and he was off into the summer dusk, and the groom was left listening to the tick of the old clock.

Only half a mile down the road, Gilbert met Hester, going home on her pony. When he said he was off to Barnaby, she jumped down and gave him a quick hug. He was nearly crying, she could tell.

'So this is it, then. I've always known you had to go!'

Hester was sad, but her mind was still full of poor Josh, whom she had left sleeping after a day of pain. 'I wish you all the luck in the world.' She grinned at him like a sister. She felt a faint tug at the heart as he turned that pure profile to her in the starlight, and smiled the diffident smile. And Hester realized then that there are many different kinds of love.

Reuben sat there until Bishop's knock roused him, to take the guests to Thorpe. Standing in front of Dolly to slip the collar over her head, Reuben muttered to the little mare about folks that kept honest men and horses out of their beds. Dolly stood patiently; she was used to working at all hours and had heard it all before.

Minutes later the outfit was presented smartly at the front door. The groom jumped down to help both men up, and he even touched his hat to them. 'Look sharp, Reuben!' said the boss grimly. As with some dogs, it was as well to tell his man to do something he was already doing.

It was a beautiful night, they all agreed, as they sniffed the drowning wafts of perfume from the night-scented flowers at the door. As they skimmed through the lanes under the emerging stars, Jameson, who was sitting next to Reuben, turned and smiled at him. 'Sorry to be keeping you out of your bed!'

Something about that smile struck a chord with Reuben. He scratched his head under the cap, and straightened his back. 'Get on, girl!' The mare responded. They splashed through the beck at the ford.

Hester had to call at the farrier's in Thorpe that night, which delayed her. She was trotting past the Crown when Reuben drew up with the usual flourish, and Bishop's guests jumped out, thanking him again for turning out so late. Recognizing her from the Slaters' farm, the two men paused at the front of the inn to say goodbye to her too. Jameson looked down and smiled. 'Give the Slaters my compliments – our stay there was very happy! And please take this for yourself.' He gave her a gold coin. Hester had cheered him up.

Hester felt like dropping a curtsy, it was so old-fashioned. 'Thank you, sir!' she managed politely. Moorlanders were not used to this kind of thing.

Reuben turned Dolly round. He had started to move off back to Kirkby when Hester suddenly gave a most unladylike yell. Mounting the pony, she trotted alongside until she got Reuben to pull up. 'Too busy to have a word with me?' she demanded. And then she told him something that made him sit up very straight indeed.

It was cold in the wood. Jameson could feel his age in the aching bones as the light mist moved softly over him. It would soon be dawn, and it was just as well to be early.

Jameson looked at his watch and yawned. At five a cuckoo started off the chorus of birdsong in the wood near the Druid's Temple; gradually the birds woke one by one, and started to sing. It was so rapturous a sound, with a faint echo through the trees, that the man was uplifted. Forty-three minutes from the first call of the cuckoo, the sun should rise over the edge of the world, by his calculations.

The man moved slightly and the bracken rustled round him. The bare moor-top had changed since Danby's day, and a grove of trees had added to the mystery of the stones. The mist was not heavy enough to obscure the sun. If this measurement showed up anything interesting, he would write it up for one of the scientific magazines.

If only Anna had lived she would have encouraged this hobby. She might even have come out with him to watch the dawn.

The mist was clearing, moved by the breeze. The first pink rays of light began to peep over the Vale of York. It was so dramatic and awe-inspiring in the sacred wood that the professor held his breath.

Instead of the sun being in line with the centre stone, it was striking the huge pillar of rocks that stood on a mound, a little way from the circle.

Slowly the sun rose, blood-red and glorious. As it came the man stood to greet it, his calculations forgotten, in simple awe, with his hands at his sides. His thoughts were still of his dead wife, and how she would have rejoiced with him in this sunrise.

And there, walking towards him among the trees, was a slight figure. It looked like Anna. It gave him a great shock.

The figure walked through the circle and stopped at the pile of rocks, lit by the sun. Then it came on, and looked up and saw him. The morning light, increasing every second, shone on the upturned face.

'Bertie! My son!' The next moment the professor was leaping down the grassy bank.

Gilbert the tinker, weary and dishevelled, passed a hand over his eyes. 'Is it . . . Father?' He stopped. 'You must have worried about me!'

The sun was higher now, and all around them the birds were in full chorus. Together they stood and watched the light grow towards another day. Then there was a cough and a small, bow-legged figure appeared on the edge of the trees.

'We were right, then!' Reuben's face had a grin of pure relief. 'Trap's here when ye want it.' He melted away again. Boss would be wanting the trap soon, like enough.

But it wasn't long before the two joined him. He explained about the boss and the trap, and took them back to his cottage, only pausing to buy eggs for breakfast at Potter's Farm.

Gilbert and his father kept looking at each other and smiling, and Reuben had to explain how he'd spotted the likeness between father and son. 'But Hester saw it, too, and she knew as you'd lost your son

... and she saw you both tonight, within a few minutes! You'll have to thank Hester for this.'

Gilbert could recall school holidays spent at his mother's family home in Ireland, and the expeditions with Irish tinkers. He couldn't remember how he came to be at Kirkby.

'To think,' said Jameson, beating the table, 'that you were so near this summer, and yet we never met. But it's all right now.' Years had been lifted from him since the sun had risen that morning.

Jameson told them that Gilbert had finished a university music course, and had been doing some research. He and a friend had gone off on a walking-tour to Yorkshire, collecting some kind of folk music. 'And what you don't know,' he said to Gilbert, 'is that you have two very good offers of employment waiting; a place in an orchestra, and a university teaching position. You could probably take up both! Most unusual for one of your age, but your examination marks were the best in the country. You've a good career ahead, my boy.'

Gilbert thought for a while. Then came the bombshell.

'I'd really like to be a sheep farmer. And I want to get married ... to a farmer's daughter.'

There was a silence. Jameson looked shocked. 'Surely, my boy, you can aim a little higher than that!'

# CHAPTER TWENTY-SEVEN

'Isn't it grand to watch other people working?' It was a determined, cheerful face that Hester turned to her favourite patient as they sat looking out over the workers in the hay, visible from the garden.

Josh Bell had healed, externally at least, to the extent that he only needed intermittent nursing care. The burns had not, as Bishop had feared, become infected. One up to Hester, who was becoming formidable in her application of scientific hygiene. Everything Josh touched had been scrubbed within an inch of its life. But even with all this energy the mood was still very sombre. Josh was saying goodbye, silently, to the countryside and the people he loved.

Hester could think of nothing to say, but she slipped her hand into his.

'I won't nag at you,' she said, after a long silence. 'But it's my duty to mention this one more time . . . there is always hope, Josh. Don't give up, lad!'

Hester heard the rattle of a horse's hoofs on stone, and the medical team turned into the farmyard in their usual style, Reuben driving. Another visit from Bishop, who was keeping a close eye on Joshua.

The doctor made a thorough examination of Josh, while Hester and his mother gave Reuben tea and seed-cake in the kitchen. Hester was always pleased to see Reuben. 'And what's the news of Kirkby?' she asked.

'Boss wants to talk to you about that.' Reuben was mysterious.

Soon afterwards the doctor came into the kitchen. 'Young Hester, can you come down to the police station tomorrow afternoon? We have an appointment with PC Brown.'

Hester was shocked. What could she have done? 'Nay, doctor, I don't like policemen – ooh, sorry Josh!' and she put her hand over her mouth in the old way. Policemen were like parsons to Hester: the less of them you saw, the better.

Reuben grinned as he went out to the mare, but Bishop ignored the remark. 'You see, Gilbert and his father are coming back – they want to find out just what happened to the lad. And you were the person who found him, up there on the moor. So we'll put all the evidence we have together, and see what we can work out.'

The storm clouds were gathering on a hot, sultry afternoon as Hester made her way to the police station on the pony. PC Brown was waiting for them in the airless little office. He bustled about, finding more chairs, rather overwhelmed by the gentry. The professor and Gilbert were there, the lad looking less like a tinker than before. Rose sat close beside him, looking apprehensive. Bishop was there, foot tapping impatiently.

Gilbert jumped up when he saw Hester, and kissed her on the cheek.

A fly buzzed in the window as the doctor opened the proceedings. 'If we put all the evidence together, PC Brown will have something to work on. What do you know, Gilbert?'

'It's a long story.' Gilbert was just a quiet as ever, a little more relaxed, but still with much on his mind. 'Some I remember, some my friends and family have told me. A couple of years ago some of our university class read *Lavengro*, the book about gypsies by George Borrow. And then the tutors gave us a research assignment: to study music at first hand, write down the music of the ordinary man in the street.'

Gilbert ran his fingers through his hair, remembering. 'Jasper and I thought we'd look at gypsy music, because of the book, and we would cultivate some English gypsies. That's how it started. Jasper made the contacts, and I went along with him. And I'd known a few, in Ireland. . . .'

The professor shook his head. 'And all the time I thought they were researching. But they were learning how to mend pots and pans, snare rabbits and whittle wood. . . .'

Bishop was becoming slightly impatient. 'So! You came down to Yorkshire on this erudite quest, and ended up at Pateley . . . without your friend?'

Gilbert's head went up. 'Jasper had to go, and I planned to go back home in another week or so. I put my papers – the notes for the research – into an envelope with a note for Father, and Jasper posted them. And that was the last Father heard of me.'

'Where did the Irish accent come from?' Bishop wanted to know.

'Well . . . my mother was Irish and I'd spent time there. . . .'

And then his hearers realized that Gilbert had always damped down his educated accent, to sound more ordinary. That was how he got away with the tinker personality. A lot of itinerants were Irish.

'And when I woke up on the moor that night, the Irish tinker feeling was uppermost! I didn't know who I was. . . .'

'So there is a gap between Pateley and your finding yourself on the moor with a broken leg.' Bishop was trying to move the story on again. 'What do you know, Hester?'

'Well, I was walking to Mrs Little's, and I heard the creaking of a cart, very faint – and the sound of a horse's hoofs. Carrier, I thought to myself.'

PC Brown looked cunning. It was about time he asserted himself, here in his own office. 'And if your footsteps were crunching, how did you hear anything a great way off?' He had been given a hard time by Roger, and was not sure that you could trust a Kettlewell.

'I'd had a lot of cups of tea! So I stopped for a – to relieve myself. And when I was squatting down—'

'That's enough, my girl!' PC Brown was embarrassed.

Hester laughed and looked at Bishop. 'The doctor says that we-mustn't-be-ashamed-of-bodily-functions!' She looked round at Rose and Gilbert, who were trying not to laugh.

'And I went to see Jenny Little – and had more tea – and on my walk home, I heard—'

Bishop decided at last to cut a long story short. 'So we think that the carrier robbed Gilbert of his wallet and threw him out of the cart, and he probably broke his leg in the fall – maybe trying to save the violin.'

The professor nodded. That sounded likely.

'So this might be yours, then?' And the policeman handed over a leather wallet; no money in it – nothing.

'Who had it?' Gilbert looked at Brown.

The policeman was enjoying his first success in detection. 'Those King lads . . . I searched the Kings' house one day, and I found a lot of others folks' gear. This wallet wasn't much to go on, but Dr Bishop told us to look out for anything that might be your property.'

Gilbert smiled ruefully. 'I'd just posted my papers off home . . . didn't have much with me, but I would have had some money.'

There was a commotion outside, and Rose went to the window. 'Mum and Dad, come for me,' she said resignedly. 'Now for it!' to Gilbert, who squared his shoulders and took her hand. They all went outside.

Fred tied the horse to a rail and stalked towards them. Fred and Martha Balderstone wanted their daughter back, it was clear. They were not impressed by posh accents, either.

Fred Balderstone said grimly: 'We've no time to sit about talking, hay's to get and it's going to rain.' They stood outside the police station in a tight little group, and Hester slipped an arm round Rose, who was crying.

Fred sounded like her own father, thought Hester. Hay is more important than his daughter's future!

'In any case, there's nowt to say.' Fred's mouth closed with finality. 'They're too young to marry. Granted, the lad's now respectable, for the moment. But will he run off again? And who's to say he can support a wife? And another thing – our Rose would be lost among gentry. She'd be condescended to, and not happy. We may be small farmers, but we're independent, and we own our own land. We're as good as gentry any day, but that's not how they see it. I'll be plain with ye.' He glared at Gilbert's father.

The professor had wondered quietly to Hester, whether Rose was too rustic for his son, but he thought that time might solve the problem. They might both meet more suitable partners in time.

The young tinker looked at Rose's grim parents, and smiled at them. Martha immediately softened her expression; she'd always liked the lad.

'I will come to see you, and tell you the details when you have more time.' His voice was as quiet as ever, but it held determination. 'I would like your permission to visit Rose, and to have her visit us in Newcastle. I have several good offers of work, and in due course we wish to get married.' As a petition, it lacked humility. Gilbert had made up his mind. He took Rose by the hand.

His father added: 'Gilbert took the highest music prize in the kingdom, when he finished his degree. He has a bright future – and a farm in Ireland too, that his mother left him!'

Fred appeared to be impressed, at last, by the mention of land. 'Well, we'll have to see. . . .'

Hester went home soon after that, as the first drops of thunder rain began to fall. Fred's hay crop would get wet, but Hester knew that at least Gilbert and Rose would be happy. Their parents didn't approve of a marriage, but they would get used to the idea.

Bishop went home quite happy; he had organized PC Brown to his satisfaction, and also, another problem was solved.

The Mechanics' Institute roof was being repaired, but there was a shortfall in funds. Another fund-raising event was called for. And Gilbert had offered to put on a musical evening, with the help of Jasper, and perhaps some of the carol-singers. It was a nice thought, and another excuse for Gilbert to come back to Kirkby.

The concert-goers were busy putting away an ample supper, encouraged by those who had provided it. Ada Moore's sponges lived up to their wildest expectations; the sponge was fluffy, light and a deep orange from eggs produced on the green grass of summer.

During the interval Mary had been persuaded to play 'The Last Rose of Summer', as she had at their last concert. This time Gilbert took up the tune, and even above the hum of talk, it sounded haunting, evocative. The tinker played with his eyes on his own dark Rose, and the more sensitive villagers shivered a little, thinking that their summer would soon be over.

Dr Johnson paced by with his wife on his arm, and stopped to speak to his rival Dr Bishop. The Johnsons had a pleased air of patronage about them; it was gracious of them to attend a village function and to mix with their social inferiors.

'Are you enjoying the music?' Bishop asked politely.

Dr Johnson smiled. 'We prefer opera, of course. But the . . . students play quite well, do they not?' He'd almost called them vagrants.

The Scott-Joneses and a few other Johnson supporters agreed. 'Not bad for students.' And yes, here were the Metcalfes, in the Johnson camp. No wonder the Metcalfes hadn't called in Bishop lately.

Glaring, Bishop replied: 'Graduates, if you don't mind. And in my opinion, their standard is very high indeed. World class, in fact.'

A few minutes later the Johnson entourage swept by Hester without a glance. They looked ostentatiously the other way. She was a fallen woman, acknowledged by the Bishops – more fool them – but not fit for polite society.

'Good job we got rid of her,' Lily sniffed. 'She fair flaunts that baby in your face.'

And Ned silently thanked the Lord that it was a dark-haired child, and looked just like its mother. He had been more careful after that bad fright, and didn't want to be reminded of his mistakes.

Ada Moore asked Hester to take round a tray of food, and she was pleased to be made a part of the proceedings.

After a round of the room, Hester came back to the table and found Mabel waiting for her. 'That red dress looks right nice!' the other girl said. 'Er ... what do you think of Josh?' This was a genuinely caring question, but also had an element of self-interest. They were waiting to get married, she and Elijah. But when? It didn't seem right to celebrate, with Josh dying.

'Dunno. Sometimes he's better, sometimes he's worse. We've done all we can.'

'Ay, well, lad can play the fiddle, but does that make him likely to be a good husband?' Fred was insisting mulishly, while eating a large slice of sponge-cake.

They looked round. Rose, not even pretending to eat supper, was talking to Gilbert and Jasper. Then Gilbert took his girl by the hand and led her off into a quiet part of the hall, away from the supper tables. They saw him draw a paper from his pocket, and the dark head and the fair one bent over it earnestly.

'Rose, I've got something here that could make him change his mind!'

'Don't think so, Gil. We've talked about your offer of a teaching job and all that. Didn't make any difference.'

Gilbert pulled a crackling letter from his pocket and took it out of the envelope. 'How about this, my beautiful Rose?' He kissed her on the cheek, and a few folks looked over at them and smiled. It was nearly time for the second half of the concert.

The music took Hester into another world. The soaring

melodies, the interweaving of the two violins and the piano, stayed with her afterwards as an image of harmony. Gilbert's music was like threads of pure gold, she could almost see them in the lamp-light. It made her think of love, and the relationship of two people who loved each other . . . and she found she was thinking of Josh.

At the end, Gilbert played 'Auld Lang Syne', nostalgically. The musicians were thanked by the chairman of the Mechanics' Institute committee, namely Dr Bishop, for their contribution to the future of the building. The roof would now be safe.

After it was over, people lingered, talking in groups, reluctant to see the end of such a good night. The washers-up were clattering away in the kitchen, and the Balderstone family was in a huddle with Gilbert.

Bishop and Reuben were counting the money in the kitchen when Gilbert came bounding in. 'We're to be married in six months' time! At Kirkby church, and you're all invited!' A quick shake of the hand from Reuben and Bishop, and he was off again.

'That was a sudden change of heart!' said the doctor thoughtfully to Hester, who was stacking plates.

All was made clear some minutes later, when he encountered the Balderstones on their way home, Rose firmly in tow, Gilbert walking out with her to their trap.

'Well, that farm in Ireland makes a difference, I must say.' Fred was converted at last. 'His mother left him a right good farm. Rent is more than I earn in a year, that's for sure. There's nowt like land, I always say.'

Hester felt only a slight, a very slight, tug at the heart when she heard their news. And she kissed them both with a sweet smile, while holding Tommy in her arms. Hester felt years older and more experienced than Rose and Gilbert. She hoped they would be able to enjoy their youth for a little while yet.

# CHAPTER TWENTY-EIGHT

Josh Bell sat in the sunshine, looking at his scarred hands and thinking deeply. He wondered, as did all his friends, just why he had to die, since the burns were healed. But the terrible weakness which had not left him since the accident was increasing and he felt that he was slipping away. He was bone-weary, worn out with pain.

It was Josh's birthday. This evening the family was going to gather for high tea, and Hester had been invited. If only he could be free from pain. . . .

Josh stood up deliberately and grasped his stick. His progress was slow, but he persevered in walking down the garden path, where he could lean on the gate and look over the sheep as they nibbled the short turf.

He meant to prove to Hester that he was trying to get well, but all it seemed to do was to make him weaker. The pains got worse.

Josh got to the gate and watched a skylark rise into the blue, spiralling and twittering as it went. His eyes travelled over the ewes, which had all lambed and were feeding quietly. There was a bunch of cows in the background, sharing the same pasture. Then he noticed something amiss.

A fat ewe had rolled on to her back and was stuck there, legs waving in the air in a most undignified way. Her lamb stood anxiously by her side, wondering what had happened. If sheep stayed on their backs for too long, they died. Rig-welted, it was called, an old Dales word which originated in Norway with the Vikings.

Josh looked round. The dogs were tied up, there was nobody about. He tried whistling, but the ewe could not hear him. Sometimes a quick fright would galvanize a sheep into making an extra effort to get up. 'Come on, lass!' he shouted. It had no effect.

There was nothing else for it: Josh would have to go down to the sheep himself. By the time his brother came home from market it might be too late.

Gritting his teeth, the young farmer went through the gate and hobbled over the uneven ground towards the ewe. Pain increased with every step, but he drew slowly nearer.

The animal had given up and was lying there helplessly, but when she saw Josh, she made an extra effort. Bending down slowly, he pushed her from one side and the combined effort rolled her to her feet again. She trotted off immediately, the lamb at her side.

'Wish I could run off like that!' Josh said to her, and picked up his stick. He stood up, rounded a hawthorn bush, and found himself looking into a pair of evil black eyes.

Letty King stood in his path. She kicked expertly at Josh's stick, and he fell heavily to the ground. She stood over him and he expected a rain of curses, but all she did was smile gloatingly.

'What are you doing here, on our land?' Josh used his police voice, even though he was at a grave disadvantage, lying on the ground. He felt annoyed that he had not spotted her. It was going to be hard to get away; he'd never felt so helpless.

The woman spoke in a quiet hiss. 'Not yours for much longer, is it? You'll be off to churchyard soon. I have the second sight . . . I can see it all.' The quiet voice was more sinister than any cursing would have been.

The old woman could kill him, but he wasn't going to believe in her predictions. He felt round for the stick, but the bitch kicked it out of his reach. The she kicked him on the knee, for good measure. She had very strong boots. And she stood back and gloated, uglier than ever. Why wasn't she in prison, with the rest of the King brood?

The pain in his knee was increasing. Josh twisted in agony, and heard a loud click in his back. More damage – would he ever be able to get up? He would be paralysed – it sometimes happened, he knew. If your back locks, you are done for.

'Don't talk rubbish, woman!' he said in desperation. 'And get off our land!' Josh was not going to let her know how terrible he felt.

'I can see it all,' she repeated, in a sing-song voice. 'There you are in church, all flowers round, your mother crying into a hanky . . . and that Kettlewell bitch is there as well, but she's got no tears . . .

she's smiling! A hard bitch that one, all she wants is your money . . . and that stupid White woman . . . I can see them in churchyard, standing together . . .' the voice died away in a wail.

The woman was under the influence of something. Her eyes were bloodshot and she swayed on her feet. She ought to be arrested. Josh felt for the handcuffs, and then remembered.

Josh wasn't a policeman any more; he would never be a policeman again. He had no power, not even enough strength to stand up. A great grief swept over him, a longing to have his youth and strength back again. His fate had never seemed so bitter as now. Josh was at his lowest ebb and the woman knew it. He closed his eyes.

There was an old footpath leading across the pasture, which villagers had once used to move across country. Letty King was on a legal right of way, and she knew it. She was also on a traditional 'corpse way', leading to the churchyard and burial ground. A grim road, used to convey the dead from the outlying hamlets down to Kirkby church, used for the last 800 years. 'This is the road you'll travel!' her voice seemed to be fading into the distance.

Josh had known of the tradition, but it hadn't meant much to a strong young man.

Then Josh opened his eyes, and found she was gone. All that was left was a smell of some drug.

The tables were turned, and Josh was now helpless himself, just as the sheep had been. His muscles were so weak that he could not pull himself up without help. 'Where are you now, when I need you, Hester?' he said sadly, looking round the horizon. But there was no trim little figure on a Dales pony to be seen. There was only the group of cows, coming in their usual way to see what he was doing.

Cows are full of curiosity, and humans don't usually sit on the ground. The older milking-cows all knew him and they formed a circle round him, heads down, sniffing. 'Ivy, Heather, Bluebell . . .' He called them all by name. Josh liked cattle and before he joined the police, he had milked this herd for years.

Bluebell was the boldest, and now she put her big head down beside him. 'Hold fast, girl!' He rubbed her head between the horns, as she used to like him to do. And gradually he pulled himself up by those wide horns, until he was standing again. Bluebell snorted, but she didn't pull away. Moving gingerly, he was able to pick up the stick before he let go of her support. 'Good lass!'

He must be paralysed . . . Josh felt numb. The absence of pain made him afraid. People said that, at the end, the dying often lost the feeling of pain and went peacefully. Perhaps it was true.

Slowly, Josh stumbled back to the house. Apart from the bruise on his knee where the woman had kicked him, there was no pain anywhere.

As Josh sat in the shade under the tree his mind seemed to clear, and he could think. The pain had been so insistent over many weeks that it had confused him, and the pain-killing drugs had deadened his brain. But now his mind was racing. There was so much he wanted to achieve before he died. Hester, Elijah, his mother . . . he wanted to help them all. By the time his mother called him in for the midday meal he had formed a plan.

'Josh is in the parlour, dear,' said Mrs Bell when Hester arrived, somewhat breathless, dusting down her skirts after the ride on the pony. 'Go in and see him, he's very quiet today.'

Hester went into the parlour, which was lit by the evening sun, and was much more cheerful than parlours were supposed to be. They were going to eat in the parlour tonight, for the birthday tea, and the table was spread with good things. 'Happy birthday!' Hester sang out, from the doorway.

And there was Josh, by the fireplace. He was on his knees.

Pushing back her hair, Hester rushed forward. 'Josh dear, what's happened? Did you fall?'

Josh looked up at her, and his face was full of pure joy. The lines of pain were fading and he looked younger, more peaceful. 'Nay, lass. Stand there. That's right, just there, in the sun. Now . . . I am going to ask for your hand in marriage.'

Hester went white with shock. 'Josh!'

The young man shuffled on the rug. 'Hurry up, please, because my knee is aching. Will you wed me, lass? For better or for worse? I know it's a lot to ask, and I said I'd never bother you again. But I'm going to buy that farm at Thorpe, for both of us and . . . I want your hand in marriage. Right away,' he added firmly, in the police voice. 'I love you, Hester lass. You and I belong together.'

'I thought you'd want a bit more than just my hand. . . ?' Even in this situation, Hester could see the funny side. 'Get up Josh, there's a dear. Well!' Hester was unusually flustered. She put a hand on his brow. 'No fever, is there? But Josh, I thought . . . you've got someone in Leeds, haven't you? What about her?'

Josh climbed up stiffly and sat down with her on the sofa. 'No, I haven't got a lass in Leeds. You must mean Sarah Jane. She was the landlady's daughter, came home with me out of kindness. She didn't want me to travel so far on my own, in the state I was in.'

Hester looked at him carefully. 'But she must have thought a lot about you, Josh?'

'We were good friends . . . and she's going to marry a missionary next year!' Josh smiled at Hester's anxious expression. It was good that she'd been a little jealous. 'You're the only one for me, Hester, always have been. Please say you will!' He sounded firm and assured.

'Of course I would love to belong to you, Josh. Can we wait until you're better?' Wait until we are sure you're going to live, Hester thought. I don't want anybody to say that I married a dying man, to get his farm.

Josh put his arm round her gently. 'My idea is to get wed when Elijah does, have a double wedding, nice and quiet like. We can go off to our little place at Thorpe and Elijah can live here – he deserves a place of his own – and my mother can go to live with her sister in Kirkby, she wants to do that. So everybody will be happy! Especially thee and me!'

And then there was no more planning for a while, because Josh very carefully put his arms round his nurse and kissed her.

The music of two violins in harmony was running through Hester's head. In Josh's arms she felt she had come home. Hester couldn't believe how happy she felt, with a settled happiness that was quite new to her. 'And Tommy?' She had to remind him about her other commitment.

Josh laughed, an easy laugh that Hester hadn't heard for years. 'Folks always did think he was mine – now they'll be sure! We'll be a grand little family, and we can train Tommy up to be a right good farmer.'

When the others joined them round the big mahogany table for the birthday feast, Josh put forward his plan. There was a shocked silence, then Elijah began to see how convenient it would be if it worked out.

'But what about your health, lad?' he asked quietly, as they were eating the enormous ham salad. They'd been planning a funeral until today, but it seemed tactless to mention it.

Josh had thought of the answer to that one. 'I'm in good fettle to what I was. Pain's going away, and I want to do all this as soon as we can. Hester'll look after me once we're wed, and I'll be right in no time.' I wonder how long I've got, went his thoughts. I hope I won't be too much of a burden to her.

'If anybody can get him through, it's Hester.' Josh's mother moved painfully on her chair; the rheumatism was getting worse. She'd formed a very good opinion of the nurse, in spite of her Kettlewell background. And it would be a relief to give him over to somebody else. Mrs Bell loved her son, but she had been looking forward to an easier life in Kirkby.

Things moved swiftly in the next few weeks, propelled by Josh's determination. The farm at Thorpe was inspected minutely by Josh, Hester and Elijah and also by Meg and Tommy, who came along and thought it was most exciting. After the ritual haggling, it was bought, with immediate possession because the owner had already moved out.

The weeks passed in a blur of cake-making, dress-making and planning. A quiet wedding, just a few people, they said. But in the end the guest list was quite long, because Josh wanted all the people who wished them well to be there in the church when they got married.

The Reverend Grimshaw said quietly to her, when they arranged the wedding, that there might be a hope of Heaven after all for Hester, if she became a dutiful wife. She would have to attend church regularly, of course.

Dr Bishop, when asked for his opinion, questioned Josh closely. He suggested that the internal pains might have originated in a twisted spine, the result of carrying heavy people out of the fire. 'And that day in the pasture, you twisted – did you say? And it righted itself. I hope I'm right, my lad.'

In the end, everything came together in time, and it was a perfect village wedding, on an early autumn day with plenty of sunshine.

Hester looked beautiful that day. The cream-coloured dress set off her rich, dark colouring and her eyes sparkled with happiness. Mabel, the other bride, had slimmed down a little with hard work, and looked quite fetching in pale blue. They had both agreed that they didn't want traditional wedding dresses. And the Bell brothers looked handsome, almost elegant in well-made new suits.

Josh still had a walking-stick, but he stood straighter now; the pain had not returned, and he was feeling almost normal. He looked round the church and saw that their friends were there: Reuben in his starched collar, Bishop and Mrs Bishop, Meg White with little Tommy. Gilbert and Rose were there too, sitting close together, with Fred and Martha Balderstone in their best clothes. Even Hester's mother and little Susan were there, looking much better than Josh had ever seen them. Lizzie was earning a living as a dressmaker.

Joshua looked again. There they were, surrounded by flowers. His mother was crying tears of joy into her hanky, and his dear Hester was smiling into his eyes. And he remembered the old woman's prophecy. It was so like, and so unlike. Letty King had got it wrong!

How he hoped she had got it wrong.